THE LAST LIE

DANA KILLION

\

Obscura
Press

1

"He's peddling poison!" A man in his early sixties shouted, his face gray and haggard, as he struggled against the grip of two burly security types in black suits and ear wires. "You tell that damn coward he can't hide behind his money! The world will know what he's done if I have to spend the rest of my life making that happen!"

Men in dark suits and women in silk dresses gaped, as guards held the man firmly by the arms and hustled him down the wide carpeted hallway, past gleaming chandeliers and decorator-selected art, and away from the ballroom.

I stepped to the side allowing the entourage to pass. The agitated man stared at me with eyes gone dark and I shivered, feeling his fury deep in my chest. He wore his devastation like a black hole ready to swallow anything in its path. With his rumpled polo and battered jeans hanging slack on his hips, I didn't imagine he was a guest at the Drea Foundation fundraiser, an organization devoted to supporting sexually, physically, and emotionally abused girls.

I watched the three men round the corner, curious about the backstory, and then moved toward the banquet hall. I could hear patrons whisper to themselves about the vulgarity of the unexplained outburst as another security guard opened the large double doors that had been shuttered, screening the commotion from the attendees. I paused, uncertain whether to continue into the room and what I might find inside. Curiosity and obligation moved me forward. Surely the moment of drama had been suppressed.

I stopped at the table and gave my name to the door attendant.

"Good evening Ms. Kellner. I don't have you on the press list. Is Link-Media covering the event tonight?"

"No, I'm here as a personal sponsor."

"Wonderful. Thank you for your support," she said, her voice appropriately perky, then handed me a program. "Enjoy your evening."

Stepping into the Peninsula Hotel's Grand Ballroom, I scanned the room of designer dresses, carefully coifed hair, and four-inch heels, looking for my date, Seth Bowman, and more importantly, Wade Ramelli. He was the chairman of the Link-Media board, which made him my boss. He'd also dodged my last three phone calls, and I was pissed.

City lights glittered through sixteen-foot windows, bouncing off the crystal, as the downtown Chicago skyline shifted into evening. Lush arrangements of peonies, freesia, and orchids, painted in shades of magenta and coral graced the skirted tables, mirroring the colors of the sky. A jazz trio filled a corner to put the crowd in a mellow mood and waitstaff circulated with trays of champagne flutes. The perfect environment to get well-to-do patrons loosened up enough to open their wallets for a good cause.

No sign of either man, so I made a beeline for the bar, winding around the clusters of twos and threes as they nibbled shrimp dumplings and stuffed endive. Cabernet in hand, I made another pass around the room, wondering which of the men in tailored Italian suits had been the subject of the screamers ire.

"Wow. Andrea Kellner you look stunning this evening. Tell me again why I can't get you into bed."

Seth Bowman stood at my elbow, a smirk on his face, as he leaned in for a peck on the cheek.

"Because I find you horribly unattractive."

No one, including me, found this Adonis, lacking in physical appeal. Chiseled cheek bones, abs of steel, arms sculpted of mahogany. May as well oil him down and pop him up on an underwear billboard. At 42, he was still a muscle machine with a two hour a day dumbbell habit. As the founder and CEO of VTF Industries, a nutritional drink company, his body was his billboard and perfection his only standard. Too much gloss for my tastes. Seth and I were pals, platonic pals, not pals with benefits. Despite my newly single status, I wasn't tempted and never had been in the eight years we'd known each other. And a night of playing dress-up in this elegant environment wasn't about to loosen my panties.

We'd met one frigid Sunday in October at a Chicago Marathon party, back when Seth was in the heady pre-launch days of VTF. He'd been so eager to share his excitement with the world that I became fascinated with his entrepreneurial spirit. We'd gotten so engrossed in conversation that morning that we'd missed the first round of elite runners as they crossed the finish line. In the years since, we made a point of getting together every few months. I'd watched his business blossom and he my career shift.

"Well, lucky ass me that you'd suffer through an evening with my beastly face. Drink up. Maybe I'll be cuter by bar time." He laughed and grabbed my shoulders. "Glad you could join me. It's been way too long. How've you been holding up since all that business with Erik? I don't think I've seen you since the funeral."

His eyes were clouded, his face tired and sad, but I had a feeling it wasn't entirely out of concern for me.

"Dazed and confused is the best way to describe it," I said. "I don't know if I should call myself a widow or a divorcee? Technically we were still married when he was killed, but the divorce was imminent. Emotionally, I'm still bouncing. Trying to manage the business, my grief, life... I have a cat to keep me company. Do I need more?" I laughed, hoping that would give the illusion of normalcy. Few people really wanted more than a surface level response that made them feel they'd done their duty and asked.

If I was honest with myself, I was still numb. Erik's death had buried me in emotional turmoil and saddled me with a business I didn't know if I was prepared to run. Promoting an employee to managing editor of the digital media company had helped keep the chaos of day-to-day content at bay, but I was a journalist early in a new career, and a former attorney, not a finance geek. Other than the disclosure documents for our divorce, I'd never even seen Link-Media's balance sheet prior to stepping into the big chair.

Four months had passed since I'd taken the helm and pressure was beginning to build from the company's board of directors to stabilize the business in the wake of its founder's death. Sensing vulnerability, our competitors were also ratcheting up the pressure and stealing market share. The weight of the grief and the responsibility pressed down on my chest in the middle of the night until it was hard to find my breath.

I put my hand to Seth's chin and wagged it back and forth. "What's up with the bags under your eyes? Is all this insane success pushing you to your breaking point?"

In fact, he looked worse than I'd ever seen him, bloodshot

eyes, skin gone ashy, his face thin. Only three years in and the meteoric rise of his unique line of herbal energy drinks had been impressive. Sales had quadrupled, endorsement offers and partnership proposals were flooding in, and media profiles appeared almost weekly. I couldn't be happier for my friend's success but seeing the toll it was taking on him had me worried.

"Just a little flu bug I picked up. So, shall we get you another drink?" He laughed and shot his eyes at my cleavage. "Hmm, you should wear that dress every day."

"Back off Mr. Testosterone." I smiled, hooked my arm into his and steered us toward the dais as the lights flickered and a man up front called for our attention.

The room quieted. The tuxedoed MC thanked the crowd for their support of the charity, summarized the years accomplishments, made a vigorous plea for donations, and then introduced two of the young recipients of the Drea Foundation's services.

As the announcements ended, Seth pulled me toward a buffet table loaded with artfully prepared canapés. An elegant woman I guess to be in her late forties approached as we examined the selection, greeting Seth warmly with a kiss on both cheeks. I recognized her from photos on the charity's website. She was slightly shorter than my 5'4", with a birdlike body. Her glossy, dark hair was pulled away from her face into a French twist. She wore a burgundy Grecian column that skirted the floor, caressing her tiny frame.

"Andrea, I'd like you meet Candiss Nadell, our hostess and president of the Drea Foundation."

"I was thrilled to see your name on the guest list, Andrea. Thank you so much for your ongoing generosity." She clasped my hand gently in both of hers and launched into her sales pitch. "Our counseling center is opening in two weeks and we hope to raise enough this evening to provide twelve additional college scholarships. We can't undo the abuse that has already happened to these young girls, but we can give them tools that allow them to rise above their attackers and not be destroyed."

"It's important work and I'm delighted to help. The trauma the girls have experienced is unimaginable," I said, unable to ignore the hundred thousand dollars worth of sapphires and gold that circled her neck.

"Yes, it breaks the heart." A shadow flickered across her face. "Oh, you must meet my husband. Darling..." she waved over a man standing at the buffet loading a plate of cheese puffs for an elderly woman draped in ropes of pearls.

His thick, wavy gray hair was combed back over his head and he sported a deep golf course tan. I guessed him to be ten, maybe twelve years older than his wife and double her weight.

"Aaron Nadell." He held out a hand adorned with several chunky gold rings. "Thank you for coming. I hope my wife isn't pushing too hard to drain a little more from your bank account. She has quite the tenacious streak where these girls are concerned."

"Only for worthy causes darling." She squeezed his hand and turned back to us. "Aaron is still pouting over the fact that I spend my time managing the Drea Foundation instead of his firm, Nadell Capital. I was there with him in the beginning helping set up the bedrock, so to speak. It's been up to him to keep business humming." She glanced over at her husband, her face a little quieter. "So far, he's handled everything as I expected he would."

A young woman stepped over and whispered in Candiss's ear. She nodded.

"You'll have to excuse me. Duty calls. Please enjoy the evening." Candiss planted another kiss on Seth's cheek and the couple disappeared into the crowd to continue their glad-handing.

"Had enough?" Seth asked. "We could ditch the crowd and pop into Shanghai Terrace for a little dim sum and sake."

"There's someone I have to buttonhole before I leave," I said, spotting Ramelli over at a dessert table. His lanky frame towered over two men he had engaged in conversation. I didn't want to miss my opportunity.

"Want me to wait?"

"Shouldn't you go home and concentrate on feeling better? Bad advertising." I winked and gave him a kiss on the cheek.

"Not a chance. Meet me at the bar in ten minutes. Another vodka and I'll have eradicated the last of this virus."

Ramelli's smile deflated slightly as I approached his party. He introduced me to the others. I managed an irritated stare and asked the men to excuse us for a moment, leaving Ramelli with no reasonable escape.

"You've been avoiding me, Ramelli. Why is that?"

"No, not avoiding. I wanted to wait until I had spoken to the entire board about your request. I expect that we can have a detailed conversation about the budget in the next two weeks."

"And you could have said that on the phone instead of ignoring me. I need approval on this software upgrade. It was yanked from last year's budget and our page load speed is no longer competitive. We don't have time to procrastinate anymore."

I could see my agitation wasn't moving the needle and softened my tone. The budget wasn't the real issue.

"I know our situation isn't ideal from your point of view, but like it or not, I'm still the majority shareholder and a board member myself. I expect the board of directors to give me a chance. A year to prove myself without the obstacles you're already throwing in my path. If I don't meet our financial goals, I'll happily be part of a realignment but until then don't handcuff me."

Ramelli's face pinched, and he tugged on his cuff. "Let me buy you out," he said. "You've had a tremendous trauma this year. Link-Media deserves to thrive. And in this competitive environment, it needs a seasoned pro at the helm. Take the money and make your life easier. You don't need this headache."

"A year, I want a year. After that we can talk."

I turned and walked away, annoyed but not surprised by Ramelli's suggestion. The idea had hung in the air, hinted at but unspoken, within weeks of me taking over the company. Not that I blamed him. The board had every right to show concern. Obstruction on the other hand...

An angry shout rose over the din of the room as I neared the bar. People shifted away from the commotion, jostling me as I plowed ahead. The throng blocked my view but I could hear a male voice on the edge of hysteria.

"She was only 19! Doesn't that matter to you, you heartless son-of-a-bitch? What did you give her? What did you put in that stupid energy drink that killed her?"

I pushed through a circle of bodies. Seth stood silently in the clearing, pressed against the bar. His eyes were wide, and he appeared frozen with fear. The man who'd been escorted out earlier paced in front of him unleashing his tirade with each step, oblivious to the alarm he was causing.

Somehow he'd managed to get back in to the event through the service entrance. Two members of the waitstaff were trying to cajole him out through the kitchen. Where in the hell were the security guards?

I ran my eyes around the room as the crowd rushed toward the exits, anxious to extract themselves from the mounting tension and trapping the guards at the door. Seth locked his eyes on mine, sheer panic in his face. A flash of fear and my own recent history passed through my mind but no one was stepping in to deescalate the situation.

I took one more look for the guard then stepped toward the man and placed a hand on his shoulder.

"Sir, would you like to come with me and Mr. Bowman and talk this through? I'm sure you'd be more comfortable—"

"*Comfortable?*"

He turned toward me and I saw the fury in his eyes. And the gun in his waistband. My breath froze in my chest and I stepped back.

"Is my dead daughter *comfortable*?" Spit shot from his mouth as he raged at me. "He killed her! He killed my baby! He doesn't get to be comfortable ever again."

With one turn he pulled the gun from his belt and shot. My own scream rang in my ears as Seth crumpled to the floor.

2

I leaned against the cold tile wall of the hospital corridor, eyes closed, feeling the rough texture against my bare shoulders. Forcing the antiseptic smell out of my consciousness, I pushed the dings and chirps of the PA system aside and focused on my breath. Seth had been rushed into surgery hours ago and panic was taking over. Someone gently took my hands.

I opened my eyes and looked up at Detective Michael Hewitt. His rugged face was twisted with worry and I threw myself into his chest. He held me tight, kissing my forehead and wrapping me in his strong arms until I calmed.

Taking hold of my shoulders, he stepped back, running his eyes over the blood smeared on my arms, my chest, and staining my silk dress.

"Tell me this isn't yours."

I shook my head. "I'm not hurt."

"What happened?" he asked, his voice tentative, his eyes filled with confusion. I wasn't sure if he was asking as a cop or as my lover.

"Can we check on Seth before we talk? They haven't told me anything."

Michael brushed his lips over mine, then turned toward the nurses' station as a doctor approached.

"Ms. Kellner? I'm Dr. Lassiter." He looked at me with kind brown eyes.

"Yes." I held out a hand. "This is Detective Hewitt, with CPD. He's also a friend. What's Seth's condition?" I asked.

"He's going to be fine. The bullet tore through his deltoid muscle and shattered a portion of his acromion. That's the bone at the tip of the shoulder. Because of his overly developed delts, damage to the bone was minimized. He's going to have some pain and physical therapy will be the extent of his workout routine for the near term, but there shouldn't be any permanent damage."

"That's such a relief." I felt the tension start to melt away. "Thank you, Dr. Lassiter."

"He's a very lucky man. You can see him now, but keep it short," he said, looking at Michael. There would be time tomorrow for a detailed police interview.

———

SETH LAY in the hospital bed, head raised, his face the color of smoke stained walls. His right shoulder was padded to the size of a cantaloupe and his arm was immobilized. A young nurse in bright blue scrubs was adjusting his IV bag. I stifled a gasp at the sight of him. His eyes fluttered open when we entered and he gave me a weak smile as I took the seat beside him. Then his eyes shot his eyes at Michael as I introduced him.

"Sorry about the dress, kid." He squeezed my hand.

"Gives me an excuse to shop." I smiled, trying not to show my fear. Seeing him vulnerable and broken was a stark reminder of how lucky he was to be alive. Mere inches would have meant a different outcome. I couldn't say it, but the panic I'd felt the night Erik had been shot was coming back at me in waves, gripping my chest. But Seth didn't need to hear that. I pushed the emotion down as best I could and held his hand, hoping the simple act would infuse us both with strength.

The nurse reminded us that her patient needed rest, then left the room.

"What's going on Seth? Who was that man?" I asked, my voice soft but unable to hold back. Questions had tumbled through my mind over the last several hours and I couldn't make sense of it.

Before Seth could answer, Michael inserted himself, switching into cop mode. He stepped in closer to the bed as two uniformed officers entered the room. They nodded a greeting at Michael, then took positions at the end of the bed.

"Mr. Bowman, I'd love to hear the answer to those questions," Michael said.

The set of his jaw and the way his eyes moved to the low neckline of my dress, told me he was formulating a few questions of his own about what I'd been doing with Seth this evening that had nothing to do with police work.

"His name is Luke Cavanaugh," Seth said, his voice shaky. "Three months ago his daughter died. She's all he had in life and its devastated him. The guy's not rational right now."

"How did she die?" Michael asked.

"A heart condition. Undiagnosed. One of those freak things. But Cavanaugh's been out of his mind ever since. He's blaming everyone and everything, including my energy drink. He just can't accept that she's gone."

The officers jumped in questioning Seth on the details of the attack. As I listened to the exchange, my thoughts ran back over

Luke Cavanaugh's words, his accusations, and the anger in his voice.

"Seth, he came after *you* personally. Is there something more to it?" I asked. Maybe it was the lawyer in me, but I couldn't help but wonder why Cavanaugh wouldn't have sent a mountain of litigation in VTF's direction instead of personal vengeance. Perhaps he had?

Michael looked at me quizzically, gauging the undercurrent in my question but whatever was going through his mind he kept it to himself.

Seth shifted in his bed, grimacing with the effort before responding. The pain and the medications were taking their toll.

"The man's grieving." Seth looked at me as he spoke and I saw the weight of that anguish in his sunken eyes. "Can we do this another time? I'm tired."

"Just a few more questions," Michael said, then continued the barrage, ignoring Seth's weakening condition.

Michael and I were both pushing Seth too hard, our career instincts taking over. It was important to get these get questions in while the incident was fresh, but Seth was fading fast.

"Please, don't charge him," Seth spat out. "He went crazy, anyone would. The man worked for me. He's a good guy who just can't see past his pain."

"It's not that simple, Mr. Bowman," Michael said, giving me a look that told me Cavanaugh was unlikely to walk away unscathed.

"Alright, you're done for the evening ladies and gentlemen. Move along." The doctor was in the doorway. "My patient needs his rest," he said. The officers filed out. I told Michael I'd meet him outside.

When the men were gone, I sat on the edge of the hospital bed and looked at Seth. This wasn't a man I'd known to be generous when attacked. Typically his ego shot back mortar fire when threatened yet he was asking for lenience for Cavanaugh.

"What is this Seth? Cavanaugh blames you. I saw the fury in his eyes." He cleared his throat, wincing as he did so.

"Not tonight."

"Okay, I'll let you get your rest. But there's something you're not saying."

A nurse entered the room, scowling at me as she checked the blood pressure monitor. I gave Seth a kiss on the cheek and promised I would check on him in the morning.

Michael was speaking with the officers when I stepped into the corridor. As I approached, he asked the men to meet him in the lobby and we were alone.

"You scared me again tonight. When I saw all that blood I..."

"I know, I was having flashbacks too." Flashbacks to the night Erik was killed and the night Michael and his partner Karl Janek, had saved my life.

Earlier this year I'd sleuthed out a conspiracy by a group of high-powered men trying to build the first casino in the city of Chicago, not knowing my estranged husband was part of the crew. My discovery sent six men to jail, including an alderman and Chicago's Deputy Mayor, netting me an award-winning story, and ownership of Link-Media when Erik was accidentally killed as his partner tried to silence me.

Michael lifted his hand and lightly caressed my shoulder. "I'd like nothing more than to spend the night holding you tight but the guys are waiting," he said, his eyes locked on mine.

I nodded and looked down, conflicted about what I needed tonight. The newness of our relationship and the emotional turmoil of my life over the past six months meant I still wasn't sure what I felt. I'd been keeping Michael at bay, asking for his patience, and so far he'd been willing to give me the space I needed.

"Was there something you didn't say in there? When you asked Bowman why Cavanaugh would come after him, I thought I saw something in your face. Was I mistaken?"

"I'm not sure. I think I'm just overwhelmed. Can we talk tomorrow?"

I needed time. I needed sleep. And I needed the clarity of morning before I said anything more. But the look in Cavanaugh's eyes was etched in my mind.

3

"**P**roduction meeting in five." Art Borkowski said as he popped his head into my office on his way toward the conference room.

I grabbed my Pellegrino and headed down the hall after him. Borkowski had been serving as the managing editor of Link-Media since Erik's death. Despite our rocky start as co-workers a year ago, we'd mended fences after he provided a crucial piece of information on my highway shooting story. In the four months since his appointment, I'd been impressed with his sound judgment and relentless focus on unbiased reporting. Placing Borkowski in the lead on day-to-day decisions, despite my ownership, had given the organization a sense of stability and me time to adjust. Unable to wrap my head around manage-ment of the digital news organization in light of the tragedy, I'd passed operations on to Borkowski, kept my pulse on the top line numbers, and my daily journalistic duties. I'd hoped that having a pro steering the ship would calm, not only the staff and our board of directors, but would also give me time to figure out a longer-term strategy. It was an unconventional arrangement and occasionally fraught with confusion, but we were managing.

I took a seat, and my mind drifted back to the day where at this very table, I was sent down the path to the highway shooting story. The story that would lead to the death of my former husband, my first journalism award, and the circumstances that landed ownership of this company in my lap. I took a drink and pushed the thought aside. The staff needed me to project stability and confidence whether I felt it or not. "Fake it till you make it" was my new motto. My world had been turned upside down in more ways than one. Putting one foot in front of the other and pressing on was the best thing I could do for all of us.

A text popped up on my phone. Cai. *"Are you ok? Just heard about last night. Call me!"* I sent back a short response that I was fine and would fill her in later. Was I? Images of last night and the night Erik was killed were suddenly jumbled in my head, and more accurately, the flashbacks of panic and fear. The stories I'd told myself about having moved past the trauma of Erik's death, were obviously just flat-out lies. Somehow we always told ourselves the biggest lies.

"You looked hot last night." Brynn Campbell slid into the chair on my right and tossed a newspaper in front of me. "Minus the blood I mean." She smiled. Peony pink glossed her lips, flattering her dark skin. Lipstick? Hmm, that was new. I'd only known her to be a Chapstick girl.

Brynn was my former intern and research assistant. She'd recently been promoted to associate reporter but still filled in as researcher whenever I needed her. Thus far, the highlight of her published work had been a margarita contest on North Avenue Beach. I knew she detested the lifestyle beat, but she was attacking it as if there were a Pulitzer at the other end.

I picked up the paper but couldn't resist a grimace. Somebody from the Sun-Times had gotten lucky. Thought he was there to shoot posed shots for the society column and instead he'd landed the front page with me sprawled on the floor, holding a bleeding Seth in my arms.

"Yep, Kellner just can't keep herself out of the middle of other peoples shit. You got the dirt on the lunatic with the gun? An exclusive we can use to boost eyeballs?" Borkowski grabbed the paper out of my hands and looked at me over the top of his tortoiseshell glasses.

"His name is Luke Cavanaugh," I said, as Cavanaugh's anger floated back into my mind. "He lost his 19-year-old daughter a few months back and grief has done a number on him."

"So, he busts into a swanky shindig to shoot up the place? How many marbles has the guy lost?"

I cringed. There was marshmallow deep, deep, down inside Borkowski but sometimes it was hard to look past his prickly shell. He stood, arms crossed, shirt sleeves rolled, looking at me like he was a school principal not believing my story.

"He's having a hard time accepting that she had an undiagnosed heart condition." I knew firsthand how that level of grief could upend reality. I'd known when my mother was killed in an auto accident and again when Erik was shot. Images of his broken, bleeding body flashed through my head. Heartache, sorrow, and anger, all swooped in and consumed me at moments I couldn't control or predict. The world simply shifted into a place you no longer recognized after a trauma.

"Odd place to lose your shit. I know Bowman's your guy, but those ads for that stupid, over-priced drink of his are irritating me. I'd love to see them go away. Whatever happened to using a good old cup of java to goose your engine? Why does everybody need an eight-dollar bottle of liquid herbs to make them feel good? Probably tastes like shit," Borkowski mused.

The group snickered awkwardly. Bottles of the stuff had been showing up around our own office. The staff was largely in their twenties and thirties and based on Monday morning kibitzing, playing as hard as they worked. A bottle of liquid energy had its appeal as did the trendiness of the hot new product that everyone was talking about.

"Martinez, you're on the follow-up," Borkowski said to one of my fellow reporters. "Short and sweet. Go with the grief angle and give me good background on Bowman."

I opened my mouth to object but didn't get out the words before Borkowski was on me.

"Kellner, don't give me that look. You're tight with the vic. And, I don't want your love life center stage. It's been done already."

Brynn stifled a laugh while I resisted the urge to kick her under the table. And to clear the record that Seth and I weren't romantically involved, but that would be protesting too much.

"What's on your plate?" Borkowski asked.

"There are a couple firms in the tech incubator getting some traction," I said. "I've got a meeting with Janelle Platt to discuss their performance."

"Everyone loves a Chicago success story. I hope at least one of them has a product that doesn't require fifteen acronyms and a PhD to understand. And don't pass up the opportunity to ask her how the hell she thinks she'll ever get elected mayor with her husband in jail."

"Ex-husband," I corrected. Janelle Platt's former husband Owen was serving a ten-year sentence for public corruption charges stemming from the reporting I'd done which uncovered a casino scheme. My investigation had brought down Owen Platt, who at the time, was Chicago's deputy mayor. Janelle and I had formed a unique bond that only two women who had been jointly betrayed could have. But I too wondered if the city would attach Owen's dirt to his spit-fire ex-wife.

Borkowski continued through the group and we kicked around concepts until he was satisfied that there was an adequate amount of new material in the pipeline.

"That's a wrap people. Pick up the pace. I need new content." His tone had taken on a level of urgency. With viewership falling, his plea was no longer a request. "Kellner, hold up."

As the crew filed out, Borkowski leaned his forearms on the table. "Have you been able to sweet talk Ramelli?" I shook my head. "What the hell is the hold up? We're going to miss our slot in the schedule if I don't have approval on the spend by early next week."

"I know. The board is dragging their feet on this."

"Well, figure out how to get skates on those feet because if we lose our time slot, we're looking at a six-month delay, minimum. And a hit to our revenue in the next fiscal year. You own 51%, can't you just write the damn check?"

"No, the number is too big. We need board approval. Look, I understand the urgency. I'll find a way to make it happen."

"Good, 'cause I'm starting to wonder if they want this thing to fail," Borkowski said without a hint of irony.

Unfortunately, so was I. Returning to my office, I picked up my phone determined not to let Wade Ramelli brush me off again.

"Wade, we need to talk," I said, when he picked up. "By that I mean sit down face-to-face and hash this out. Whatever hesitation the board has about my ability to run this company needs to be separated from our current needs. This software upgrade is essential."

"Then Erik should have made it a priority in his budget."

I had no answer. It was tough to defend a dead guy.

"I can't speak to what Erik did or didn't do," I said, tapping a pencil against my desk, frustrated that our conversations always came back to what Erik should have done. I let out a breath and redirected. "What I know is that we need to be forward-thinking and not react to the market after the competition moves to the next level of technology. The industry is moving past us. Borkowski and I have laid out the circumstances as they exist today, the ROI, and our revenue projections if we don't stay ahead of this. We presented this to the board six weeks ago. It's time to act."

"Andrea, I appreciate your passion but we're just not convinced that the circumstances are as dire as you've made them out to be. Or as urgent."

I paused, considering my next move. May as well cut to the chase. "We both know that this isn't really about the investment. It's about strategy. The company needs a plan of attack and Borkowski and I are trying to provide that. Nothing is going to work if management and the board can't come to a shared perspective on the future of the company. Haven't we been through enough? A year. I need the board to commit to giving me a year to prove that I can make this work. You owe me that." I paused, listening to the uncomfortable silence at the other end of the phone. "You owe Erik that."

I had pulled out my guilt card. As Erik's mentor, and a board member since he'd founded the company, I had to hold on to hope that emotion could sway him. And if I could sway him, then the rest of the board would fall into place.

"That was a cheap shot. You know I can't make any promises. This isn't as simple as my obligation to Erik. We have obligations to our investors as well. Readership is trending down, ad revenue is not holding up to last year. A software upgrade is not the fix. I'm not sure we have the time to let you be indulgent," he said, his voice riddled with condescension. "We'll speak soon, but that's all I'm willing to commit to."

I ended the call, flopping back in my chair in frustration, angry with his tone and the implications about my abilities. Borkowski's comment about the board wanting us to fail rushed back. I didn't know what irritated me more, the sexism or the mistrust.

4

———

W hy hadn't Seth waited for me to pick him up from the hospital? Another dumb, cocky decision no doubt. After the staff meeting I'd called Northwestern to check on Seth, only to be told he'd been released. So, I left the office, picked up a grocery bag of prepared meals from the deli, and jumped in a cab headed over to his Lake Shore Drive condo. The only question was would I find him passed out on the floor?

When I arrived, the uniformed doorman put in a call, then sent me up. I rapped on the red lacquered door and waited confused once again by male bravado that let a shooting victim feel it was smart to leave the hospital alone. Footsteps sounded moments later. The door swung open and Seth stood on the other side, his arm in a sling. He held a towel in his free hand. Wet splotches dotted his light gray T-shirt. His muscular legs were hidden by a pair of sweatpants. He motioned me in, mopping his close-cropped hair as he shuffled barefoot down the hall.

The hallway opened into a glass-box living room. Sunlight streamed in, bouncing off the hard, slick surfaces. Marble, glass, chrome. Seth wasn't a throw pillow and dried flower kind of guy. He'd hired a name brand designer a year ago, and she'd transformed what had been a lovely apartment into a showstopper. The glistening water of Lake Michigan and a dead-on view of the Navy Pier Ferris wheel framed the extraordinary views from the 28th floor.

The condo served as a perfect backdrop for the type of entertaining Seth liked to do—cocktails with well-heeled, well-connected types, or one-on-one's with young, female, flavors-of-the-week. Romantically, commitment wasn't his thing, but at least he was honest about it.

In many respects, we were an odd pairing as friends. He was all about flash, and the belief that you had to look successful to be successful. I was quiet determination. What linked us was fierce loyalty. Neither of us made friends easily, acquaintances, yes, but friendship was reserved for the handful of people we knew had our backs. And Seth had earned my friendship years ago when he stepped in to help my sister Lane after she'd had a run in with an abusive boyfriend. To this day, I still didn't know what he'd done or said to the guy, but he'd never bothered Lane again. Our schedules kept us from seeing each other more than a few times a year, but we both knew we'd drop everything if we needed each other.

He tossed the towel on the coffee table and folded himself slowly into the black Italian leather sofa.

"This thing is driving me nuts already." He patted the thick wading on his shoulder. "And I smell like hospital."

He looked like hospital too. Even more gaunt and sallow than last night. A prescription bottle sat on the glass-topped table along with pages of post-op instructions. Knowing Seth, he likely assumed the medical instructions were optional or that he knew more about his own physiology than the pros.

"You know I would have picked you up." He shrugged,

already impatient with being an invalid. "I brought you some food. Can I get you anything now? You're looking drained."

"Grab me a protein drink out of the fridge. But watch your step. Had to stick my head under the kitchen sink sprayer and the whole damn floor is wet."

I put the grocery bag in the fridge, mopped up the floor, retrieved the drink, and then grabbed a pillow out of his bedroom. Twisting open the cap, I handed the bottle to Seth. He looked up at me through bloodshot eyes as I tucked the pillow under his elbow.

"How are you feeling?"

"Achy, tired, like I'm moving through sludge. Par for the course they tell me. But no way I'm keeping this harness on for six weeks. Would you please sit down? All this hovering is making uncomfortable."

"Well, having a near-death experience causes that. Get used to it. Now's not the time for macho-ing your way to health."

"You're overreacting. Keep it to facts, not headlines. I know my body. The one-size-fits-all recovery plan is for couch potatoes who don't know the difference between a ketone and ketchup."

I sat next to him on the couch and leaned my elbows on my knees. "You forget, I'm the one that held you bleeding on the floor."

He tipped his head back and closed his eyes. "Whatever. Send me a bill for your dress."

"I know you're in pain, so I'll resist telling you what an asshole you're being."

He opened his eyes and pulled his head back up. "Sorry. You're right. Not surprisingly, I'm a terrible patient. Thanks for being there, I appreciate it." He sneezed my hand. "Last night wasn't the evening either of us planned. In addition to all of this," he said, lifting his shoulder slightly, "The timing is shit. All I can think about is how I need to be at work right now."

"Forgiven. Now tell me about Cavanaugh before I take your pain meds away." I'd been unable to think of little else since last night. "What do you know about him other than his daughters' death?"

Seth paused and stared out the window. "He worked for me for four years. Ran my production team. When his daughter died, his worked started slipping," he said, his voice low. "He'd forget to place orders. Staffing wasn't getting ramped up. Demand was accelerating, and we needed to up our game, but with all the fuck-ups Cavanaugh was making, distribution had been crippled."

"Did you suggest he get help? Therapy?"

Seth nodded and let out a sigh. His face was wracked with sorrow.

"We talked several times, I told him that he needed more time to process everything, suggested he take some off at full pay. But he wasn't having any of it. Eventually I had to intervene." He paused. "I'd run out of options. So I passed most of his responsibilities on to someone else. We'd have been dead in the water otherwise. When I told Cavanaugh about the changes, he lost it. Started tearing up the place, screaming that it was my fault his daughter was dead. I had to fire him. I hated to do it, but he didn't leave me with any other choice. I have a lot of respect for the man but I couldn't take the risk. I told him I'd happily give him his job back when he got his act together, but I don't think he heard anything that day."

So maybe this wasn't just about a dead child. Sounded like Cavanaugh's whole world had crashed around him. I knew what that was like. My own mother had died suddenly when I was a teenager and the trauma had changed all of us, my father in particular. It had forced me out of childhood long before I should have been.

"Is that why you don't want to press charges? You feel sorry for him?"

Seth hesitated. "I also don't want the publicity. I've got an IPO planned for early next year."

"And negative publicity would bring unwanted attention and scare away investors."

He nodded. "You know how I am, I'm protective of information. As far as I'm concerned, company details are a need-to-know issue. The fewer ears involved, the less opportunity for rumors and backstabbing. So, this isn't for public consumption, but right now orders are coming in faster than I can finance them. A high-class problem I know, but I'm struggling with cash flow. We can't have one more thing go wrong. If Cavanaugh continues on this misdirected rant about his daughter, I'm screwed. Millions of dollars are on the line. He wants someone to blame for his daughter's death. He's angry that I fired him and conflating the two."

"Surely he's seen autopsy results? Science doesn't lie," I said.

"Then maybe it's just flat-out revenge? I'm not sure he can separate the two. I'm in the cross hairs. He knows about the IPO. What better revenge than scaring off my financial partners? Andrea, I can't let his grief destroy my company."

Seth's voice had taken on an urgency that I hadn't seen in him before. He sat forward. Perspiration now beaded his upper lip. I didn't know if it was the pain or fear of losing his company that had him terrified.

He looked at me expectantly. "I need to know what Cavanaugh has said to the police. And whether they're taking his accusations seriously. Can you help me?"

I hesitated imagining Michael's reaction but also my reporter antenna was up. Something felt incomplete as if Seth was holding back. I didn't doubt the financial vulnerability but my gut told me this explanation was too neat and tidy.

"Something I don't understand is what connection Cavanaugh's daughter had to VTF?" I asked, needing a few more questions answered. "Why does he think her death is related to the drink?"

He shrugged. "She was around the plant all the time. Kind of grew up there. Every time I saw her she had a bottle in her hand. I assume that continued at home. We basically sell it to employees for next to nothing. Beyond that, you'd have to ask him."

I still wasn't feeling at ease, but Seth was clearly unsettled by the uncertainty. "I'll make some inquiries, but I can't promise anything. My questions could bring attention you don't want."

"I understand. Whatever you can do would help. Thank you."

I said goodbye, feeling uncomfortable for some reason I couldn't put my finger on.

5

I walked into Intelligentsia Coffee fifteen minutes late and craned my neck looking for my sister Lane. No sign of her, not that I should have been worried. Timeliness was not one of her virtues although I might have trouble defining *one*. I ordered a pot of Pearl Jasmine and grabbed a table, wondering what the hell she wanted now.

Our relationship could only be described as complicated. She was three years older but had none of the classic firstborn traits. After our mother died, we watched helplessly as our father slipped into depression. Lane moved into denial, pushing every teenage boundary she could find, while I was forced into the role of parent to them both. I still hadn't forgiven her.

It didn't help that our old pattern had continued into adulthood. Lane was a realtor whose choice of projects, men, and general life-style seemed to swing her from crisis to crisis. Unfortunately, I was her back-up plan when those life choices fell flat. She'd borrowed my car, my couch, my money, and yet was always one deal away from paying off her debt. And dummy me had let it happen.

Pedestrians rushed past the coffee-bar window as cold easterly winds tugged at their jackets. It was mid-afternoon and traffic was still brisk on Randolph Street. Millennium Park was steps away, as was Michigan Avenue, which meant shopping, restaurants, and a dozen different bus lines all converging. As I sipped my tea, my conversation with Seth flooded back. The stress of his business had been showing on his face even before the shooting. A fitness buff like him should know he'd jeopardize his recovery if he didn't take it easy, but I suspected dollar signs were going to cloud his judgement. For the first time in our relationship, I was worried about his health and the situation with Cavanaugh wouldn't help.

Cavanaugh's face still haunted me. The pain, the anguish, *the blame.* What had caused him to accuse Seth after he'd been given a valid medical explanation for his daughter's death? He'd tried to kill the man. I understood grief, but attempting to take someone's life was personal. Threads of doubt gnawed at my stomach. It was as if I was looking at a puzzle with no picture and therefore could only see the obvious corner pieces.

Lane breezed in as I finished my first cup, looking like she'd run the last five blocks. Loose locks of hair sprung from her topknot and her blouse had managed to come loose from the waistband of her skirt. She waved as she saw me. Few who knew us saw much of a family resemblance. She was tall, blond, and sturdy. I was short, brunette, and petitely built. The one thing that connected us was our turquoise eyes.

"Did you order me a coffee?" she asked, then gave me a peck on the cheek.

"It would have been cold by the time you got here."

She rolled her eyes, tossed her overflowing tote bag on the chair, then went to the counter to order. A woman juggling a stroller and her coffee walked by, bumping Lane's seat in the process and sending the bag crashing to the floor. She mumbled her apologies and kept going as her toddler started to wail. I shrugged it off and bent to picked up the satchel. Lipstick, pencils, a smattering of business cards, and a half-drunk bottle of VTF energy drink went rolling. Hmm, even Lane drank the stuff. I returned her items unceremoniously to the tote.

Order placed, Lane joined me at the table. A large mug of cappuccino was her drink of choice today, although if it contained ample caffeine, she drank it. She stirred cinnamon into the decorative foam, warming her free hand on the cup.

"Hey, the reason I wanted to see you is we have to talk about what we're going to do with the three-flat in Englewood."

"What do you mean? Why would we do anything?"

After Erik's death, one of my surprises was learning that he and my real estate agent sister had purchased an investment property together without telling me. More accurately, Erik had served as the banker, with ulterior motives of his own after I shot the idea down. Like it or not, I'd been thrown into being a landlord. Intertwining myself any deeper into Lane's financial dealings had not been an appealing thought, but I hadn't had the energy to do anything about it yet.

Unfortunately, I also had a long history with Lane's convoluted business sense and lack of fiscal restraint. I'd bailed her out of more jams than I cared to admit and the ledger was still not in the black. As any therapist would say, I needed to firm up my boundaries where Lane was concerned, but it wasn't a battle I was ready for.

"It's profitable," I said, taking a drink of my tea. "We're fully rented. Is there a problem I don't know about?" I asked, dreading her answer.

"Well, I've been thinking about selling. Now that everything has calmed down for you, it might be a good idea. Buying the place was Erik's idea. You made it clear you never wanted to own it."

"No, I didn't want to own it. You and Erik made that investment in secret and over my objection, if you recall. However, the problem with selling now is that we've owned it less than a year. We'd lose money if we sold now. There's been no time for appreciation."

Despite her bad judgement, Lane was always into these deals for the profit. There was an ulterior motive. I put my elbows on the table and gave her a hard look, distrust filling my mind.

"But you keep saying you want to simplify your life. Right? Isn't this one way to start?" she asked, lifting her coffee to her lips.

"What's this all about Lane?" I said, hearing the impatience in my voice. I knew my sister well enough to know that my well-being was rarely her top priority. She wanted something, and it probably had nothing to do with me.

She started to speak, saw the look on my face and closed her mouth. Good choice.

"Ok, I've gotten into a little trouble with one of the tenants. He's a few months behind on rent. I started eviction procedures, but he's gone hostile. Now he's turning the other tenants against me and they're threatening a rent strike."

"And you haven't felt you needed to tell me about it?" I pinched the bridge of my nose and shook my head. "What were you thinking? This is exactly the kind of situation I was afraid of."

My former career as a prosecutor had trained me to control outward displays of emotion. It was a helpful skill as an attorney and as a journalist, but Lane had a way of pushing my buttons that made that discipline fade into the ether.

"I thought I had it handled." Lane shrugged, sipped her coffee, and avoided looking at me.

"What are their demands?"

"They want a new furnace. He said they have to heat their

apartments with the oven in the winter. But my furnace guy said the equipment has a couple more years in it so I think this is retaliation for the rent increase. You used to be a lawyer. Can't you just write a scary-sounding letter and make it go away?"

"Being a landlord is just a pain in the ass," I said, ignoring her poorly reasoned legal argument. "A new furnace is going to cost us twenty grand. Its either take the hit, or we find ourselves on Channel 5 when someone freezes to death. What a choice." I let out a sigh and turned away. Damn.

"I know it sounds bad, but that's why I was thinking it's a good time to sell. Eliminate the problem. Pull out our cash."

"A new owner is not going to want to take on a tenant problem or a major expense right off the bat. I know your realtor optimism is endless but have a little common sense. Even if we did find a buyer willing to walk into a legal mess, the price cut we'd need to take would put us underwater on the loan. Look, get a couple estimates on a new furnace, run the comps, talk to a real estate attorney, then we can figure out what to do. In the meantime, I'll start praying that this cold snap is short-lived."

I poured the balance of my tea in a to-go cup at the counter and said goodbye to Lane, leaving her to come up with a better solution. She'd promised repeatedly that this building would require nothing of my time. Instead, it looked like it would require my checkbook. Yet again I was being left with another crappy situation to clean up and an untrustworthy sister.

6

I was still fuming when I returned to my co-op. Lane had gotten us into yet another mess. As if I needed one more complication in my life right now. When the hell was any normalcy going to return? Walter, my blue-eyed Ragdoll cat, greeted me at the door. I picked him up and he went limp in my arms as I stroked his fur. His purr comforted both of us. I filled his bowl with kibble, refreshed his water, then went to my bedroom to change.

Boxes of Carrara marble tile were stacked in the corner awaiting my go ahead on bathroom remodeling. I'd bought the apartment as my marriage was failing and fought tooth and nail to keep her. It was on the 11th floor of a grand old 1920s building with tall ceilings, herringbone floors, and a stunning wrap-around terrace. I was in love with the place. It also hadn't been remodeled in fifty years and needed a top-to-bottom refresh.

The kitchen had been nearly complete when Erik was killed and I simply hadn't been in the mood for the chaos of more remodeling. Luckily my contractor had been patient with me but if I didn't get started soon, I'd be back at the bottom of his schedule. In the meantime, I'd chosen to live with the boxes.

Michael and I had made plans to meet for dinner at Fig & Olive, so I laid out a silk blouse, pencil skirt, and a new set of lace lingerie that hadn't made it out of the drawer since I'd purchased them. As I showered, I thought about how I was going to broach Seth's request with Michael. I'd seen Michael's look last night. Knew he was wondering about my relationship with Seth. Peppering him with questions wasn't going to calm the water.

My phone was ringing as I turned off the water. I tossed on my robe and picked up.

"Hi Andrea, this is Candiss Nadell. I'm calling to check on our friend Seth. How's he doing?"

"His injuries are relatively minor, compared to what could have happened." A shiver escaped as I was brought back to the terror I'd felt when Luke Cavanaugh pulled the trigger. "Luckily, it appears there'll be no permanent damage."

"I can't tell you how upset I am over this. It's been so traumatic for all of us at Drea. Of course, we're cooperating fully with the police, and the Peninsula Hotel is as well. It's been quite the onslaught of calls and emails. Our members are beside themselves with worry."

I imagined Candiss had been on the phone ever since the ambulance left the hotel late last night. This wasn't a crowd afraid of giving their opinions. And the local news was absolutely giddy with the drama.

"Is there anything I can do for Seth? I've put in a call, but I suspect he's keeping to himself today."

"Hopefully he's turned his phone off," I laughed. "I'm sure he'll get back to you in the next few days."

"This makes me feel better. Andrea, could we get together for coffee tomorrow morning? I'd love to speak to you further about the Drea Foundation. You've been very generous financially but I'm hoping we might find other ways to get you involved. I'd hoped to speak with you more last night but..."

I agreed to the meeting, but I suspected Candiss would be looking for more of a time commitment than I was able to give right now. However, it wouldn't hurt to get to know someone as well-connected as Candiss Nadell.

———

MICHAEL WAS at the bar when I arrived, a scotch in front of him. Soft lighting glowed from underneath the thick marble counter. R&B played gently in the background just loud enough to mute the conversations in the modern two-level space. I watched him for a moment, admiring how his dark hair curled at the back of his neck. Gotta love a guy who could play tough all day and still knew to put on a decent sport coat for dinner. I walked over, placed my hand on his shoulder and he turned. A large smile spread over his face.

"You looked beautiful tonight." He gave me a kiss, then ran his eyes appreciatively down my body, sending a wave of heat up the back of my neck. "Although I liked last night's dress better, minus the blood of course." He smiled. "Come on. Our table is ready." He picked up his glass, and we followed the hostess to the window overlooking Oak Street. At this point in the season, only a handful of lonely pedestrians hustled by on the street below. The row of high end shops that lined the street were dark except for front lighting, but it took a lot to stop a window shopper this time of the year. Avoiding the brisk wind blowing off of Lake Michigan was a bigger priority.

I ordered a Cabernet, and we settled in.

"It's good to see you," Michael said, taking my hand. "I'm sorry I couldn't spend more time with you last night. Are you alright?" He reached over and pushed back a strand of hair that had fallen over my face.

"I'm okay. A little shaken that's all. What happened with Cavanaugh?"

I wasn't sure why I was switching the conversation so quickly off of the personal, particularly after seeing the longing in his gaze. I had so many conflicting emotions about this budding relationship—desire, fear, the need to protect myself by slowing things down—that I was certain Michael had to be as confused moment-to-moment as I was. I fell back into distancing him whenever it started to feel comfortable. One of these days, I knew he would need more or perhaps nothing more at all. For now, this was the best I could manage.

"He's in custody but refusing a lawyer," Michael answered, but I could see his eyes tighten at the question. "And Bowman's still insisting he's not going to press charges. I don't know what the hell's up with these two."

"Assault with a deadly weapon?"

Michael nodded and took a sip of his drink. "There were enough witnesses to make that stick."

"And defense will focus on his state of mind given the recent death of his daughter. Probation. One year, tops." I couldn't help but try the case in my mind. It was still force of habit.

"Should we order? Work can wait." He smiled and grabbed my hand.

I nodded, and we discussed the appetizers, choosing zucchini carpaccio, mushroom crostini, and prosciutto to share.

"Has he talked about why he shot Seth?" I said, the moment our server left the table.

Michael's jaw tensed before he answered. "Essentially he keeps repeating that he blames Bowman for his daughter's death. Says there was something in her energy drink. Guy seems on the verge of a psychotic breakdown if you ask me." He paused, taking a sip of his scotch. "But Bowman probably told you that already."

I ignored the innuendo. I didn't owe Michael an explanation for our friendship. But my ears perked up. "Is he accusing Seth of putting drugs in her drink?"

"It isn't clear what his accusation is, I'm not sure he knows. The girl's dead, she drank a lot of the stuff, therefore it must have caused her death."

"What about the pathology report?"

Michael put down his glass and gave me a long stare. "You know the drill, if there's no sign of foul play the ME does an external exam and a basic tox screen. Nothing out of the ordinary was identified. Cavanaugh pushed, they opened her up, found she had an enlarged heart. Other than that, the report also showed high liver enzymes but that could be from partying too hard. She may have only been nineteen, but Cavanaugh says she was a party girl. Well, his actual words were 'she hangs with people she shouldn't'."

"Would you look into her history?"

"I thought we were here to have a nice dinner, just us, a quiet personal evening. I'm sitting across the table from a reporter tonight. What are you asking me?" Michael pulled back, his arms now crossed over his chest.

"Well, if there's more information from the pathologist, or the medical examiner, would you tell me? After all, I was in the middle of this incident."

"Is this about Bowman? How about you tell me what's going on between the two of you?" His voice had lowered a notch. "You said you wanted to take things slow. Things with us, I mean. But if it's because you want to see other people, you need to say so right now. I don't share."

Shit. One question too many. "No, that's not what I meant at all. Seth's a friend. There has never been anything else between us." I reached over, laid my hand on his arm and looked into his eyes. "With everything that's gone on over the last few months, there's a lot we haven't talked about, like our respective marriages. I need some time, but it's not because I'm seeing anyone else."

Michael relaxed a little. He'd told me that he and his ex-wife had reached an impasse over his career, but that's about all I knew. I hadn't wanted to go down this path. Somehow sharing the painful details of my marriage would have moved our status from dating to relationship, so I'd avoided the subject. It seemed Michael wasn't going to let me wallow in denial any longer.

I paused and let out a breath. "Mine was ending because of infidelity. I've been deeply hurt by a man I truly loved, a man who kept secrets and told lies. I'm wounded, not only by his death, but by the hurt he caused while we were together. I guess I'm trying to trust again and I've pushed you away because I'm scared. But that's about me, not you. I'm afraid I'll be hurt again."

I could feel the tears slip over onto my cheek. Michael wiped them away, not taking his eyes off mine until he leaned in for a kiss.

I was confused and angry with myself. And in the process, I'd treated Michael as if he were simply a source. But I'd also learned there may have been something in the energy drink, something that Seth hadn't mentioned, and that opened up a whole host of new questions.

7

I walked into the restaurant at nine a.m. and checked in with the maître d'. The wood was dark, the leather rugged, the mirrors antiqued. I could smell the faint whiff of sandalwood and cloves. Money, the room smelled of money. How many millions of dollars in corporate deals had changed hands in this room?

I was unaccustomed to the obvious maleness of it all as I was escorted through a sea of middle-aged men in dark suits to a booth in the back of the restaurant. Candiss had asked me to meet her at Margeaux Brasserie in the Waldorf Hotel and the power breakfast meetings were already in full swing. It seemed of another era, where men brokered their business meetings against the backdrop of a dark, expensive, steakhouse vibe. If it were later in the day, scotch and cigars would have felt at home here, women on the other hand, did not. I could only assume Candiss did not share my discomfort.

I had just ordered a pot of Earl Grey when Candiss arrived. Her red St Johns suit and the serious rope of pearls around her neck drew all eyes her way. She glided into the room, carrying her tiny frame as if she were royalty. Not a hair out of place.

Every element of her appearance perfectly chosen. True wealth didn't need to shout. The fineness of the tailoring, the cut of the cloth, all spoke volumes.

She gave me a buss on the cheek when I stood to greet her.

"I see you've ordered tea. Coffee for me, black," she said to the waitress.

Candiss settled into her seat. "Tell me, how is Seth? I've been worried sick. I called Northwestern Hospital to check on him but they were reticent. I understand of course, but it's been maddening."

"He's home now. They released him yesterday. He's not one for staying away from work, but hopefully he's following Doctor's orders."

"I'm so glad. I'll send over some goodies from Eataly, although I suspect he lives on protein shakes, vitamin packs, and red meat."

We both chuckled and ordered fruit plates. The Seth I knew didn't count calories, he measured, charted, and graphed every morsel that went into his mouth for its nutrient content using an app on his phone. He would pull up his numbers and adjust his diet if he wasn't happy with his potassium intake that week. I had moments of admiring his discipline. Eating well was important to me too, but who the hell wanted to live never allowing yourself the occasional cookie?

"I'm sure he'd love to hear from you," I said. Although I wasn't sure how she and Seth had gotten to know each other, or how well.

Candiss was looking down the aisle behind me, her eyes narrowed and her mouth tight. I paused for a moment, watching her, curious about what had shut her down when suddenly, as if a switch had been flipped, her face softened and her eyes regained their sparkle.

"Marcus, so good to see you," she said, holding out her hand to a man who'd approached our table. He was elegant in a navy suit and French cuffs, with sparse gray hair slicked back over his head. He smiled tentatively at Candiss.

"I saw you sitting here, so of course, I had to come say hello. I don't mean to interrupt, give my best to Aaron. Perhaps we can all have dinner one of these days," he said.

Candiss flashed an effusive smile. "Of course, that would be lovely. I'll be sure to tell him you asked about him."

He nodded and turned back toward his table. Candiss's face went flat again the moment his back was turned.

"Is everything okay? You look upset," I said.

She turned to me, shaking off her dark mood as quickly as it had washed over her. "No, just some old history. Marcus made the mistake of lying to me once. I don't tolerate liars. Ever."

Despite her smile and the soft tone in her voice, there was steel in her eyes. I sensed that she was a woman who never forgot a slight.

"So, where were we?" She sipped her coffee and then patted the corners of her mouth with her napkin. "Andrea, we at Drea are quite beside ourselves over this incident. Members have been calling in droves, immensely upset to have been so near harm. That Seth was injured is tragic, but I shudder to think what could have happened. The images going through my mind are truly appalling."

I imagined Drea's wealthy patrons did indeed have a few choice words for Candiss, some of which were probably unkind. It was also likely that the incident had put a serious damper on her fundraising efforts.

The waitress returned, setting fruit and croissants on the table. Candiss gently adjusted her plate, apparently unhappy with the angle of the presentation.

"Of course, I had quite a stern meeting with the manager of the Peninsula," she said. "Their security team completely fell down on the job." She leaned in, lowering her voice. "There is no excuse for that level of incompetence, and at the Peninsula of all places."

Candiss spoke as if counseling a wayward student. She was one of those women who could cut with a raised eyebrow or a slight turn of the head. Every move of her body seemed deliberate. I imagined her contact at the Peninsula was still quaking from her dress down.

"Have the police spoken to you yet?" I asked.

"Yes, not that we know anything other than what I'm sure they've been told by others. Such a loss of self-control. Have you heard anything about this man or why he wanted to harm Seth?"

The question was logical given that her organization sponsored the event, but something told me to hold back. Beyond instinct, I wasn't sure why. Was she fishing for news of a scandal? Perhaps she knew of Seth's IPO? They were acquainted after all.

"I understand that the gentleman recently suffered a loss in his family, a child," I said, keeping to the obvious facts. "Apparently, he's dealing with some psychological issues as a result, as we all would be."

"Ah, I see. I guess we're all capable of extreme measures when something important is taken from us."

She looked across the room, her gaze distant. I found myself wondering what this wealthy, pampered woman knew of extreme measures.

"Well, on to more positive things," she said. "Andrea, I'd love for you to consider taking a more active role in Drea. Money, of course, is important, and you've been quite generous over the past few years, but we need female role models. Particularly women such as yourself who are making inroads in male-dominated fields."

The sales persona was back. I could see immediately that

Candiss was completely at home in the role of female charmer. Her face lit up, she spoke with enthusiasm. It had to be her philanthropic secret weapon. I paused, took a sip of my tea, letting the aroma of bergamot and croissants waft over me. I wasn't hesitating over the organizational mission, but I was uncertain of my ability to commit the time.

"I'm honored that you would think of me," I said. "I'm very supportive and committed to the work the Drea Foundation is doing, but I need to be sensitive to over-extending myself. Currently the board is about 50% women. What do you feel you need from me?"

"I knew you would have done your homework prior to our meeting." She smiled, picked up her fork, and skewered a raspberry from the fruit plate between us. "Yes, we have strong support from women. But to be blunt, there is simply too much of the ladies-who-lunch crowd. Don't get me wrong, I'm immensely happy for the time and money our members put in, but we need more women who can contribute from a business perspective. We need women such as yourself who can be role models for the young women we support. These young people need to see there are women who make their way in the world, beyond marrying well."

"Candiss, I appreciate your candor. Let me give this some thought and we can speak again. As you can imagine, my energies are focused on Link-Media at the moment. We've still got so much work to do to stabilize the organization and build for the future."

"I understand. I'd be thrilled to have you involved in whatever capacity you feel is appropriate." She paused and took a sip of her coffee. "Did you know that Wade Ramelli is a dear friend of mine?"

I shook my head, caught off guard once again by the connections this woman had.

"Yes, Aaron and I play bridge with Wade and his wife Barbara once a week." She leaned over and placed her hand on mine. "I'll urge him to give you his full support. That way you'll have fewer demands on your time."

I felt myself draw inward. Had Ramelli spoken to her of our situation at Link-Media? I suddenly had the sense I was part of a hidden chess game.

8

W alking out of the Waldorf after my meeting with Candiss, I was annoyed, and had the vague sense that I was being manipulated without knowing how or why. I'd gotten the distinct impression that Candiss knew something about the tension between Ramelli and me. I imagined Ramelli with a condescending smile as he dealt a hand of bridge to her and her husband and then gossiped about our struggles over sherry. Surely he knew better than to disclose material nonpublic information, but the idea of him flapping his mouth with friends, even innocently, made me uncomfortable.

As did Candiss's readiness to stack the deck to get what she wanted. It suggested an agenda broader than the one she'd outlined to me. Was there another reason she wanted me involved with Drea? I made a mental note to see if I could explore the board dynamics a little deeper before making a decision about joining.

I buttoned my coat against the wind as the doorman hailed a cab. It was a cold gray day, and the temperature seemed to have dropped while I'd been in the restaurant. Once inside the cab, I instructed the driver to take me to the Merchandise Mart.

Janelle Platt and I had arranged for an interview this morning. Wanting to promote her support of Chicago's growing tech entrepreneurs, she'd asked me to meet her at the heart of the movement, the city's technology center.

As her mayoral bid started to pick up steam, she was more than happy to give me a front-row seat to the campaign. And I was just as happy to take it. There had to be some benefit from our corrupt husbands' intersecting history. I'm sure she thought I'd go easy on her. Borkowski would slap me upside the head if I went too soft, but for now I thought of it as simply having a better understanding of her past.

Exiting the cab on Wells, I walked through the side entrance. Given the state of my bathroom remodeling project, Ann Sacks and the Graff showroom pulled at me. But shopping for tile and faucets would have to wait. The first two floors of the building were design showrooms open to the public. They were great places to browse and gather inspiration, but deep pockets were generally needed if you wanted to buy. This building was the mecca of Chicago's interior design world, especially if you were into modern Italian anything, and I was.

My heels clicked on the marble floor as I made my way toward the main entrance lobby but the sound was muffled by the high ceilings in the corridor.

Also known as theMart, the building was so large it had its own zip code. Built in 1930 by Marshall Field & Co., it stood at 4 million square feet of space and housed Chicago's wholesale showrooms. As Chicago's apparel and gift industries had died, the buildings tenants had consolidated around the interior design industry. In 2012, a portion of the building was redeveloped to support the digital technology community. Named 1871, after the year of the great Chicago fire, it was home to 400 early-stage start-ups and housed satellite offices for a number of local colleges. Janelle had some specific businesses here she wanted shown off which I assumed were to hold up as examples of more to come should she be elected.

I was whisked up to the sixth floor where a receptionist directed me down a wide hallway to a conference room. The space was mildly industrial with bright, enticing graphics decorating the walls, open workstations, and multiple small pod-like seating areas set up for impromptu collaboration. Janelle was on the phone when I entered the glass box room. She motioned me in and wrapped up the call.

"Andrea, so good to see you," she said, giving me a big embrace. "You look well. Please, let's sit."

Her navy jacket and skirt were more toned down than what I'd seen her wear in the past, but I guessed they were still Armani. A gold lapel pin with the Chicago insignia graced her collar. Ah, it was her new campaign wardrobe.

"Congratulations on your announcement. It's quite exciting news." I took a seat next to her at the conference table.

"Ha, is that the best you've got? Come on Andrea, with our history, I know you're thinking 'what the fuck is she doing?' Everyone else is. Based on what we've gone through together, you and I should at least have the balls to be straight with each other."

We laughed, and she grabbed my hand.

"Why don't we get the personal stuff out of the way, then you can grill me on the business shit. Tell me, how are you holding up?" She shivered. "Sorry, I hate that question. It's a polite way of asking, 'are you drinking yourself into a stupor? Or have you tried to slit your wrists yet?'"

"Neither, thankfully, although there have been moments." I laughed, a little quieter this time. "I'm managing, some days better than others. Like you, I'm doing what good Midwestern women do—carrying on. I keep using the word 'numb' which seems to be the only appropriate word I can come up with. I feel drained of emotion. What about you?" I asked.

"Still fucking pissed off. But I'm using my anger in the best possible way, for revenge."

"By going after the job Owen wanted."

"Exactly. The job he thought was rightfully his as deputy mayor. Instead, the greedy son of a bitch can watch me kick dirt in his face, from jail."

"What do you think your chances are against Mayor Rendell in February?" I asked, touching the icon of my recording app.

"Oh, into work mode are you? Darn, now I have to watch my language." She tugged at the lapels of her jacket, sat up straighter, and brushed her bangs off her forehead.

Chicago had an unusual no-party mayoral election process. All candidates who met the requirements were on the ballot in February regardless of party affiliation. If no candidate took a majority, the top two participated in a run-off election in April. Current Mayor Rendell and Janelle Platt were the leading contenders at this point in mid-November, but sensing vulnerability, the field was now at ten candidates. A number likely to tighten as the year came to a close.

"Well, as you know, Chicago has been in turmoil since the casino scandal. Although Rendell was not directly implicated in the backdoor casino wrangling, his administration and his judgement have to be under question. I would argue that his hands-off approach allowed this maneuvering to happen. Chicago needs a mayor who is unafraid to pushback against aldermanic fiefdoms, who will restore confidence in city government, and who is unafraid of getting her hands dirty."

"Critics would argue that your hands are already dirty, given that the mastermind of the casino deal was your husband." I watched the slight tightening of her eyes. It was a tough question for me to ask, since my estranged husband had also been involved, but a question I knew Janelle expected.

"I would remind voters that not only did I have a hand in exposing the scheme, but I gladly provided extensive testimony in the court case that sent my ex-husband, and his partners, to jail. That should serve as an indication of not only my fortitude, but my willingness to put the city first."

She leaned forward and looked directly into my eyes as if daring me to counter. Or maybe she was just practicing for a more hostile audience.

"Look," she said. "We've seen enough of what men have brought to the table as leaders, and it's often been ugly. It's time for a woman's perspective."

"Beyond restoration of trust, what would your priorities be as mayor?" I asked.

As we spoke, it was hard to suppress thoughts of the personal undercurrent running through this conversation. Janelle, even more so than I, had had a front row seat to the abuse of power inflicted on the city by her husband. We'd spoken since the issue had become public, but didn't know each other well enough to have gone into full-disclosure sharing. I presumed trust was a hot-button issue for both of us.

She twisted a ring on her right hand, pausing to collect her thoughts. "One issue I believe in strongly is that Chicago has an opportunity to support women-owned businesses. Not just an opportunity, but an obligation. We're here at 1871 because I wanted to bring light to two companies based here in the tech incubator that are poised on the brink of an IPO. I applaud them for their success and hard work. Millions of dollars in investment are flowing into Chicago's economy. Innovation and entrepreneurship is vital to Chicago's future. I'll be working with the business leaders and education community on job training initiatives.

"We've had eight IPO's out of this wonderful incubator alone in the past year and a half. Chicago is becoming a serious entrepreneurial force. What isn't being discussed is that, all of them were male-owned companies. Where are the women? We can't let women miss out."

"Is that a function of the tech industry or other factors?" Seth's comments about his IPO plans immediately came to mind and I wondered what the financial upside was for him personally.

"Like most issues, the solutions are multi-part—recruiting, financing, training, press—are all factors, but factors we can influence. This doesn't have to be a boys' game. For long enough, we've seen how they handle themselves and it's not pretty. Now, why don't we go meet the hotshots."

Janelle stood, so I turned off the recorder and followed her out of the conference room. As we walked down the hall to meet the troops, I also wondered what Seth stood to lose if his IPO didn't go through. If Cavanaugh scared away Seth's money guys, it wasn't just the IPO windfall gone; it was damage to the existing company's bottom line.

"Do you happen to know Seth Bowman? He owns VTF Industries, they make energy drinks."

"Of course, I know of the company, but haven't met Bowman. Isn't he the guy who was involved in that shooting at the Peninsula?" She smiled and nodded at two bearded men in T-shirts walking past.

"Yes. There was an incident earlier this week at the Drea Foundation gala. A grief-stricken former employee decided to take out his anger on Seth. Luckily he's doing well." I kept my summary brief seeing no reason for me to add any color to the incident.

"That had to add a little entertainment value to the event. I bet Candiss was wetting her pants," Janelle chuckled. "That kind of tawdry attention doesn't play well in her crowd."

"You know her?"

"She, and her husband, Aaron. Speaking of tawdry…"

I stopped walking. "What do you mean? Has he been involved in something?" I asked, my curiosity piqued.

Janelle looked over her shoulder. "Other than playing fast and loose with other peoples money?" she said, her voice low. "There've been rumors for years about his firm being on shaky ground. Risky investments, overstated returns. Even an illegitimate child."

I wracked my brain for anything I'd heard over the years that would have suggested Nadell Capital was a troubled company, but came up with nothing. I wasn't tied in to the city's financial movers and shakers, but Chicago wasn't as big of a town as some would believe, not where reputations were concerned. It should be easy enough to find someone who could corroborate this. I could feel excitement settling into my stomach the way only a hot tip with home page potential could.

"Sounds like fraud. Did he not get caught? Or wasn't there enough to hang him?" I asked, putting on my poker face.

"I don't have details. Like I said, it's the rumor mill. I doubt it reached Ponzi scheme status or the guy wouldn't still be operating, but he's always struck me as someone who would sell his mother if it meant making a buck. I'd put my money in my mattress before I'd give it to him."

Well, that little tidbit wasn't what I'd expected to hear, but thank you Janelle! I was already running through potential sources in my mind.

9

"So? Did she dish on the ex?"

Borkowski shouted at me as I returned to the office. He was standing in the aisle next to Brynn's cubicle, his arms crossed over his chest, tortoise shell glasses pushed up to the top of his balding head. Apparently I wasn't going to have a chance to take off my coat before updating him on the interview. What did he want, a Tweet or a story? I was feeling prickly after seeing Janelle again. It had yanked the Band-Aid off the wound I kept pretending had healed, until something slapped me upside the head with reality. Right now all I wanted to do was hide in my office and go back into denial mode.

I walked over, placed the hot container of soup I had in one hand and the Pellegrino I had in the other, on Brynn's desk and unbuttoned my coat before responding. No sense spilling my lunch if you could call it that at nearly 4:00 in the afternoon.

Brynn leaned back in her chair and smiled but said nothing, probably grateful to have Borkowski's attention elsewhere.

"Not exactly," I said, responding to Borkowski. "But don't be surprised by her very pro-female agenda. I don't know if she's always been such a strong feminist, but it seems she intends to use her husband's behavior to punctuate her argument for having a woman in charge."

"In other words, her challengers will portray her as a militant man-hater. Good. That will bring us eyeballs."

"So sexism sells?" I said, my voice rising an octave. "Do you have any idea of the double standards women face? If she's tough, she'll be told she doesn't smile enough or will be called angry. If she's softer, then she doesn't have the *cojones* for the tough decisions. Women are torn apart for their hair, their clothes, how old they look, as if appearance is more important than the contributions they make. When was the last time any male politician was criticized because of his turkey neck or ill-fitting suits rather than the behavior he displayed?"

I was offended by his comment and allowing myself to get worked up in anticipation of the battle Janelle Platt would be facing even though I knew his comment was dead on. Just the thought of the narrow-mindedness that would be on display was irritating me.

"Whoa, cool it," Borkowski said, his hands up in surrender position. "Nobody called you any names here. You don't need to defend the entire female gender just because I speculated on the ugliness of the contest."

I let out a breath. "Sorry I jumped down your throat. Sensitive subject." As much as it had given an interesting news angle to explore, my interview with Janelle had also brought me back down into the depths of the ugly side of my former marriage. I was deflecting. The unresolved anger and confusion I felt over Erik's behavior and death had been brought to the surface. Janelle was coping by using her anger; I was still suppressing. Screaming at a dead man didn't accomplish much.

"I'll take that as a sign of Platt's persuasiveness." Borkowski raised his eyebrows and shot a look at Brynn wondering if she was going into attack mode too. She remained quiet and sipped her coffee, more interested in watching the show than partic-ipating.

"Get me the draft by Monday." He shot me another look, shook his head, then trotted back to his office.

I gave Brynn a weak smile and picked up my lunch from her desk. "I have a project for you but give me a few minutes to regroup."

She nodded, and I made my way to my office ignoring the amused glances from the rest of the staff. Setting my food on the desk, I then tossed my coat on back of my chair, and opened email. I scanned the subject lines for anything important as I ate. A note from Lane was in this afternoon's stash with an esti-mate of temporary fixes to our three-flat furnace issue but no mention of replacement estimates. Nothing from Ramelli. I added both issues to my Monday to-do list.

"You human again?" Brynn was standing in the door.

"That bad?" I asked, motioning her in.

"No. Of course not. Just trying for a little levity." She took a seat across from me. "I have to say your timing was spot on, however. Borkowski had just come over to give me a hard time about a missed deadline when you showed up. Funny, but he didn't seem swayed by the fact that my source got hit by a bus and couldn't talk to me."

"Misdirected priorities. The nerve of the guy," I laughed, noticing the pink lip gloss again today. "Do you have a date tonight?"

"What? Where did that come from?"

"Just wondering. It's Friday and you don't normally wear makeup. I thought maybe you had plans after work. It looks nice on you."

"Geez, something wrong with trying to look professional?" she said. Despite the sarcasm, I saw a little pleasure in her eyes.

"Was there something else you wanted to talk about or did you ask me in for girl talk?"

I laughed. "I'd like you to look into a company called Nadell Capital, it's a venture capital firm. Owner is a guy named Aaron Nadell and I've heard rumors that the organization is a little shaky. Risky investments, perhaps exaggerated investment returns."

"How deep a dive?"

"For now, I'm just looking to corroborate the rumors. If we're lucky, you'll someone with first-hand knowledge."

"You got it. I'll touch base again when I have some leads and you can decide from there where you want me to focus." She stood. "And get some rest this weekend. I hear it cures every-thing." She winked.

I smiled and turned back to my computer, typing Aaron Nadell into the search bar. In addition to charity events and other publicity fluff pieces, a list of companies he'd invested in rolled up. Thoughts of Erik and the financial scheme he'd gotten himself tangled up in ran through my mind. Had Aaron Nadell also allowed greed to drive his decisions? As I scrolled through the pages, a knot formed deep in my stomach. Greed always had consequence.

10

I could hear Walter's funny little chirp as I put my keys into the lock on my apartment door. The noises he made seemed to come from a bird he had hidden in his chest. Somewhere along the way he'd come to recognize the sound of the elevator and routinely greeted me at the door. I scooped him up, feeling his entire body purr.

I tossed my bag on the sofa and Walter and I continued our routine by heading into the kitchen for his dinner.

"How about tuna?"

He blinked and flicked his tail in agreement as I popped open the can. Wet food in his bowl, fresh water, and a scratch behind the ears, all his needs were met. Too bad mine weren't as simple.

I leaned against the counter while he ate at my feet and marveled again at my newly remodeled kitchen. My first project had been to tear out the avocado 1970s kitchen. But that was before I learned my husband was a philandering pig.

My contractor, an old-world saint-of-a-man originally from Poland, had patiently worked around my tighter finances and then my grief, completing the kitchen shortly after Erik died. I had chosen modern white oak cabinets, quartz counters, and integrated appliances. It was a stunning contrast against the vintage backdrop. The contractor thought I was nuts. Wait until he saw what I wanted to do with the bathrooms.

I poured myself a Pellegrino and headed back to a spare bedroom where I'd set up a makeshift office. Folding chair, a table that wobbled when I typed, and boxes in various states of openness that I'd paw through whenever I need paperclips or a stapler. I'd lived in this disarray for nearly a year, uninterested in tackling anything that wasn't essential. But the annoyance of the shaky table was starting to get me. I turned on my laptop and vowed to shop for a proper desk over the weekend.

I was meeting my dearest friend, Cai, for dinner in an hour, but wanted to put in a little more work on my interview with Janelle Platt before I went out for the evening. As I formulated my thoughts on Janelle's candidacy, and the two tech companies we had toured, I couldn't help but think about Seth. There were millions of dollars on the line for the men I spoke with today. I could only imagine what Seth's windfall might look like if it went forward. That was life-changing money.

With a rough structure in place, I set aside the article and changed for the evening.

Tavern on Rush wasn't our usual hangout but our favorite, Nico Osteria, had been booked with a private party. Friday night at prime time in the Gold Coast, we jumped on the alternate reservation, lest we get shut out. The popular sidewalk terrace was full, despite temperatures in the forties. Heaters tucked into the awning framework blasted down on the patrons. Computer monitors also hung overhead along the expanse projecting a slideshow of photos of patrons, celebrity clientele, and complimentary Tweets.

I followed the hostess to the quietest table they had where I was content to watch the street scene from inside. I ordered

Cabernet for both of us. Cai and I had been friends since our first year of law school at the University of Chicago. Her drink of choice was the easy part. There was little we didn't know about each other. She'd been there through my former career as an assistant state's attorney, the painful decision to leave the law, and the breakup of my marriage. She'd been my rock over the last four months.

Ten minutes later Cai strolled in, her pale skin flushed from the cold, her dark hair worn long and straight. Cai's mother was Japanese, her father Irish, and she'd gotten the best of both in looks and in personality, although neither parent admitted to that.

"Hey doll," Cai said, swooping in for a quick hug. "Hope we can hear each other over all the hook-ups being maneuvered." She looked over at the bar and rolled her eyes. "When do we get too old for that?"

"Emotional age? We're long past. Sit. Have a drink and tell me about latest your case. I'll fill you in on the drama with Seth after I've had a little more of this." I tapped my glass.

Cai was an attorney with one of Chicago's top law firms, specializing in corporate law. She, and the nearly 700 attorneys at the firm, put in enough billable hours to fund a small country. Legal work had been too soul draining for me. I left after a young man I'd prosecuted took his own life, and then I arm-twisted my husband for a shot as a journalist with his digital media company. Hard to believe that had only been a year ago.

"You know how it is," she said, tipping back her glass. "Another arrogant client who's bullied his way to business success by bending the law. When it catches up with him, he still thinks he's going to win by being a blowhard. And I get to be the one to give him tough love and pull a miracle out of my ass."

"Sounds like marriage."

Cai let out a cackle, nearly spitting her wine. "Exactly. I babysit men all day, who wants to do it at night too? Cheers."

We clinked our glasses and started to dig into the details of our week starting with my conversation with Janelle Platt.

Over the din of the busy restaurant, I heard a familiar high-pitched laugh. Lane was at the bar, one arm draped over some guy I didn't recognize, the other holding a martini. By the sway of her body I could tell it wasn't her first. I watched for a moment, then turned back to Cai.

She was watching my sister too, a look on her face that mixed incredulity with disgust. I probably had the same expression.

"Really? Haven't I seen this movie before?" I said, feeling my body tense. I looked at Cai and shook my head.

"Are you going over to save the day?" Cai asked.

"Not if I don't have to."

The crash of glass hitting the tile floor drew me back to Lane. She let out a shriek of laughter, and then I watched as her friend struggled to catch her as she went down too.

"Shit. I have to play Mommy again." I finished off the rest of my wine and maneuvered through the crowd to the bar.

"Hey, Andy what are you doing here?" Lane mumbled.

"Jesus, Lane. You can't even talk. I'm her sister," I said to the guy attempting to hold her steady. "How much has she had to drink?"

"Hell if I know. She's had two while I've been talking to her. I just met her half an hour ago. She seemed sober then."

He propped her on the stool, but she continued to sway. As he held her shoulders, I raised her chin and looked at dilated pupils that couldn't focus. She lifted her hand and started pulling at the top edge of her turtleneck as if it were constricting.

"She looks sick. Maybe you should take her to the bathroom," he said, happily abdicating responsibility to someone else.

The patrons on either side seemed to be having the same thought and had stepped back. I couldn't blame them. She looked like she was about to toss her cookies.

"Is she okay?" Cai had joined us, our coats and purses thrown over her arm, having jumped to the obvious conclusion that our evening was over.

"Nope. Help me get her to the ladies room."

Cai and I stood on each side and coaxed her to her feet. Lane's hands went back to her neck, and she pulled violently on the shirt as if struggling to breathe. As Cai and I fought to steady her, Lane lost her footing and went down hard, out cold on the floor next to the bar.

"Call an ambulance," I yelled to the bartender, then looked down at my sister and cursed.

11

"Second time in three days I've been in this damn hospital," I complained to Cai. "And now I have to sit here because my 37-year-old sister doesn't have the sense to keep her drinking under control. It feels like high school all over again."

I was beyond irritated with Lane. We were sitting on a bench in the emergency room waiting area of Northwestern Hospital, fighting impatience and trying to distract ourselves with vending machine tea. Dinner hadn't happened and stale cellophane-wrapped peanut butter crackers were starting to look appealing. Codes and pages pinged over the PA system while we sat. The room was already buzzing with what I assumed was a typical Friday night crowd—fights, overdoses, and accidents that wouldn't have occurred if the victim hadn't been inebriated. I shuddered at the image of what the medical staff might be dealing with at the height of the evening.

"We've both been too busy to talk about it, the shooting I mean." Cai said. "I can't imagine how frightening it must have been."

I felt myself shudder. Images of the hate in Cavanaugh's face, the sound of the gun as it discharged, the terror of hold Seth's bleeding body in my arms, all played through like a horror movie I couldn't turn off.

"I spoke to Seth this morning," she said. "I swear he's too obstinate to die." She chuckled.

"You spoke to him?"

"Yeah. Actually, he's a new client. Something else we haven't had time to talk about." A shadow crossed Cai's face. And she paused as if she were suddenly uncomfortable. "You were there with him when he was shot?"

"It all happened right in front of me. Seth and I went to the gala together. Obviously, I wasn't hurt, but yes, I had a front row seat."

"You went together? A date?"

"No, of course not." I shook my head. "You know I'm not interested in him romantically. I hadn't seen him since right after Erik died so when he asked me join him, I thought it would be a nice change. Some evening that turned out to be..."

Cai was intimately aware of my romantic history, both the issues in my marriage that had led me to file for divorce last year, and the unease I was feeling about my budding relationship with Michael.

As I sat lost in thought, I watched a woman across the room consumed with tears, and wondered what had brought her to the hospital. It was an instinct for me now to be curious about people's stories, particularly those that brought pain. And what better spot for a story than a hospital emergency room.

She looked back at Cai who seemed lost in thought herself.

"What's up? You're being a little cagy. What's that about?" I asked. An idea popped into my head and I leaned in, lowering my voice. "Are you representing Seth in his IPO?"

She tilted her head and raised an eyebrow. "You know I can't talk about my clients," she said, straightening up as a nurse walked by.

"Seth told me himself that he hopes to go public this year. That's not a deep dark secret," I said, taking a sip of the luke-warm tea.

"Fair enough," she shrugged. "Yes, I've been retained. But that's going to be the extent of our conversation on this subject. This is way too complicated. And you're a journalist for god sakes." She tipped her head back against the wall and sighed, then a smile. "I bet the shooting made Borkowski's day. Nothing better for a headline than an incident among Chicago's elite"

"I'll make sure to save the photo that ran in the Sun-Times if you haven't seen it. They got me with boobs hanging out and a bloody Seth in lap. I'm sure it's still online. I'm thinking with a little cropping it could be my new headshot." We both laughed.

"Ms. Kellner?" I looked up. Dr. Lassiter stood in front of us. His face still full of warmth despite the later hour. "Back again I see. I'm afraid we don't give friends and family discounts." He held out a hand and smiled. I stood and introduced him to Cai.

"It's nice to see you, but I'm starting to worry about your choice of friends." Cai and I chuckled at his joke, but unfortu-nately, he wasn't far off.

"Is my sister ready to go home? I assume you've pumped her stomach and lectured her on the dangers of alcohol poisoning? She's prone to over-indulgence, but this is the first time a visit to your fine establishment was required. Lectures from her little sister never seem to break through, perhaps this will."

I rambled on not normally willing to share my sister's chal-lenging personal life, but under the circumstance, it seemed like the sensible thing to do. Perhaps another voice could get Lane's attention. Mine certainly never seemed to.

"Actually, although there was alcohol in her system, it was insufficient to cause this episode."

"What? Then what happened? She was stumbling, slurring her words. I don't understand." Possibilities ran through my mind but nothing came to me that could explain the behavior I witnessed earlier in the evening.

"Frankly, I don't know. Not yet anyway, but I'm concerned. She's experiencing cardiac arrhythmia, in layman's terms an erratic heartbeat. Does she have any history of a heart issue? Or is there any family history?" he asked, concern showing in his eyes.

"No, nothing," I said, my mind searching for anything that might have gotten buried in my memory. For the first time, I was scared.

"Could someone have slipped something in her drink? She was at the bar with a guy I think she'd just met." I asked. A hazy image of the man came to mind. And every story I'd ever heard of a woman being slipped Rohypnol or other date-rape drugs. Why hadn't I thought to get the guy's name? Could I pick him out if I saw him again? Unlikely.

"Possibly. But don't jump to conclusions yet," he said, hearing the alarm in my voice. "It could simply be a virus. I've ordered some additional testing. We're giving her fluids to help push the alcohol out of her system. Right now she's sleeping, and that's the best thing for her. Check back in with me in the morning. Hopefully, we'll know a little more."

I looked at Cai, feeling a cold sweat break out on my neck as he walked away. A heart issue? Hadn't Seth said Cavanaugh's daughter died of a heart issue?

12

The doorbell rang as I was pouring hot water in my teacup. Michael. We'd made plans to go out for brunch this morning and shopping for office furniture after, but my thoughts were tied up with Lane. I'd spent the evening tossing and turning, and in between, beating myself up over not getting contact info for the guy at the bar. I was also dreading the phone call I needed to make to my father. Even the smallest bit of bad news seemed to crush his soul a little bit more.

Since my mother's death, he lived as if another massive blow was always around the corner. Not that he said much, men of his generation didn't talk about their feelings, but gone was the easy smile that lit up his eyes, the one I could still picture from my childhood. Now he seemed hollow, a physical clone of a man that went through the motions of being alive but had no joy.

I set down the cup and went to the door. Walter meowed and followed as I walked, nervous that I was leaving him alone.

Steeling myself against the fear welling inside me, I opened the door, but instead fell into Michael's chest before he'd even walked inside. Despite my uncertainty about a relationship, in this moment I needed him, I needed to be held and told everything would be okay.

"Hey, what's going on? What's wrong?" He whispered into my ear as he stroked my hair. Taking hold of my shoulders, he stepped back, his face full of concern.

"It's my sister. She's in the hospital."

"Let's sit down and talk." He closed the door and took my hand leading me to the sofa. Walter jumped onto my lap when I sat, eyeing Michael with suspicion as he always did. It was hard to know what went though that little cat mind of his, but it didn't seem he was ready to share me with anyone, especially Michael.

"Tell me what happened." Michael said once we were settled.

I filled him in on the evening at the bar. "I thought she'd just had too much to drink. Lane's never been one to turn down a party, but the doctor is saying something else is wrong. She was incoherent, stumbling. He's not sure what it is. Her vitals are wonky. It could be a virus, but he also said her heart beat has been erratic. He wanted to know if she had any history of heart issues." I was vomiting out the information not pausing to breathe or bothering to add any context.

"Have you checked on her this morning?" he asked. His voice was full of concern but at the same time strong, reliable, soothing. I was filled with relief just having him here to talk to.

"I called the hospital about half an hour ago. She was still asleep, but that's all the nurse could tell me. The doctor will be able to speak with me in a few hours."

Michael pulled me in for a hug. Walter hissed and jumped to the floor. But I stayed there relishing the feeling of safety in his arms. It wasn't an emotion I'd often felt over the past year. And I recognized how much I missed it. I thought of the days not that long ago that I had blindly assumed safety would always be part of my life. But trust and safety had abruptly been yanked from me. First when I learned of my husband's infidelities, and then again when I realized how deep into the casino scheme he'd been.

I drew in a breath and worked to calm my racing heart. If for no other reason, I needed to pull myself together for the call to my father.

Michael kissed my forehead and pulled back. "Don't start assuming the worst. The doctor said a virus was a possibility. Maybe she took something that didn't mix well with the alcohol."

"She wasn't sick on Thursday. We met for coffee." I paused, my mind racing down rabbit holes.

"What? What are you thinking?" he said. "You're obviously going to a bad place."

"I'm thinking about Luke Cavanaugh's daughter."

He looked at me intently before responding. "Wait a minute, that's a huge leap. Just because two people show an erratic heartbeat doesn't mean they have the same illness," he said, his voice soft and reassuring. He knew I was alarmed and was trying to pull me back.

"Cavanaugh believes his daughters heart issues and death were caused by Seth's energy drink. When I saw Lane yesterday, she had a bottle of the stuff in her bag. How can I not think about that?"

"Look at me." His voice was demanding. "Cavanaugh's daughter had a genetic condition. This doesn't mean Lane is going to die too."

I squeezed his hands and tried hard to dispel my fears. I knew he was right. I'd let my imagination suppress my normally logical thought process. I nodded, trying to convince myself it was just a coincidence. "Okay." I shook my head in agreement. "I'm going to need a raincheck on brunch. I have to call my father and then go pick up a few things for Lane before I go to the hospital."

"Of course." He traced the curve of my cheek with his finger. "Call me as soon you know more."

We stood and walked to the door. He pulled me in for another hug, whispering, "it's going to be okay." We stayed there feeling each other's warmth, basking in the comfort until I pulled away.

"Thank you. I'm glad you were here today." I said, giving him a weak smile and a kiss goodbye. I picked up the phone as soon as the door was closed.

My father sounded calm but then I hadn't expected anything else. He handled his pain by letting it eat away at his insides.

My mother had died in a car accident with her lover when I was in high school. Leaving my father a widower, a single parent to two teenage daughters he didn't know how to raise, and with the aftereffects of a betrayal he couldn't understand. He'd died emotionally in that moment and was no longer the man I'd grown up with.

Although I'd told him it wasn't necessary, he insisted on coming to Chicago, intending to drive the hour and a half down from his home in a suburb of Milwaukee. I gave him the address of the hospital and told him I would meet him there. Then I grabbed my bag and headed over to Lane's apartment.

Lane had given me a set of keys two years earlier after losing hers for the second time in a month. I'd grown tired of her sleeping on my couch and insisted on the backup set of the keys. I let myself in.

She'd purchased the condo in a River North high-rise during the frenzied boom of the pre-crash years when realtors were buying multiple units pre-construction with little or no down payment. Ever the optimist, she'd jumped on that bandwagon as well, and at one point owned four units in this building. Luckily she'd been able to dump everything but this one at a small loss. She didn't say much these days about her financial situation, but she hadn't fully repaid the money I'd last loaned her either. Perhaps that was the real motivation behind her suggestion that we sell the three-flat.

Despite its sleek modern bones, the interior furnishings had the look of Grandma's castoffs. I found it odd that a realtor, keenly aware of the value of visual appearance, didn't seem to care about her own home. But then again, there were many things about Lane that I didn't understand.

Her bedroom was down the hall in the back. I pulled open the heavy drapes that blocked her city view and got to work. Dust motes danced in the sunlight. Grabbing a shopping bag, I threw in a robe, a cardigan, and an assortment of toiletries. Seeing a couple trashy romance novels sitting on her nightstand, I added them to the bag. I made one more pass around the room but didn't see anything else I imagined she'd need for the next few days, but what the hell did I know?

Moving back to the kitchen, I bundled trash that was getting ripe. Then decided to open the fridge and make sure nothing was going to turn into a science experiment before she got home. I opened the door and stared at the shelf. A dozen bottles of VTF.

13

"I s he in?" It was 8:00 a.m. Monday morning and I was standing at the reception desk at VTF's River North office, playing the odds that Seth hadn't been able to resist getting back to work. And I needed to talk to him.

I'd spent the balance of the weekend at the hospital with my sister and father pretending I wasn't scared to death by where my imagination was taking me. Wild theory was the last thing my father needed to hear, so I'd kept the crazy thoughts to myself, but that hadn't kept me from obsessing on the idea. Michael had done his best to keep me grounded, staying in touch via text and phone, and reminding me that Lane was in great medical hands. I'd also made sure Lane's doctor was aware of her high caffeine intake, but stopped short of making any connections I couldn't prove.

I'd been tempted to call Seth a number of times over the weekend to press him on Cavanaugh, but instead restrained my dialing finger by forcing myself to remember my legal training, waiting until I could grill him in person. Had Seth told me the truth? Was it possible that Luke Cavanaugh's daughter had died because of something in the VTF drink? And if she had, was my sister next?

Company signage screamed at me in neon. Vigor. Tone. Force. The tagline for VTF Industries. The receptionist smiled, nodded, and told me to go on back. I made my way down the hall past walls peppered with images of intense faces and tight, sweaty bodies. Marketing images all intended to suggest that VTF could make anyone who drank it look that good. Upbeat dance music played lightly in the back ground.

The employee population seemed to be made up of pouty young things who all looked to be fitness models. Leggings. Tank tops. $400 sneakers. There was enough Lycra in this building to keep four knitting factories busy. I made my way through the maze of cubicles until I reached Seth's office, a box tucked away in the back of the brick loft building, one much like the one that housed Link-Media. I rapped on the glass side panel and Seth motioned me in.

He looked like hell. Pale, sunken eyes, a slight tic at one side of his mouth. At least his arm was still in a sling.

"Seth, we need to talk," I said, softening my tone. After a weekend focused on my sister, and letting fear control my emotions, I'd lost perspective. The man was recovering from a gunshot for god sakes.

He looked at me confused by my unannounced visit but closed his laptop and offered me a chair.

"If you're here to lecture me about getting back to work so quickly, save it. No choice." He patted a stack of files on his desk. "I'm taking care of myself. Only a half-day, I promise." He shook the bottle of antibiotics he was taking, then lifted a bottle of VTF to his mouth and took a drink.

Words caught in my throat as it occurred to me to stop him. I held back. If the drink was the problem, wouldn't Seth and his employees have been affected? Surely they drank more than anyone else? I relaxed a little with that realization.

"What's going on? You're upset."

I took a breath and composed myself. Nothing would be accomplished if lashed out irrationally and emotionally. I needed to be logical, detached, to pick up on any inconsistencies, and I couldn't do that unless I went back to my prosecutorial past.

"I haven't been able to get Wednesday evening out of my head. Cavanaugh was consumed with anger and I can't wrap my head around that. Tell me again about Luke Cavanaugh's accusations. What exactly does he think happened to his daughter?"

Seth shifted slightly in his seat and stared down at his desk before responding.

"I told you the other night. His daughter had a heart condition," he said, his voice was softer now but I could hear pain in it this time. Pain I hadn't heard, or hadn't listened for, in our earlier conversations.

"It was undiagnosed. And he's looking for an explanation, grasping at straws and hoping to explain how this poor young woman lost her life when he hadn't seen it coming. He's been despondent. Irrational. You saw that. And I completely understand. She was a lovely young woman. She didn't deserve anything that happened to her. I'm heartbroken myself. As far as I know that's all there is to what happened at the Drea gala."

My logical brain understood how grief changed us. Turned us into versions of ourselves we couldn't conceive of. Inspired actions that were foreign and strange and hurtful. But Cavanaugh seemed to have targeted his anger and that hadn't been made from whole cloth.

"Seth, I saw Cavanaugh's face. I heard the urgency in his voice. He blames you. I want to understand why." I shifted my weight but stood firm, watching his face, his body language.

Seth narrowed his eyes and leaned forward, resting one elbow on the desk. "Obviously there's something you're not saying. Why don't you tell me what's really going on here so we can get this resolved? I don't know what else I can tell you."

"Nothing is going on. Just concern," I said, but I didn't believe him. My gut was telling me there was more.

He looked at me angry, or maybe hurt that I was questioning him, but didn't respond. I couldn't read his face. Was he stalling? Was he in pain from the trauma of his own injury? Every instinct I had told me there was something he wasn't telling me. I felt myself getting agitated again, but shook it off. I needed to stay analytical and calm, even though right now all I wanted to do was to jump over the desk and shake him.

"Is it possible that your energy drink was a factor? Have you considered the possibility? Investigated anything?" I asked, grasping for ways to explain away Cavanaugh's accusation. And hoping that my friend had done the right thing.

"I can't believe you're asking me these questions. Do you think that I wouldn't have done everything possible if I thought for a moment VTF contributed? It's absurd. Cavanaugh's grief is talking, nothing more."

It was a move taught to first-year prosecutors. Watch for deflection. Watch for individuals who pivot around an answer by delegitimizing the question or the person who asked it.

"My sister collapsed. She's been in the hospital since Friday night. They don't know what's wrong with her." I knew I'd throw him with my own pivot, but sometimes, surprises were good strategy.

I watched the confusion wash over his face. "I'm so sorry, but does this have something to do with your visit this morning?"

"I went to her apartment to pick up a few things. In her refrigerator were a dozen bottles of your drink. Do I have a reason to be worried? Please tell me Seth."

I watched a shadow cross his face. He stared off out the window before responding.

"I'm really sorry about your sister," he said, his tone now cold and businesslike. "You appear to be jumping to the conclusion that there's some connection between the death of Luke Cavanaugh's daughter and your sister being ill. You're a former attorney, step back for a moment. I'm sure that when you can look at this objectively, you'll understand that this is pure coincidence."

He said the words, but his face was now a mask. I wasn't looking at my friend, I was looking at a CEO with an IPO on the line.

"Bullshit! Seth, I can see it in your face." I got to my feet, leaning over his desk, my eyes locked on his, pleading. "You need to get straight with me. Tell me what's going on. My sister could die and you're sitting here worrying about your business. Aren't you? Have there been others who've gotten sick? Do you even know what's happening?"

The accusations tumbled out. I couldn't believe where my head was taking me, but I couldn't seem to stop the thoughts. Couldn't seem to focus solely on facts.

His face crumpled, his body slumped deeper into the chair. Leaning forward, he rested his head in his hands unable to look at me. I gave him a moment. But every fiber of my body wanted to scream at him.

I softened my tone. "Seth, please talk to me. What's going on?"

Finally he looked up. "I think that a batch of my product was tampered with. I think someone is trying to sabotage me."

"Tampered with? How?"

"I don't know." He shook his head, clearly not having the energy for further speculation. "We had a couple of reports of people getting ill around the same time that Cavanaugh's daughter got sick. We didn't see anything at first, couldn't explain on our end anything that would've caused problems. Our standards and our quality control have always been beyond reproach. But we've had trouble with one supplier, well, one ingredient really, and had to go to a new vendor. I think maybe a batch of the product may have been tampered with. If there's a connection, it's the only thing that makes sense to me."

"And who would do that? And for what purpose?"

"You said it yourself, the IPO. There's a lot of money on the line. Investment that I've already made in the company. And with this IPO, the stock potential is enormous. Anyone with significant holdings is going to be very wealthy. Not everybody wants that for me, for us, for VTF."

"Are you saying an employee sabotaged you?"

Another shrug. "Best guess, I think it was a competitor. Someone who wants me to fail. Someone who wants VTF to be publicly humiliated so that we either cancel our IPO or the exposure will kill us later and we'll no longer be a threat."

"Corporate sabotage?"

"I can't think of a better reason. Money and lots of it. There are a number of companies that aren't happy to be losing market share."

"How would they have tampered with the ingredient?"

He paused, hesitating. "Well, two possibilities come to mind; they've got a vendor willing to have his palms greased or one of my employees is helping me fail."

We looked at each other. "Cavanaugh?" He shrugged.

"So, who have you talked to about this? What have you done to ensure safety? Your product hasn't been recalled, has it?" Surely, he wouldn't have been able to keep that quiet. I racked my brain but couldn't remember anything other than glowing press coverage.

"We were able to isolate the batch and work with our

retailers to pull it off the shelves quietly. All of our quality control standards have been re-evaluated. We've made sure we're clean and we're no longer working with that supplier," he said. "But I can't trace every bottle that's sitting in a retailer's back stock."

"And you didn't want to make it public if you didn't have to." Classic self-preservation. I was disgusted, but understood the impulse given what the company stood to lose.

"You know I wouldn't jeopardize people's health." He looked at me, his eyes pleading, desperate for me to believe him.

Did I? "This sounds really far-fetched. Corporate espionage of a small energy drink company? Really? Are you sure it wasn't just a human error?"

"Andrea, you of all people know the extent to which people will go for money."

He sat back up in his chair and looked at me. Challenging me to argue. Damn. How dare he bring this back to Erik? But despite my flash of anger that much I did know to be true. Greed had no bounds. But what now? Lane's face just before she collapsed flashed in my mind. There was no room for error.

14

I stood outside a red brick Victorian two-flat on Waveland Avenue fear knotting my chest. The weather had turned, and the wind was now fierce and cold and the sky gray with moisture. I could barely feel the temperature given the cold-sweat running down my back. Instinctively I turned up the collar on my wool coat and climbed the stairs. Scanning the name tags, I saw Cavanaugh listed for apartment number one.

After my meeting with Seth, I'd found myself compelled to speak with Cavanaugh. Tampering, sabotage, a grief-stricken father—whatever was going at VTF revolved around production and that meant Cavanaugh was at the center one way or another. Seth's speculation, such that it was, of a malicious competitor was a hard one to swallow. It was just too complex to pull off. I could imagine half a dozen ways to damage a company's reputation that didn't involve the convoluted maneuvering he was suggesting. The only thing I could safely say I agreed with was that there was a large enough chunk of cash on the line not to dismiss it out of hand. But if the product had been adulterated, my bet was on an angry employee or a dumb mistake, and who better to speak to about that than Luke Cavanaugh.

Given our last exchange, showing up unannounced was a risky move and possibly one of the stupidest things I'd done recently; after all, the guy did draw a gun and shoot Seth in the middle of a crowded room. For all I knew, he had a full arsenal stashed in his coat closet. My gut said Wednesday night had been a one-off, and therefore the danger minimal, but I had Mace in my pocket and Michael one tap on my phone away. Neither would be helpful if there was a semi-automatic weapon on the other side of the door, but I had to take the bet. With any luck, the worst that would happen is I'd be met with a door slammed in my face.

My body tense with unease, I pressed the doorbell and seconds later I heard footsteps. Then the door was flung open and Luke Cavanaugh stared at me, looking even more jaundiced in the light of day than he had the night of the gala. Barefoot, sweatpants, a T-shirt covered with paint. His sallow skin hung on his body as if he hadn't eaten in weeks. His bloodshot eyes told me he wasn't sleeping much either.

"Yeah, what the hell do you want?" he said, looking at me as if I were about to hand him a religious solicitation.

"Wait, a minute. I know you. You were there the other night, at that fancy party. What the hell are you doing at my house?" He shuffled a bit as the wind slapped him in the face, lifting his hair.

"Mr. Cavanaugh my name is Andrea Kellner. I'd really like to speak to you about Wednesday night. I'd like to understand what happened to your daughter."

"And why the hell would you want that? Clearly you're friends with that bastard Bowman. He send you over here? Is he trying to shut me up again? Telling you to make me go away?" He gripped the door handle, ready to make his point.

I backed up slightly, watching his hands for sudden movement. "No, Mr. Cavanaugh it's not like that at all. I'm not here to shut you up. You're clearly devastated by your daughter's death. I want to know what happened. Can you talk to me about her?" I held out a business card.

He took the card, considering what to do. His eyes told me he was desperate for someone who would listen to him but he didn't know that I could be trusted.

"My attorney doesn't want me talking to you people, but he's about as worthless as the cops. What the hell, come on in."

I followed him into a narrow hallway my eyes running the perimeter alert for danger. Dark stained wainscoting ran the length with burgundy wallpaper above. The walls were lined with coats, winter boots, and stacks of old newspapers. It opened into a cozy living room. Family photos in mismatched frames hung in artful disarray on the walls, crocheted afghans rested on the back of an overstuffed sofa, and an assortment of throw pillows dotted both the sofa and the side chairs, waiting for someone to sink in. Nothing matched. Nothing looked planned. But it all looked loved and comforting. Not a gun in sight.

Cavanaugh stopped behind a leather La-Z-Boy. I was drawn to the oak fireplace, the focal point of the room. It probably didn't work any longer, but it was intricately carved, its varnish now crackled and darkened. More framed photos filled the mantle. Photos of Cavanaugh in better days and photos of a young girl.

"Is this your daughter?" I asked, watching him nervously, and keeping a direct line of sight.

I was looking at a photo of Cavanaugh with a high-school aged girl. They smiled brightly, arms around each other, posed in front of the entrance to Disney World.

"Yeah, that's me and my Kelly. About three years ago."

"You both look happy." I turned and faced him head on. He was staring at the floor struggling to hold back tears.

"What is it you want?" he said. "You didn't come here to look at family photos and tell me how cute my kid was. I've had enough of my time wasted. Say what you need to say and move on. You don't really give a shit, anyway. Nobody does."

My heart broke seeing his pain, his isolation. Or was this a man wracked by guilt? I let myself relax a little but kept my hand on the mace in my coat pocket.

"Mr. Cavanaugh, you seemed convinced that Seth Bowman had something to do with your daughter's death. Can you tell me why you believe that? Can you tell me why you hold him responsible?"

He looked up at me, his face expressionless except for a slight softening around his eyes. I could feel his urge to talk, to be heard.

"I understand that you haven't seen a lot of support," I said. "I imagine that you're feeling ignored. You don't know me. And I'll be honest, I do find it difficult to believe, that Seth Bowman, a man I call a friend, could be associated in any way with the death of another human being. But Mr. Cavanaugh, I'm also a journalist. You clearly believe that your daughter's death is going uninvestigated. I commit to you that I'll listen with an open mind and an open heart. I'm not here at Seth's request. He doesn't know I'm here."

Cavanaugh adjusted his stance. His arms gripped the back of the chair as he clenched his jaw and tried to figure out whether to speak to me. I took his silence as a good sign and continued.

"I very much want to understand what you believe happened to your daughter. I can't imagine the pain you're feeling. I can't imagine the heartache this is causing for you. But I'm absolutely willing to listen openly to anything that you can tell me about how she died."

I stood, silently waiting for him, every word I'd said true and heartfelt. Hopefully, he'd been able to hear that.

After a moment, he let out a breath and said, "Okay I'll talk. But if Bowman's your friend, you're not going to like a goddamn thing I've got to say." He held out his hand and motioned toward the upholstered chairs flanking the fireplace.

"Deal. I'm prepared to hear whatever you've got to say." Cavanaugh didn't appear to be a threat, so I unbuttoned my coat and took a seat. Then pulled out my phone. "Is it okay if record this?"

Cavanaugh nodded, then ran a hand over his unshaven chin as he sat across from me. "My daughter Kelly started working at VTF about two years ago. You probably already know that I was the production manager. I was there for about six years. Kelly kinda grew up there. I'm a single dad, Kelly's mom left us when she was two, so that meant Kelly ended up being alone a lot of the time. Not a great thing for a high school kid if you know what I mean. So I'd have her come over to the factory after school now and then. You know, just to make sure she stayed out of trouble. High school kids can run pretty wild if you don't watch them carefully."

I nodded, remembering Lane's turbulent high school years. And the furtive phone calls I'd have to make to her friends trying to get her home so my father wouldn't have to worry. I resisted the urge to pepper Cavanaugh with questions knowing that this was his story to tell and his pace to tell it.

"But what I didn't count on was that she'd have a thing for Bowman."

"A thing? As in she had a crush on him?" Interesting. I wondered if Seth had known.

"Exactly. She followed him around like a puppy dog waiting for him to dole out treats. Didn't bother me at first. What 17-year-old kid doesn't develop a crush? As far as I could tell Bowman was always a decent guy. Least I could keep an eye on her there. But once she turned 18, things changed."

He looked up at me, shaking his head. "I don't know, must've been all that hanging out at VTF. All everybody talks about there is what workout they're doing. How many reps they did last night. All silly stuff to me. I don't do any of that shit, but Kelly was into it. She started working out, getting in with that crowd of young people at the facility who are obsessed with how they look. Everybody wearing those tight leggings and stuff. So, she decides that she wants to be a model. A fitness model. You know one of those one of those girls that jumps around and sweats in her workout clothes." He shrugged.

"And how did you feel about that?"

"Mixed feelings. I knew she wasn't interested in going to college but I thought maybe if she was into that fitness stuff, maybe she'd be a trainer or teach some yoga class or something. I didn't mind that. She was a pretty girl, but I didn't think all that focus on how she looked was healthy. For her mind, you know? All I really cared about was that she was happy."

His eyes seemed to soften.

"So what happened from there?" I asked, a picture of the relationship between Kelly and her father starting to form.

"Bowman started talking to her about modeling for one of the campaigns. Some big ad campaign he wanted to do. I wasn't involved in that stuff. I think it had to do with the expansion or some new product release. I don't really know. Kelly didn't care. She saw this as her big break. And I suppose it could've been with the company going national."

"And Seth was encouraging her?"

"Sure seemed like that to me. It's all she talked about. Started working out four hours a day if I let her. She said she needed to be "buff" for the photo shoot. I don't know what buff means exactly, she looked good to me. But it didn't seem to be hurting anything, so I didn't hassle her too much.

"But then the advertising campaign started getting pushed

back. A few weeks, then a few more. Bowman kept telling her just to be patient, it was going to happen. It made Kelly crazy, she thought she'd done something wrong. That she hadn't been working hard enough."

"Did the photo shoot happen?" I asked, jotting myself a note to look at dates.

Cavanaugh got to his feet and stepped over to the mantle, picking up the photo I'd been looking at earlier. He looked at it wistfully a tiny smile on his face, and then returned the photo to its place of honor.

"No, but that's when things started getting a little too messy. Messy because I found out things had started to get more personal between Kelly and Bowman."

"Personal? As in romantic?" I tucked my hair behind my ear as I processed the thought.

He nodded. His face was tight with anger. "Kelly kept it from me. She knew I'd go apeshit. The man's old enough to be her father. What the hell does he want with a kid? But Kelly was over the moon. She was convinced not only that she had a big career in front of her, but that Bowman was going to help her get there. I don't know what he told her, but something happened and all of a sudden, in her mind, she was already the new body of VTF. I warned her that Bowman probably didn't give a damn about her, that she was just the flavor-of-the-month, but she didn't want to hear it. Not from me. She had it bad for him."

What the hell had Seth been thinking? An 18-year-old kid? I suddenly saw a side of Seth I hadn't known existed, a side that disgusted me. I didn't know if Cavanaugh was inferring a connection between Kelly's death and the fact that she may have dated Seth, but I let him talk.

"Do you know if they were still dating?" I said, but the question that came next was why had Seth hidden the relationship when we spoke earlier?

"I think so, but she stopped talking about it after I gave her shit. Who knows with 18-year-old girls? There hadn't been any big meltdowns that much I know. She was still hoping that this modeling thing was going to work. I think he was probably just stringing her along."

"Mr. Cavanaugh are you suggesting that their romantic relationship was somehow a factor in Kelly's death?"

He grimaced, then shook his head.

"No, that's not what I meant, I'm just saying there was something going on there that needs to be factored in. My point is she was excited. By the possible job, having a grown man pay attention to her."

"I understand that you would be concerned about a relationship between a man of his age and your daughter, but I'm still not clear on your accusation that somehow Seth had something to do with Kelly's death." My mind tussled with the implications. Seth had behaved badly, but the way I saw it, this was another strike against Cavanaugh.

"What I'm just trying to tell you is the full picture," he said. "That's a part of it. The other part is that she was working her ass off to be this ideal. Having people at work tell her she needed to tone up here and tighten up there. Hours and hours a day were spent in the gym but she barely ate anything."

"You mean she was dieting?" I shifted in my seat and slipped off my coat. Cavanaugh was simply a father consumed by grief.

"She went even further than that. She counted her protein intake, fat, all that. Said she was trying for ketosis, whatever the hell that is. It was really out of control. She weighed everything, measured everything she put in her mouth. Charted what she ate. She wouldn't eat anything that didn't help get her towards her goal. I thought it was crazy, but she felt this is what she had to do to get this modeling gig."

Cavanaugh was on his feet again, this time pacing, seemingly unable talk about these details without moving. Even his words were coming out now faster and more urgently.

He sighed. "She also went hard and heavy with the VTF drinks as part of her program. She probably drank six or more of them a day. I would bring home cases for her."

I'd read a little bit about ketogenic diets. The theory was if you ate a low carb, high fat diet, you'd force your body into ketosis and therefor use your fat for energy production. It was popular among the extreme-health crowd and fitness enthusiasts. Seemed like too much work to me.

"Beyond being worried about her nutritional level, do you believe that this regime was in some way taxing her body or that it contributed somehow to her heart failure?" I made another note to look into the health risks.

"Lady, for a reporter you're not picking up on this too fast," Cavanaugh shot at me. "Let me put the pieces together for you. What I'm saying is the thing that changed, the thing I believe made a difference in her being alive or dead, is that she couldn't get enough of that damn drink. I know they've got all these quality control measures in place, or at least we did before I got yanked out of there. Who the hell knows what they're doing now? I'm saying that we don't know what high doses of this stuff does. Six to eight drinks a day? Do we know that? No, we don't."

He was agitated. Pummeling his argument as if I were a jury. And his question was valid. Could Seth or anyone say without a doubt that high doses of the drink were safe? What was the safe limit of caffeine intake? How much did Lane drink?

"And the sales of the stuff were coming in so fast we couldn't keep up," he continued. "We were grabbing new vendors left and right. Running three shifts a day to meet the demand. This stuff has ballooned in popularity and we didn't staff up. We didn't have the money to staff up. Maybe something happened with the quality of the product? Don't know. I'm not there. What I do know is that my daughter started drinking six or eight of these damn things a day and the next thing I know, she's dead."

15

I pulled up to the squat red brick building that was VTF's production facility at 9a.m. Finding the parking lot nearly full, I squeezed my small Audi into a slot between the dumpster and a tricked-out Chevy Silverado. Grabbing my bag, I sidled out of the tight space careful to avoid brushing against the trash, and then headed toward the door.

Cavanaugh's pain had gotten to me. My initial instinct was that he was telling the truth, or at least the truth he believed. But his pain could also be guilt. Could he, as Seth suggested, have tampered with the product, and now believe it had accidentally caused his daughters death?

I hadn't been able to let go of the thought, so I'd phoned Seth late yesterday afternoon and asked for a tour of the manufacturing facility. He'd agreed, assuming he now had an ally that could throw some positive publicity his way. The best buffer against bad press was lots of good. I didn't correct him.

I still wasn't sure of the timeline of the alleged tampering or how Seth was certain it had been a one-time event, but I intended to find out. Now the question was, what would I tell Borkowski? Nothing, yet.

I walked in to a bare-bones reception area. Wood paneling, molded plastic chairs, and threadbare carpet. Designer furnished it wasn't. An elderly Hispanic woman sat at a desk behind a sliding glass partition as if it were a doctors office. I introduced myself and told her I had an appointment with the plant manager. She told me to take a seat then buzzed my tour guide.

Knowing that Seth was wired to turn on the PR spin at every opportunity, I'd asked him not to be here, but my request was dismissed out of hand. Seth fervently controlled his company message. Aside from the parade of bodies, which were nothing more than props in marketing images, no one else gave voice to VTF. Seth *was* the brand and not about to slack off now, even while healing from a gunshot wound. I had hoped for unfettered time to ask questions, to explore what might have happened without Seth guiding what I saw or heard, but that looked unlikely. After speaking with Cavanaugh yesterday, I was feeling confused and uncomfortable. Seth was a friend, and I wanted him to be successful, yet he'd chosen to hide his suspicions about product tampering and hadn't disclosed his romantic involvement with Kelly. Why?

A Hispanic man in his early forties opened the door to the left of the reception window and stepped into the room. He was short and round with an easy smile, a refreshing change from the hyper-toned gym rats in the corporate office.

"Good morning Ms. Keller. I'm Martin Vasquez. Welcome to my second home." He laughed.

I held out a hand. "Thank you so much for meeting me on such short notice Mr. Vasquez."

"I'm always happy to show people around the place. Everyone seems so surprised that producing a drink is so involved." He smiled. "Why don't you follow me to the back?

What I thought we'd do is run through production in the order we make it."

"Perfect. Has Seth arrive yet?"

"He just phoned. He's hit a small traffic delay and will meet us soon."

I smiled to myself and followed Martin down a spartan hall-way. At the end, he opened heavy metal doors, and we stepped into a cavernous space. It was well-lit and bustling with a low din of machinery. I stood for a moment taking in the flurry of activity.

We walked to a small office on the left, nothing more than four partitioned walls, three desks, a few whiteboards, and some battered file cabinets.

"This is my office," he said. "I'm both the plant manager and the head of production. This is where we handle ordering our raw materials, do projections based on seasonal demands, and manage our inventory."

"How many products are you producing?" I asked.

"VTF's primary product is our energy drink. Six different flavors. Based on the success of the core product, we have three other product lines in research and development. That's done at the corporate office but I work with the team on formulation, sourcing, and production planning."

"Will those products be produced in this facility?"

"Since we're still in the R&D stage, we probably shouldn't go too deep into that. Don't want to give away any company secrets." He smiled and winked.

"So currently you produce only the energy drink."

"Yes, that's correct."

"And 100% of the production is done here?" There was too much background noise, even in the enclosed office, to make recording possible so I resorted to old-fashioned pencil and paper, scribbling cryptic notes as we spoke.

"Yes, although orders have tripled over the last year. At some point, we'll need to add another production line. We haven't determined if we'll go outside or expand this facility, but for the moment we're managing. It's gotten a little hectic but we can handle it." He smiled, the pride obvious.

"And the raw materials, where are they sourced?" I was having trouble imagining how Seth's theory of deliberate tampering could be true. Contamination, spoilage, accident, were all far more likely. Was Seth getting a little paranoid because of the IPO?

"We make every effort to source our raw materials domestically. We have a handful of dedicated suppliers."

A young woman, in a plaid flannel shirt over her T-shirt and jeans, walked into the office and shut the door. She was in her early twenties with long dark hair pulled into a loose ponytail and a butterfly tattoo on the side of her neck. She eyed me suspiciously as she took a seat at one of the computers.

"This is Olivia," Martin said. "She's my production assistant."

I held up my hand and introduced myself.

"You doing a story on the place?" she asked, looking me up and down.

"Possibly. I'm doing a little background work. Research," I said, being as vague as possible. Martin hadn't asked for specifics of my story and I didn't need him to start now.

"And Ms. Kellner is a friend of Mr. Bowman's," Martin chimed in.

She stared at me unsmiling as if trying to figure that out. What was up with the attitude? I chalked it up to her age group and turned to Martin.

"Let's go see how the stuff is made," he said.

"Nice to meet you," I said to Olivia as we passed. She looked up, nodded, then went back to her computer screen.

I followed Martin out to the production floor. Metal shelving rimmed the left side of the space stacked with tubs and jugs and bottles. Rows of inventory of what I assumed were the raw materials used to make the drink were stacked nearly to the ceiling.

"As you can tell, this is where we store the ingredients. Items are pulled from this area and used to fill the machines that we use for bottling."

I scanned the labels on the packaging, but it was hard to tell what I was looking at without a scientific journal in front of me, nor could I figure out the organizational system. The shelves were chock-full, tubs stacked sideways and on the floor, as inventory overflowed it's assigned space. It wasn't clear to me how they found what they needed.

"Is there a master inventory marking system that tells you what you have on hand or where it's stored?"

"You may have noticed tags on each shelf. Each item we purchase is identified with an SKU, a stock keeping unit." He pointed out a six-digit number on the nearby shelf. "Things have been a little crazy, given the demand, but we know exactly what we have and where it is," he said confidently. "I'm hoping we'll have time to do some reorganization after the first of the year. Although, I could probably use another 200 square feet for ingredient storage. Let's go over to bottling."

The main cavern of the room was a hamster maze of conveyor belts moving empty bottles along the path where they were each filled with liquids.

Martin's phone pinged him. "Sorry, I've got a situation I need to check on," he said, after reading the text. "Wait here for a moment and I'll send Olivia over to finish things up. Stop in my office before you leave."

I stood watching in awe at the efficiency of the technology. Large silver drums containing the mixture squirted out rationed amounts of elixir. A single bottle moved to four stations before being capped at the end.

Olivia joined me as I watched. "So, what's in each of these hoppers?" I asked.

"Sorry, trade secrets." She smiled, crossing her arms over her chest. "I'd have to kill you."

I ignored her clichéd joke. At least she seemed in a better mood now.

"Each hopper contains its own mix of ingredients. The large one is water."

"Careful." I smiled at her and cocked a brow.

She rolled her eyes. "Oh yeah, water, our big bad trade secret. The others contain botanicals and flavoring. Once the liquid ingredients are added, the bottles are capped and labeled, then they proceed down the belt where the mixture is shaken."

"And are the core ingredients of each of the flavors the same?" I asked, thinking about Seth's theory that one shipment had been adulterated.

"Mostly. Some of the botanicals change for flavor. Right now, we have six, with two more being released next month."

"So this production line handles one flavor at a time. Correct?"

"Yes, we swap out the hopper when we need to switch to another flavor. Obviously that takes coordination so that the proper labels are applied to the proper drink. Line gets shut down when we switch out flavors, so it's not too bad."

I wasn't hearing anything about the process that helped me understand how a bad ingredient would be traceable unless it was exclusive to a specific flavor. I made a note to ask Seth about the time frame and how he'd discovered the problem.

"What is the lead time from order to delivery?"

Olivia leaned in as the fan from the ventilation system kicked in, drowning out her words. "Right now we're running about eight weeks, order to out the door. We prefer to keep it closer to four, but we've been having trouble keeping up. I guess there are downsides to success," she shouted, then tilted her head and moved further down the line away from the noise, joking with one of the employees as she passed.

"What about refrigeration?" I asked when we could hear each other again, wondering whether spoilage was a concern.

"Technically, that's not necessary unless a bottle has been opened. If not, shelf life is a year. Some of our stores stock the product in refrigerated cases, but that's just their marketing. I guess they think it seems fresher that way."

"I understand the ingredients are sourced domestically. Are you involved in that?" Thinking back to my conversation with Seth, he'd indicated one vendor and one ingredient, as the problem. I made another note to ask him for those details.

"I don't go out and meet with vendors, if that's what you mean," Olivia said, pushing a loose strand of hair out of her eyes. "Martin does that. I complete the purchase orders, follow-up on delivery. And make sure Martin knows if something is not going to be here on time or if somebody short ships us."

Olivia seemed knowledgeable, competent, perhaps even a bit passionate about the work she did despite her initial attitude. Employees on the line had smiled or waved at her. She seemed comfortable here, liked even. I was curious about her background.

"How long have you worked for VTF?" I asked.

"About two years. I was working in food service, hostessing at the Waldorf for minimum wage." She rolled her eyes at the memory. "One of the regular customers hooked me up here. It's a much better gig and I'm not working for slave wages. But it's been crazy. Who knew this stuff would catch on the way it has?" She shoved her hands in the pockets of her jeans and shrugged.

"I'm imagine your family is very proud of you. You're young to have so much responsibility."

"My mom would be, if she were still alive." A shy smile crinkled her eyes. "My dad, he's just some loser who walked away before I was born. I'm on my own now." She looked at me, resilience in her stance.

"I can imagine how difficult it's been."

She shrugged.

"Yeah, well that's life," she paused and took a few steps down the line. "We're nearing our capacity in this plant," she said. I guessed she was done with questions on her personal life. "And not all of our vendors are up to it."

"You mean speed or quantity?" I said, switching with her back to business.

"Both. We've needed to expand our vendor base to meet the demand. And not everybody has been able to ramp up."

That was a slightly different spin than Martin had given me.

"What about quality control? Can you trace a batch back to a date or a lot number once it's in the retailers' hands?"

"Of course." She walked down to the end of the line where a group of women were pulling bottles off the line and packaging them in cardboard cases. I followed.

She picked up a bottle, saying something in Spanish to the woman packing, then showed me the label. "The back of every bottle has a ten-digit code, a lot number. I can trace this back to the exact day and batch."

"What about ingredient testing? How do you know what you're getting from your supplier is exactly what you ordered?" The issue was at the heart of Seth's argument.

"We've worked with these people for a long time. It isn't complicated."

"Didn't you say that you've been forced to take on new vendors and suppliers? Do you have some kind of testing program that would authenticate the quality of the ingredients? Do you tour their facilities?"

"Well, that's Martin's area," she said. "We've been so over-loaded, I'm not really sure."

"So, it's possible that a vendor could slip something in that been diluted or adulterated."

"Why would they do that? And piss off a big customer?" I sensed her mood changing a little with my question, and I wondered whether I'd insulted her or if the process had gotten a little slack. Were the demands of their success putting strains on the organization beyond what I could see in capacity to store ingredients and finished inventory? While the process itself seemed militaristic in its precision, disorganization was showing in the inventory control.

"Hey, is Olivia giving away our secrets?" Seth. Dressed in his uniform of tight workout gear and sneakers. His shoulder was still padded under the Lycra and thankfully he had the sense not to give up the sling. He gave me a peck on the cheek as he joined us. It made me uncomfortable, but Olivia looked at me with a new curiosity and at Seth with alarm.

Although a little color had returned to his face over the past few days, the whites of his eyes had taken on a jaundiced yellow and he appeared shaky. He hadn't looked well the night of the Gala. Was this the aftereffects of his injury or his energy drink? He ran his hand over the stubble on his chin as if he were unfamiliar with the feeing. He shouldn't be at work at all, let alone here traipsing around a factory.

"Don't worry, your secrets are still safe. Olivia has been quite professional." No reason not to give the girl her props.

"Good to hear." He smiled at Olivia and grabbed my arm. "You don't mind do you, I just want to reinforce some of the highlights." Olivia rolled her eyes and returned to her office while Seth shuffled me over to the staging area for finished product.

"Morning Splash is our top seller, a kiwi-blackberry

mixture." He picked up the bottle, holding it like he was a model at a trade show. "It's refreshing and not overly sweet, gives a nice energy boost. Would you like a case?"

"Thanks Seth, but no." He started to pitch the health benefits of the drink.

"I can get the PR speech from you on the phone. You should be at home resting or since you're being stubborn, sitting at your desk in your office with your feet up. Your staff can manage a brief factory tour without you."

He put the bottle back and gave me a weak smile.

"Can't help myself. You're always a salesman when you own the company. But don't you think your readership would want to know about the health benefits?"

"You tell me all about them when I call you later." I was feeling guilty and conflicted. He wasn't up to this even if he didn't know it, but the sooner I had some answers the sooner we'd both feel better. "I think I have everything I need for now."

"Okay, then I'll walk you out," he said, wearing his disappointment.

His gait was slow, although steady, as we walked back to the production office so I could thank Martin and Olivia for their help. Then Seth escorted me out through the reception area.

I stopped for a moment trying to sort through my impressions of the plant and Seth's commentary yesterday.

"Is there something else you want me to know about what's going on here at the plant? I said, giving him one more opportunity to fill in the gaps.

"It's all good. I'm just happy to be back to work."

"Then do you want to tell me why you didn't mention that you dated Kelly Cavanaugh?"

16

Seth's insistence that there was no romantic relationship between Kelly and him was still on my mind as I returned to the office. According to him, she had a teenage crush that was completely one-sided. He was simply being a nice guy to his employee's daughter. Yes, they'd spoken about a possible photo shoot, but he'd made no promises. Loathe though I was, my instinct was to believe Cavanaugh over Seth. And I knew I'd never look at Seth again with the same respect.

I waved at Brynn who was deep in a phone conversation as I walked into my office. Plopping my bag on the file cabinet beside my desk, I did a quick scan of email, deleted the junk mail that filled half my screen, read a note about payroll numbers I'd been cc'd on between Ramelli and Borkowski, and then reached for my phone. I hadn't spoken to my father yet this morning. He'd been staying at Lane's apartment at night when the nursing staff kicked him out of her room, but it was just a place for him to shower and get a few hours of sleep on her couch.

I'd suggested he go back to Milwaukee, told him I'd call if

there were any news, but the idea had been rejected out of hand. His protective streak wouldn't allow it.

Lane was still asleep when I got through, however, my father informed me that the doc had stopped by, indicated he wasn't finding anything in his testing, and her heart rate seemed to be was normalizing. He was considering sending her home in the morning. It was great news and I could hear the relief in my father's voice. I told my him I'd stop by after work.

I'd also gotten two call messages from the vocal tenant in our three-flat. Sounded to me like Lane had done nothing to appease him before falling ill. Why wasn't I surprised? I threw my pencil down in disgust. Unable to track her down, the tenant was now moving on to me. I called the companys who'd provided repair quotes, arranging for estimates on a new furnace system for the building, then phoned the tenant to assure him it would be handled. My bank account wouldn't be happy, but Lane and I could fight this out later. For now, it was close my eyes and write the damn check. After that, I was done. I needed to untangle myself from Lane's messes and sell the place, even if it meant a loss.

"Knock, knock."

I looked up to see Brynn and motioned her in. "Please don't make me cover another daycare center opening. I don't understand how women do that mother thing. All those dirty hands grabbing at you and wanting to sit on your lap. Ick." She leaned against the door frame, shuddering as she spoke.

"Don't ask *me*. I haven't been there either. Although I do have an older sister that occasionally qualifies as a child. Do you need hand sanitizer?" I laughed. "This is just Borkowski trying to see how tough you are."

"No, he's trying to see if I'll quit." She pushed up the sleeve of her oxford shirt, otherwise known as her uniform. She dressed like she spoke. Straight forward, functional, easy to understand. She shared none of my fashion taste for drapey architectural cuts from little-known designers. If Brynn's attire described her personality, what did mine say about me? Something to ponder another time, perhaps after a few glasses of wine.

"I know you two have mended fences," she said. "But he's still a jerk in my book even if he is the boss. So, what's got you running around? Sorry, I meant to ask about your sister. How's she doing?"

"Stabilizing apparently. I just got off the phone with my father. She might go home tomorrow."

"That's good news."

The fact that Lane was showing signs of improvement was comforting. However, not knowing what had caused the episode, or if it would reoccur, still had me holding my breath. Replaying the mental tape of Cavanaugh's anguish wasn't helping either. My thoughts about the whole damn situation bounced between panic and this-is-too-crazy-to-be-real. But I couldn't seem to get it out of my mind.

"I took a tour of the VTF plant this morning," I said to Brynn.

She looked at me, confused. "Does Borkowski know about that?"

I shook my head. "I have to play this out a little bit. I also spoke to Cavanaugh yesterday. He insists that this drink played a role in his daughter's death."

Brynn shook her head, closed the door, and sat down.

"Don't give me that look," I said, seeing the amusement in her eyes. "I'll tell Borkowski if there's a reason to tell him. Well, maybe." I laughed. "Do you drink it? The VTF stuff? Everyone else around here seems to."

"No," she said, looking a bit disgusted. "I'm not giving up my coffee. I like my drinks the color of my skin. Green is for grass, mint ice cream, and the Chicago River on St Paddy's day. So, are you going to tell me what you're hearing? You can't bring me under the tent and then leave me hanging. Especially if it involves something fun like working around Borkowski."

Brynn leaned forward in the chair and I gave her the Cliffs-Notes version of my conversation with Cavanaugh, and my impression of the VTF facility.

"You're making one of those faces you make when your mind is fifteen steps ahead of everybody else," she said when I'd finished. "Is something bothering you about the plant?"

"I'm not certain. Something feels off but I can't pin it down," I said, images of the disorganized raw material storage in my head. "I saw a facility starting to feel the strain of its success. I guess it's not hard to imagine cutting corners or people making mistakes. But beyond that..." I didn't share with her Seth's comments about sabotage. It still seemed too sensational and over the top to be taken at face value, nor had I discounted the idea of a pissed off employee making a statement.

My phone rang and Michael's name popped up on caller ID. I'd sent him a text earlier this morning asking if he'd seen Kelly Cavanaugh's autopsy report. He was probably annoyed that I'd asked but oh well.

Brynn stood to leave. "Yell if you need anything."

"Thanks for calling me back," I said to Michael, hoping to make this sound like a business call. "Were you able to look at Kelly's autopsy?"

I also wasn't being fully transparent about my relationship with Michael, at least not with anyone other than Cai. The obvious messiness of a romantic involvement between a cop and journalist had both of us feeling sensitive. It was a constant elephant in the room that influenced, or more often stifled, our conversation. We both had professional history keeping our cases at the office, but given the start to our relationship, it was hard to imagine work as a taboo topic. And harder to imagine anyone else thinking there wouldn't be pillow talk. Better to pretend nothing was happening.

In reality, the bigger issue was me. Talking about a relationship with Michael made it real, and I wasn't ready for real.

"I hope you have someone in your office because this isn't a girlfriend talking." His voice was tight.

"Sorry. I'm in the office. I should have called and updated you on Lane rather than barking an order. There's been some minor improvement." Saturday seemed like ages ago and a good night sleep even further away. "I'm a little frazzled. Can we talk more about it tonight? Maybe meet for a drink?" All I was really in the mood for was a hot bath and an early bedtime, but that wasn't Michael's fault.

"Sure, we can talk about it later. I know you'd call me if there were any news."

"Thank you for that. I'm just tired and distracted."

"So, Kelly's autopsy. I reviewed it again yesterday, and it reads exactly as we talked about. Heart failure. The ME believes she was born with a defective valve. There was no way of knowing she had a problem until the incident happened."

"Do we know anything about the timing? Were they able to determine if there was anything that exacerbated the condition? Something that caused her heart to fail, now?"

"Like what?"

"I don't know. Exertion, sports, something she consumed that caused her heart to race?"

"Something she consumed? Is this about Kelly Cavanaugh or your sister? Are you still thinking there's a connection?"

I could hear frustration in his voice. I took a drink of tea before responding afraid my tone would be sharp. Snapping at him because I was obsessed wasn't fair, nor did he have all the information.

"Lane is in the hospital with an undiagnosed illness and an erratic heartbeat is a primary symptom," I said. "What you don't know is that her refrigerator was full of the VTF energy drink. So that's two data points between the women. Coincidence? May very well be. But I'm not going to pretend it's not worthy of consideration."

Michael was silent on the other end of the phone. I assumed he was contemplating how close to the line we were stepping. "Okay, I'll get you an appointment with the ME. But I want to be there when you speak to him."

I agreed, and we made loose plans to meet for a drink.

Ending the call, I then dialed Cai. "Are you free for a quick cup of coffee?"

"I can be. Now?"

"I'll meet you downstairs in fifteen." More detail wasn't needed. We both knew the shorthand.

Cai breezed into the Starbucks in the base of her office building five minutes after I had arrived. Her dark hair was pulled back in a low, loose knot. She was in work mode, an ivory silk blouse and navy pencil skirt. But the four-inch Louboutin stilettos said something else. Cai would prefer to endure weekly visits to her podiatrist rather than wear flats. She waved, ordered her drink, and joined me at the window counter.

"What? Nothing to do today so you decided to visit me?" She uncapped her dark roast and brought it to her lips, smiling. "You interjected yourself at the perfect time. I was reading a counteroffer that had my blood boiling. This is much more fun than storming around the block of few times to work off my annoyance."

"I visited our mutual friend Seth this morning." I said, leaning against the counter and watching her face. Cai must have had meetings with Seth about the IPO prior to the shooting. Had she noticed that he didn't look well?

"Oh?" she said, not raising her eyes. "How's he feeling?"

I doubted that she didn't already know the answer, but let it slide.

"He looks like shit. And you know that's not normal. How long has he looked like death warmed over?"

"Is that why you asked to meet?" She put down her cup and looked at me quizzically.

"Don't tell me you haven't noticed how thin he is? Or how pale and sickly he looks? Something's going on with him and it started before the shooting. I'm worried about him."

"He's been under a lot of stress. And by the way, it's not unusual to lose a little weight when you've just been shot. Of course he looks like hell. Wouldn't we all?"

"Come on Cai. Don't go lawyer on me. I'm concerned about my friend. I think he's sick and not talking about it. And I think you know it and that you're both pretending everything is okay because of this IPO."

Cai raised her eyebrows and looked at me over the rim of her coffee. "That's quite the story you've fabricated. Do you think the guilt trip works on attorneys? You know I can't discuss my client or his business with you. Are things so rough at work that you need innuendo to sell subscriptions?"

I'd pissed her off. The attorney voice was back. She was a master at well-placed inflection. My phone pinged a text from Michael.

Call me ASAP. I dialed while Cai recapped her coffee and picked up her wallet. I laid my hand on her forearm, asking her to wait a minute, so I could apologize. I was doing a lot of that today.

"Did you get the appointment?" I asked Michael.

"No, I got distracted." He paused. "We have another dead kid. Male, 22, fitness buff. Roommate says he'd been doing a three-day fast, drinking nothing but VTF. I thought you'd want to know."

I stared out the window, stunned at what Michael had just said. My worst fears were coming true. "I'm heading to the hospital now."

I hung up with Michael my thoughts immediately on my sister.

"What's wrong?" Cai asked. "You look like you're going to pass out."

"I think your client's going to need a different type of attorney, and soon."

17

I left Cai standing at the counter with her coffee, a confused look on her face, as I ran out of Starbucks. She'd hear the details of the latest incident from her client, perhaps even from police headquarters. Right now the only thing that mattered was getting to my sister. I hailed a cab and got over to Northwestern Hospital as quickly as I could.

"I need to see Dr. Lassiter. It's urgent," I said to the nurse managing the station. Seeing the look on my face, she hesitated only a second.

"I'll track him down and send him to your sisters room," she said, reaching for the phone.

Lane was awake when I entered her room, her hair in a loose bun and her bathrobe over the hospital gown. She was having a conversation with my father about a book he used to read to her as a child. A midday talk show host added commentary in the background. Something inane about the rising price of Thanksgiving turkeys this season. The normalcy of their conversation immediately felt incongruent.

I looked from Lane to my father feeling my heart race. I'd been so intent on speaking to the doctor that I hadn't figured out what I was going to say to Lane. Seeing her awake and conversational lessened my anxiety, slightly.

"Everything okay?" my father asked. "You rushed in here like something was wrong."

I made a quick decision not to say anything until I'd spoken to the doctor. The additional stress wasn't going to help anyone, especially since we couldn't tell her we had a remedy. I walked over to the side of Lane's bed and grabbed her hand.

"You look a little livelier today. Are you feeling better?" She didn't really, but I felt the need to sound a little more upbeat.

She looked down at my hand on hers and lifted her eyebrows. "That bad, huh?"

Our relationship was complex to say the least and public displays of affection between the two of us were reserved for extreme moments. Oops, caught in the act. I laughed it off as if she were being silly. I slipped off my coat and set my tote bag on an empty chair. Inside was a bottle of VTF I'd picked up downstairs in the hospital food court to give to the doctor. At the very least, maybe the ingredient list would give some ideas.

Lane sighed and adjust the pillow behind her back. "I'm getting sick of this damn place. I'm so tired of the mush they call food around here that I'm *almost* willing to try one of your disgusting green drinks." She gave me a weak smile.

"Now I know you're still sick." I laughed. "Had you asked me for a caramel macchiato I would've known you were feeling better."

"Oh, come on, the food ain't that bad," my father added, picking up the Chicago Tribune he had on his lap.

Since he was content with anything wrapped in plastic, he could throw in a microwave, I told Lane I'd run downstairs and get her something from Beatrix. After overdosing on Spaghetti-O's and Campbell's soup during high school, I didn't wish canned food on anyone other than my cat.

The doctor came into the room. He looked around, appearing confused by the relaxed mood he'd walked in to.

"You wanted to see me, Ms. Kellner?" he said.

"Yes, I do." Then to Lane. "I'll go get you two some lunch." May as well continue being evasive.

I didn't say any more but stepped out of the room, Lassiter following behind. I turned the corner and walked down the hallway until I felt we were out of earshot.

"The nurse said it was urgent." He looked quickly at a text that had popped up on his phone. "What's going on?" he asked.

I took a breath. "I may know what's wrong with my sister. Or at least a direction that we can investigate. I know we spoke about her high caffeine intake, but I believe it's possible that something Lane has been drinking may be the cause of her illness."

"I'm listening." He looked at me, brow furrowed, anticipating what I had to say.

"My sister has been consuming an energy drink produced by a local company called VTF Industries. You may be aware of them. They've had quite a bit of media coverage recently. However, I have reason to believe that two individuals have died suspiciously after heavy consumption of the drink."

I could see I had his attention. I pulled the bottle out of my tote and handed it to him. He looked carefully at the label.

"Beyond a heavy dose of caffeine, I don't see anything concerning on the ingredient list. What do you know of these two previous cases? What links do you believe exist?"

As I was filling him in on Kelly Cavanaugh's death, I saw Michael rushing down the hall. A slight sheen of sweat glossed his forehead. I hadn't been this happy to see him since the night Erik died.

The men exchanged greetings.

"I was updating Dr. Lassiter on Kelly," I said to Michael. "Why don't you fill us in on today's situation."

"A fitness center employee came back to his apartment this morning after being out all night and found his roommate dead," Michael said, his voice showing none of the anxiety that was in mine. I listened intently as he spoke, soothed by his nearness. "A Jeremey Wolanski, age 22, a personal trainer at Equinox. According to the guy we spoke to, there'd been no evidence of illness, but he said Wolanski had complained of feeling like he couldn't catch his breath. Like his heart was beating too fast was the exact quote. The young men worked together."

"And the deceased drank this energy drink?" Lassiter asked.

"Yes. He was on his fourth day of what he called a juice fast. And by juice, he meant this." Michael nodded at the bottle in Lassiter's hand

"Can I assume an autopsy will be performed?"

"We've been able to speak with Wolanski's mother and she's granted permission. She also confirmed that as far as she knew, he had no health issues and was not taking any medication. She isn't sure if he had a primary care physician. I've been in contact with the medical examiner's office and a copy of the autopsy report of the first victim is being sent over to you. Clearly this is conjecture, but it's worth looking into." Michael said, watch me for a reaction.

"I agree," Lassiter said. "How long ago did the first victim die?"

"Three months," I said.

"That means we should approach toxicology differently. Perhaps there's a bacterium we missed or possibly a contaminant. I'll speak with the ME. If we can isolate any other common elements in the pathology, it can help us with the direction. I'll get this bottle in for analysis, but if there's a contaminant, that doesn't mean it will be present in this batch." The doctor looked from me to Michael, then tapped notes into his phone.

"I understand. Does that give you any ideas about how to treat my sister differently?"

"I'll order some new toxicology tests, see if there's anything out of whack." He lifted the bottle. "I'll speak to you soon."

Lassiter left, leaving Michael and me alone in the hall.

"She's going to be okay," Michael said, pulling me into his arms. "We'll figure this out."

I clung to him, willing his words to be true, drawing on his strength. I pulled away keeping my hands on his arms. "It's time I told Lane."

"What happened to my salad?" she said as we returned to the room. "He's cute, but not what I meant when I said I was hungry."

Lane and Michael had met after Erik died. But at the time, he'd just been a cop doing his job who happened to have a little bit of a crush on me. I could see her mind whirling, but couldn't tell if she was curious or nervous. Regardless, the cat was going to be out of the bag on my love life soon enough.

I introduced Michael to my father. It felt odd. But this was hardly the time to be concerned about father/daughter protocol.

"What's going on? You two look all serious," Lane said, suspicion winning out.

"Lane, how frequently are you drinking VTF energy drinks?"

18

I'd lied to Lane. Well, that is if you call omission a lie. Michael had left the hospital to get back to work on the Wolanski case while I stayed to explain the situation to Lane and my father. I told them enough about the concerns we had regarding the energy drink to explain the additional testing Lane would be going through but left out the part about anyone dying. In other words, enough to scare them a little, but not enough to cause panic. Bottom line, they seemed to be relieved to be one step closer to an explanation for her illness. Too bad I wasn't.

Then I'd made the lunch run to Beatrix I'd promised, picking up a Supernatural Chopped Salad for Lane and a Prime Burger with Kennebec fries for dad.

Leaving them to their meal, I made a run to Lane's apartment to pull all the VTF out of her fridge, assuming Lassiter would want it for testing, then hustled over to have another heart-to-heart with Seth.

This one might lead to bloodshed. He'd lied. I could feel it and I was disgusted.

I stormed into the VTF company headquarters, blowing past

the receptionist I'd met yesterday. She was on the phone engrossed in some sales pitch. She frowned and tried to wave me down, but I kept walking. Today wasn't a day for politeness.

I found him in his office leaning over his large conference table sorting through piles of head shots. His desk phone was beeping as the receptionist tried to get in a warning call, fortunately she hadn't been fast enough. A young woman wrapped in Lycra stood next to him making some inane reference about having used a brunette in the last photo shoot. They both looked up as I burst into the room.

"You'll need to finish this later," I said to the woman. "I need to speak with your boss." She swung her eyes from me to Seth wondering what he wanted her to do. He nodded and mumbled something about using her best judgment as she shuffled the photographs into a folder. Neither one of us said another word until she was out of the room and the door was closed.

"Well, you certainly know how to make an entrance," Seth started. "I assume this phone call is my warning announcement?" He stepped to his desk and picked up the handset, assuring his receptionist that everything was fine.

Hardly. But he'd find that out soon enough.

"You do have my phone number," he said. Seth was annoyed, but his arrogant tone did nothing to redirect my focus. I'd heard enough of his evasion and lies. People were dying, and he knew it. I could feel his fear under the mask of bravado. Men were predicable that way. The bully in them came out the minute someone pushed them to admit their failings.

"Sit down," I barked.

He slowly pulled out a chair and did as he was told, but leaned back, his good arm braced over the one in the sling, letting me know that compliance was only momentary.

I had too much anger inside me to do anything other than

pace. "You need to start talking and no more of this innocent bystander bullshit you have been dishing out."

"Start talking about what? I don't have time for whatever this histrionic display is all about so please get to the punch line."

"Sexist response. Nice touch, but clichéd. It's time for confession. There are no investors in this room. I want the truth, the truth about Kelly Cavanaugh. The truth about what's going on in this company that you are hiding. I want to know why people are dying and why you've looked so sick even before you were shot!"

"So you're barging in here to call me a liar?" Seth started to get to his feet.

"You dated her. Lied about it, and now someone else is dead." I stood firm in front of him watching, waiting, gauging his body language as he let that sink in.

Seth sat back down. The little bit of color left in his face drained away and he stared at the table frozen. "What are you talking about?" he squeaked out.

"Another man died today after drinking your drink. And my sister is lying in a hospital bed. I'm not going to let her be the next victim because you're too damn worried about your IPO."

My voice had taken on a cold, controlled anger. Nothing made me more irate than when greed trumped humanity. And here, this man, a man I'd known for years, a man I considered a friend, was doing just that. He had concealed information, I could see it in his face. He knew there was a connection between Kelly Cavanaugh's death and her use of VTF.

"No, that can't be. It has to be a mistake." He looked up at me with confusion and panic in his eyes. But the only thing I cared about in this moment was getting at the truth.

"Dammit, Seth. Tell me! What really happened? What do you know?"

The office door opened and Michael Hewitt entered, escorted by the nervous receptionist I had ignored earlier.

"This is Detective Hewitt," she said, her face a mix of confusion and fear.

Seth nodded, and she scurried out, tripping on her own feet as she left.

Michael looked at me, his eyes flashing anger behind the police detective mask. He wanted to give me shit for being here ahead of him. We stared at each other, words unsaid. I opened my mouth to explain myself, but nothing would come. All my fears and emotions were jumbled up in my head. I was acting on adrenaline, not logic or protocol.

"I need to speak to Mr. Bowman," Michael said, his eyes on me.

In other words, hit the road. I returned Michael's glare, frustrated to be shut out, frustrated that I hadn't gotten answers, and frustrated to be out ranked.

"I'm not talking to anyone without my attorney," Seth said, reaching for the phone.

As Seth placed his call, Michael pulled me aside. "You need to leave. I know you're worried about your sister but you can't be here." His voice had softened, but only slightly. "What in the world are you thinking running over here to warn your friend, *if* that's what he is?"

"Warning him?" I snapped my head up. "What are you talking about? I came here to get answers. I came to find out what's in that goddamn drink so I can save my sister's life. And you choose this moment for some ridiculous conclusions about Seth and I being romantically involved? As if *that* were any of your business."

"This isn't the time or place for this conversation." Michael's voice was stone cold. "You need to leave now and let me do my job. What you're doing is bordering on obstruction."

My frustration threatened to overflow. Michael needed room to do his job, and I knew that, but he had no claims on me. How dare he throw jealousy into the situation.

"My attorney is on her way," Seth said, too distracted by his own conversation to have noticed ours.

My eyes swung from Seth to Michael. It appeared they both had ulterior motives. Michael stared at me, his eyes hard. I turned and left the room, disgusted with both of them.

I paused to control my emotions as I reached the building lobby. Leaning my head against the wall, I took a couple deep breaths. Seth knew, I could feel it. He knew about Kelly, he knew about the connection with his drink, and he hid the information to save his own ass. I seethed with anger at his greed and hubris.

Michael had been doing his job when he asked me to leave, but the accusation? He could think whatever the hell he wanted, right now I didn't give a damn who he thought I was sleeping with.

19

I returned to my office, my mind laser focused. I needed to know everything I could about VTF Industries. The image of Michael questioning Seth with my best friend serving as his attorney, made my head spin. Once she understood the gravity of the situation, I was certain Cai would help him find an appropriate criminal defense attorney. But for now could this be any more strangely intertwined?

My fingers flew over the keyboard working my browser into a frenzy. Page after page I dug into VTF's history. As a private company, it wasn't as easy as contacting investor relations or pulling up an annual report. I found a few articles on Crain's and documented the basics but it wasn't enough. LexisNexis gave me slightly more information. But who were the suppliers? What about investors? Was someone padding the bank account for all this growth? I knew Seth had bootstrapped the company in the beginning, but it seemed unlikely he could fund his aggressive growth strategy on the strength of his personal financial situation alone.

I needed help. I found Brynn holed up in an empty conference room, large noise-canceling headphones over her ears, and a pile of documents spread out on the table in front of her. Engrossed in her work, she hadn't noticed me.

I pulled out a chair and sat down beside her. She tapped off her music and pulled the headphones down around her neck.

"Are you working on anything that can be interrupted?"

"Are you kidding? I'm blasting music to keep myself from falling dead asleep on the table. What do you need?"

Brynn was a computer whiz. She could turn over rocks that I didn't know existed. "I need some information on a private company. I'm looking for investors, any outstanding loans. Basically I want a deep financial dive. You game?"

"Anything to get me away from analyzing the decline in membership in the Junior League, duh." She rolled her eyes. "What's the company?"

"VTF Industries."

She slipped the headphone off completely and laid them on the table, then tilted her head as she looked at me. "You want me to investigate your friend's company? I know it's none of my business, but why not just ask him?"

"I'm not sure he'd tell me the truth," I said, the hard reality difficult to face. "I told you about Cavanaugh's claims. Well, they may be accurate. There's been another death."

"What?" She leaned forward, her eyes wide, placing her elbows on the table.

"A young man. Twenty-two. He was a personal trainer with Equinox. He'd been fasting, drinking only VTF products for several days. His roommate found him this morning. Obviously, we don't have enough information yet, but it's hard not to wonder if those dots connect. I also don't want my sister to be victim number three."

I couldn't believe what I was hearing myself say. Seth was someone I'd have trusted with my life. Now I didn't know what to believe about him.

"They're both around my age, the victims, I mean," she said slowly, letting the idea that one of her contemporaries had faced his own mortality sink in. "Do you think that means something?"

"I don't know. Perhaps twenty-something's are simply the target market for the product?" I shrugged. Based on VTF's marketing images, it was logical to assume this was the target demographic.

"Anything specific on the financial angle? Are you thinking bankruptcy?"

"Seth told me there's an IPO planned for early next year. I'm wondering how leveraged VTF Industries is going into the deal. It also means a big windfall for him and anyone else with skin in the game. I'm wondering who else that might be."

"Done. Say no more, I'm on it. Do you want this to take priority over the information you asked for on Nadell Capital?"

I nodded. "And Borkowski doesn't need to hear about this yet either. I'll figure out what to tell him when I know more."

"You got it, boss." She smiled and winked. "I hope your sister's okay."

I returned to my office racking my brain for any mention Seth may have made of investors. He'd always been a good salesman, a glass-three-quarters-full kind of guy. I knew that he'd struggled in the early years to some degree, as everyone did, but at the time, he'd spoken about it as if it were momentary inconvenience, not a make-or-break moment. If he'd ever mentioned a financial partner or any kind of cash infusion, it wasn't coming to mind. Then again, would he have shared that with me? Appearances meant a great deal to him; would he have viewed taking on a partner as a win, or some type of flaw in his ability to make it on his own?

And what about the jealous competitor theory that Seth was floating? I wasn't buying it, but I pulled up some data. Projected to reach $60 billion dollars in the next few years, the energy drink industry was dominated by a handful of major players such as Red Bull.

VTF wasn't a threat to the big guys. It simply picked up the crumbs by targeting the under-tapped subcategory of organic. The smaller players like VTF, typically sold things like kombucha, raw-pressed juice combos, or bottled flavored teas. However, it could be viewed as an acquisition target.

If Seth were to be believed, and a competitor was coming after him, logistics were the key. I let myself mull that over. The only options I saw were tampering within the plant, which meant an employee, or tampering at the supplier level, and that would have meant cooperation between multiple parties. A pissed off employee seemed the more likely bet. And that brought me back to Cavanaugh.

I didn't think for a second the man would have done something intentionally to harm his own daughter, but bad judgement with unintended consequences was another story.

My internet dabbling was also bringing up articles about the health concerns related to energy drinks. Caffeine was the stimulant of choice in all of them, VTF's included, although none had levels beyond what was generally considered safe. References were also made to stimulant additives such as guarana, taurine, and L-carnitine.

Several individuals were alleged to have died from cardiac arrest after ingesting high caffeine and taurine energy drinks, but I couldn't find a case that had proven the causal effect. The information sent a chill of fear down my spine. Lane practically mainlined coffee. Adding in the VTF dosage, who knew how high her daily intake was. I made a note to look for specific legal case details and to talk to the hospital staff about cutting her off. The bottom line seemed to be that no one knew what the combined effect of the caffeine and the stimulants did to the body, let alone multiple bottles.

I sent Michael a text reminding him that he'd agreed to let me meet with the ME to discuss Kelly Cavanaugh's autopsy report provided we went together.

As I sat the phone down and swung my eyes back to my computer screen, it rang. I grabbed it, my eyes still on the data.

"Andrea, I'm so glad I caught you. This is Candiss Nadell. I wanted to follow up on our conversation about increasing your involvement in the Drea Foundation. Could you free yourself up for lunch so that we might speak further? We're busy with our strategic planning and I'd love your input."

"Yes, I'd love to be involved. However, there's a personal situation that's developed since we last spoke that's pressing. I'm not sure the timing is right."

I felt guilty saying no. These girls needed every bit of help they could get, but right now I wasn't sure I could afford the distraction.

"Oh, I'm so sorry. Is there anything I can help with? That sounded like I was prying, didn't it? I just meant feel free to reach out. After all that's what Drea is founded on, women supporting other women."

"No, you're not prying. It's my sister. She's fallen ill and has been hospitalized. I'm sure we'll have her situation sorted through shortly. I'll be in touch soon."

"How awful. Again, please let me know if there's anything at all I can do."

"Thank you. I'll speak to you when I can," I said, ending the call.

As always, Candiss had maintained her charm and grace. Hmm, Candiss had known Seth for a long time. Did she know anything about his investors? Perhaps even invested herself?

20

It was four o'clock in the afternoon and the diner I had just entered was nearly empty, occupied only by a couple of guys in electrician uniforms nursing their coffee at the counter. The acrid scent of a pot burned down hit my nose, reminding me that I disliked the stuff. I'd received a call an hour ago from Olivia, the VTF production assistant I'd met yesterday morning. She'd asked if we could talk. Although I was anxious to get back to the hospital, Olivia was on my list of people to circle back to, so I suggested a coffee shop in the Loop that was easy for both of us.

A waitress in a light blue polo and matching bandana around her head, told me to sit anywhere as she topped off the men's cups. I walked to the far corner and took a booth away from the window where we'd have some privacy. If Olivia wanted to talk, I was going to make it as easy as I could.

Finished with her customers, the waitress came over, and dropped a menu onto the table. I ordered a bowl of fruit and a cup of hot water, expecting the mediocre black teas most diners seemed to stock. She looked at me over the top of her glasses but kept quiet. Most likely thinking that my tip wouldn't be worth her time.

I pulled a Ziploc bag out of my purse and fished out a decent bag of tea, and a honey stick. I was always prepared for a tea emergency.

Olivia joined me a moment later. She mumbled hello and slid into the booth. After removing her canvas army jacket and knit hat, she balled them into the corner of the booth. Strands of hair had come loose from her ponytail and hung limp around her face which was pink from the cold.

The waitress returned with my order. "I see Lipton isn't your thing." I shrugged and smiled. "How about you, honey?" she said to Olivia. "Do you drink fancy tea too?"

"Coffee, cream and sugar."

"My kinda girl."

The waitress gone, I sat quietly waiting for Olivia. I had about twenty thousand questions I wanted to throw at her, but she'd been the one who'd asked to meet so I waited.

"I looked you up," she said. "You're a reporter, right? That's why you were at the plant. You're doing a story on us."

"I work for Link-Media. It's a digital news organization so we're online content. As I said yesterday, I was gathering some background research." I decided to leave it at that for the moment and see where this was leading.

"What kind of story is it?"

I dunked my tea bag and stirred in the honey before responding, calculating how to manage the conversation. I could tell she was feeling me out and had a sensitive bullshit meter, but I was anxious to get to the hospital. I made a gamble that she would appreciate someone who cut to the chase.

"Olivia, I'll make a deal with you," I said, leaning my elbows on the table. "If you're willing to tell me exactly why you wanted to see me, I'll be straight with you on whatever questions you have. I'm glad that you called me, I just don't have a lot of time today. My sister's in the hospital and I'm a little preoccupied. I'm meeting with you on my way to see her. So, why don't we both just agree to be direct. And then maybe we can speak more another time."

She thought for a moment. "That's cool with me," she said. "But I have one question first." I nodded for her to continue. "Do you have something going on with Seth? It looked like you guys were tight."

She said it as if she'd already made assumptions about what "tight" meant.

"We're friends. I've known him for about eight years. He helped my sister out of a jam with a not-so-nice boyfriend several years ago, so I respect him." I took a sip of my tea before continuing. "Despite our friendship, if you're concerned that this conversation will get back to him, or that I couldn't be objective, I give you my word that if you want this to be a private conversation, then it will be." I paused, keeping my eyes locked on hers. "Unless you and I agree otherwise."

She cocked her head and considered me. The waitress delivered her coffee, and she took her time stirring in a healthy portion of milk and three packets of sugar.

"Didn't you get the memo? About sugar?" I said, in an attempt to ease the tension. "I thought you guys had to take an oath over at VTF to live on nuts and twigs. Sugar is the bad guy, right?"

She laughed. "I just help make the stuff, I don't drink it."

Finally, we were getting somewhere. "So why am I here?" I smiled and stabbed a green grape, wilting before my eyes.

"I heard about that guy that died. Everyone's talking about it." She tucked a strand of hair behind her ear. "I even saw a video his roommate posted on Facebook saying drinking VTF might have killed him. And Seth hasn't been in the office since you left. No one knows where he is. Has he been arrested?"

Facebook? The line between journalism and self-reported media just kept getting narrower. "If you're worried about your job, I don't have any information about Seth and his plans, if that's what you're worried about," I said. "As far as I know, there've been no charges against anyone. Regardless of the roommate's accusations, it's far too early to draw any conclusions. I would expect status quo for the near future. Martin appears to have the plant working at high capacity. Don't worry just yet."

It sounded hollow, even to my own ears; of course she'd be worried. I could only imagine what the rumor mill at the plant was breeding. In the absence of information, crazy theories typically occupied far too much air time.

"Is it true? Did he die because of our drink?" Olivia looked at me. I saw fear in her eyes and heard it in her voice.

"No one can answer that right now. But I'm sure that CPD is going to do everything it can to find out," I said, hoping to help calm her anxiety. News had traveled fast and if people were already jumping to conclusions on the cause of death, then Martin had a potential morale issue on his hands and Seth, a PR issue that would need more than a boilerplate press release.

I'd certainly gone down the who's-to-blame path, but then again, I knew about Kelly Cavanaugh and Lane.

Olivia stared off at the street traffic outside lost in thought, but didn't seem calmed by my words. I made a quick decision to see if she'd trust me enough to answer a few of my questions.

"From what I saw in the plant, the bottles are sealed with a plastic wrap before they leave your facility. Correct?"

She turned back to me and fiddled with her coffee spoon. "Yes, right before they're put in the cases. If they've been tampered with, that plastic wrapper would be missing. If that's where you're going?"

I nodded. "What about spoilage? Are there inspectors that come in periodically, you know like in a restaurant?" I made a note to myself to check into the food safety regulations.

"Sure, but we only see them maybe once a year. The government is not exactly a precision machine. Bottles and caps are sterilized, we've got this super complex water filtration system. I can't imagine any bugs getting into the stuff."

"Based on what you know, is there any reason for anyone to question the safety of the product? Even if it were unintended." I was thinking of Cavanaugh. He would have been her boss prior to Martin.

She hesitated, twisting a leather bracelet strung with a charm on her wrist. "You sure this is confidential? If this gets back to Seth or to Martin, they're going to know it was me."

"Olivia, if you know something, please, you need to tell me. We don't know if this young man died because of anything VTF did, but if you hold back and someone else gets ill, we have a bigger issue on our hands." I felt bad laying on the guilt, but the truth was painful.

She took another drink of coffee and stared out the window again, trying to make up her mind. "I don't know this means anything, but we have a couple new vendors for the botanicals. Vendors that aren't top tier. Orders have been coming in so fast that we're having trouble keeping up. I think we've cut some corners trying to get product out."

"Seth told me that a few months back there'd been a batch that had to be recalled. Was that related to a new vendor?"

"A recall? I don't know anything about that. We've been working three shifts. Trying to keep up with the orders and it still isn't enough. Raw materials are disorganized, some of the vendors are unproven. I don't even know if we've been following the cleaning protocol. Cleaning these machines takes them off-line for 12 hours. I haven't seen them go down more than once in the last six months. We don't have the time. I love this job, but if we're making people sick, there isn't going to be a job."

"Sounds pretty chaotic. Given the production demands, are you saying that things just got sloppy? Or are you suggesting that maybe a supplier didn't send what you ordered?"

"I don't know. I guess I'm just saying it's possible that a mistake was made."

"You've worked at VTF for a couple of years, were you around while Cavanaugh ran the department?"

"Yeah, what are you getting at?" She was suddenly wary again.

"Well, he's had a rough year. His daughter died. That's a lot to go through and I can't help but wonder how that might have affected his work." I hated to ask the question but there was no way around it.

She looked at me and shook her head. "Don't go there. Luke's a good guy. I'm not going to trash him. I'm only talking to you because I don't think Martin will. Reality is we just can't keep up with production. We've gotten sloppy and Martin will be the scapegoat for all of this, if it hits the fan."

"No. Of course. I'm not suggesting Luke did anything intentionally," I said, lowering my voice and softening my eyes. And hoping my compassion for the for the man's situation was clear. "But no one thinks clearly when they're experiencing such grief. He suffered a tremendous loss. It's understandable that he would have been distracted. I'm just wondering if you saw anything that gave you reason to believe he wasn't at the top of his game."

She seemed to relax a little, picking up an empty sugar packet and folding it accordion style.

"Luke was pretty much a mess most of this year," she said. "It started in the summer, June I think. He and Seth had a couple of major blowups. Like I told you, we were having a hard time keeping up with production and everybody was tense. It only got worse after Kelly died."

"Do you know what their arguments were about?" My ears perked up.

"Not directly. But there were rumors about Seth and Kelly," she said, looking up over her coffee.

"About them dating?" So it wasn't just Cavanaugh that thought the relationship was romantic. Was it appearance or reality?

She nodded. "I don't imagine Luke thought much of a man nearly his age dating his daughter. Can't blame him. Pretty creepy to me too." She scrunched her nose. "I don't know if that was the problem or if they were blaming each other for production fuck ups. Maybe both." She shrugged and folded the sugar packet in the opposite direction.

"Did you ever see them together in an intimate situation or was it rumored?"

"Rumors. But enough of them to wonder."

I nodded. "Do you know anything about the financial situation of the company? Were bills paid on time? Are you involved in any of that?"

"Invoices don't get paid at the plant. We send them over to bookkeeping at the River North office after we've confirmed the order. But Luke did tell me some of our vendors were being paid late. That's part of the reason we were scrambling to line up new suppliers. Suddenly you're not on the top of their priority list for shipping if they have to beat you up for money."

Interesting. Money was tight. That was new information. "Do you know how long this been going on?"

She thought for a moment. "I'd say about seven months. We had this big spread in one of the fitness magazines and that really jacked up the business. We'd already been running at a good clip and when the article came out, we had to ramp up even more. Pushing vendors to increase their production. Calling in favors. But if you're paying your invoices at sixty days instead of thirty, at some point vendors want more than promises."

And vendors who wouldn't ship, meant escalating financial problems. Eventually it was a hole so deep you drowned in your own mess. Many a company had been taken down by success they couldn't keep pace with. Was Seth in that boat?

"Did you ever hear anyone talk about investors? Or financial partners?"

She thought about it for a moment. "We had reports we had to run every month. Inventory, payroll, stuff like that. Luke said it was for "the money guy." I thought he meant the accountant but I suppose it could have been someone else."

"Do you remember hearing a name?"

"I think it was something like Natell or Nadell."

21

A cold wind whipped at the collar of my jacket as I stood on Wabash Avenue and hailed a cab. The sky was already dark, and it felt as if the first snow of the season might arrive. I was unprepared for the temperature and rubbed my hands together once seated in the back of the taxi.

My head was whirling just as ferociously as the wind while the car maneuvered over to Northwestern Hospital. Had Olivia's reference to a money guy named Nadell meant Aaron Nadell, Candiss's husband? And that Nadell Capital was funding VTF? Shouldn't be surprising, after all that was his business, but I was struck again by the clubby nature of business dealings and wondering what else might be hidden.

Olivia also seemed to be corroborating Seth's assessment that Luke Cavanaugh had been under immense pressure. Pressure that was affecting his performance. But once again Seth had chosen to leave out information that seem pretty critical. Why? Was he simply trying to put VTF in the best light?

I was getting a picture of a business that didn't jive with the glossy photos and upbeat media coverage. Financial pressures. Production pressures. Demands for product that they couldn't keep up with. It wasn't conclusive of anything, other than being a potential breeding ground for sloppiness, but it did allow me to picture one possible scenario.

I found my father dozing in his chair when I walked into Lane's room. She was propped up in her bed, absently flipping through the local TV news with the sound off as he slept. She wiggled her fingers hello. I handed her a fruit smoothie I'd picked up in the food court before coming upstairs.

"It's not green. I appreciate your restraint." She gave me a small smile.

"It was hard, but I managed to resist." And to feed her a non-caffeinated drink in the process.

"How nice to see sisterly bonding." My father had woken. He sat up blinking sleep from his eyes. I stepped over and gave him a kiss on the cheek.

"Has the doctor been back in?" I asked. Lane shook her head. I looked at her realizing that I was seeing the contours of her face, the shape of her eyes, the texture of her skin with a level of detail I didn't know I'd ever done before. I was looking at her, really looking at her, hoping to see some sign that my imagination was worse than reality.

I saw pale skin and bloodshot eyes. Neither were encouraging signs. She seemed so groggy much of the time it was difficult for me to tell if she knew how sick she was.

"Drink up," I said. "I'm getting tired of seeing you without makeup."

"Well, I haven't seen anybody around here worth impressing. Other than that cop you brought in. Is he single?"

I ignored the question.

"According the nurse, the doctor's supposed to be back tonight," my father said. "She said something about having some test results back."

A nurse came in and checked Lane's IV. "Dr. Lassiter will be in shortly," she said. "Do you need anything right now?"

"How about a triple espresso from Starbucks?"

"You wish, honey." She smiled.

The doctor came in moments later. "How you feeling?" he asked.

"Ready to go dancing. You wanna join me?"

He laughed. "Well, your sense of humor is back. That's a good sign."

"Have you gotten any of the test results back yet?" I asked.

"They're starting to come in. At this point, I can rule out bacteria. We don't see any of the usual markers. So that eliminates one possible cause."

My father chimed in with questions which Lassiter answered, politely, but never going into any more than vague detail. As the men spoke, my mind was drifting to Jeremy Wolanski. How were his parents handling their grief tonight? What questions would haunt them over the next days, months, maybe even years?

My family had felt that anguish. I had felt that anguish. I couldn't let it happen again.

I pulled my focus back to the group. Lassiter was saying that the balance of the new test results he had ordered should be another 48 hours and that he'd check in on Lane in the morning. I followed him out telling Lane I was going to get a cup of tea, grabbing the tote bag I'd brought with some of the energy drink from Lane's refrigerator.

"Doctor, thank you for not going into detail about the toxicology test. I just didn't want to worry them without having something more than a hunch."

He crossed his arms over his chest and nodded. Before he could say anything, Michael rounded the corner. What was he doing here again?

My face must have shown my surprise. "I just brought someone in to the ER," he said, as if reading my mind.

The men shook hands. I imagined Lassiter was as confused as I was about why Michael kept popping up, and whether he was here as a friend or as a cop. While I appreciated Michael's official role, the personal side was more complicated. He was growing tired of the push-pull of the emotional barriers I'd erected, but I couldn't set aside my fear of being vulnerable again. I didn't know if I'd ever really trust anyone again, at least deeply enough for another relationship to develop, or if either one of us had the fortitude to find out.

"I understand your concern," Lassiter said to me. "But at some point, you'll have to tell her. I'm not seeing improvement in her condition, but she seems to be stabilizing. Have you gotten any closer to understanding what might be happening with this drink product?"

"Not yet," I said. Michael looked at me quizzically but held his questions.

"The fact that the lab ruled out bacteria, probably eliminates sanitation issues. I understand the company has brought in new suppliers that haven't been vetted as thoroughly as they should be. That seems like the next avenue to explore," I said.

"I'm doing what I can to get these toxicology reports expedited," Lassiter said. "But I'm sure I don't have to remind you that if there's a link between this product and causing harm to consumers, there's no way to keep it quiet. We'll have to contact the Department of Public Safety."

"Trust me, if there's any connection, I'll be the first one to yell it from the rooftops. Oh, I have some more samples for you," I said, handing him the bag. "These were in Lane's refrigerator."

Lassiter promised to call me as soon as he had more information, then left to attend to other obligations. Michael stared at me, his eyes hard, until Lassiter was no longer within hearing distance. "What are you doing, Andrea? Have you turned this into another personal mission to solve?"

I said nothing for a moment, gathering my thoughts.

"If you expect me to sit on the sidelines that won't be happening. This is my sister we're talking about. I can't live with myself if I don't do everything I can to make sure she stays safe. That's always been my job. I've been her protector since she was seventeen. It's in my DNA."

"I don't expect you to do nothing. But there's a point where you have to let the professionals do our job. But since you're so chummy with the crew over at VTF, I imagine you already have all kinds of information you haven't shared."

The jealous tone in his voice was back, but I ignored it.

"The professionals didn't listen to Luke Cavanaugh," I said. "If they had, maybe another person wouldn't be dead and my sister wouldn't be on the verge. From where I sit, I don't have a choice. But, we could work together on this. I'll share, if you do. Are you willing?"

Michael looked at me, his jaw tightening. He ran his hand through his hair as he considered the implications of my request. It was messy, personally and professionally, and neither of us had ground rules to fall back on. "Can't do it," he said. "Not if you think we'd be some crime-solving tag team. I have people to answer to, procedures to follow. Bringing a journalist under the tent at this stage doesn't fly with the guys I report to. I'm all ears if you stumble on something we need to know, and I'm happy to let you be first in line when we're ready to go public, but beyond that, you need to back off and let us do our jobs."

"Not a very satisfying answer, Detective Hewitt." My first thought was that I was being shoved to the back of the bus, and the second was that he was just following protocol. Not a surprise on either front. We looked at other for a moment, thoughts circling that were best left unsaid. He had a job to do and so did I. Nothing had changed. Nevertheless it stung.

"I'm going to go." Michael started to say something. I shook my head. "Don't. I understand. It's just been a long day. We'll talk tomorrow."

I gave him a quick kiss then headed downstairs to the hospital coffee shop. I parked myself at a table, nursing a cup of tea and an apple. My head was full of questions without answers. I needed to sort through the jumble of information that was starting to surface. Seth withholding information, the financial and capacity pressures that VTF was experiencing, the consequences of Cavanaugh's grief. It was easy to imagine that circumstances had contributed to a defective product, but these pressures proved nothing about the quality of the drink. Nor did they prove a connection between the drink and the deaths.

I was also feeling a little bit uncomfortable with how the conversation with Michael had ended. There was so much we didn't know about each other. After being thrown into a life-or-death situation at the start, he seemed ready to jump into a commitment, while my instinct was to extend the get-to-know-you stage indefinitely. I didn't know how long he'd be patient with me, but cautious was the best I could manage whether he liked it or not.

I finished off the last of my apple, capped my tea, and headed toward the elevator with a bag of snacks in hand for my sister and my father.

While I could tell that my father felt better supervising Lane's care from the armchair in her room, it was time for all of us to get a decent night of sleep. My guest room was nothing but an empty box so I'd offered him my couch for the night, since I was only a ten-minute walk. He'd declined on previous evenings, but knowing my father, it was likely because he perceived it as an intrusion in my mental space rather than discomfort with the sleeping accommodations. Maybe tonight he'd take me up on it.

As I rode the elevator back up to Lane's floor, I scrolled through half a dozen texts and news alerts that had popped up on my phone. The doors opened as I was responding to a note from Brynn. As I turned toward Lane's wing where the long hallway split, low voices down at the other end pulled at me. The sound was familiar. I turned around. Michael stood, his hands on the shoulders of a pretty blond. Only inches separated them. He pulled her into an embrace and kissed her.

22

"Are you always up this early?" my father mumbled as I tried to tiptoe past the makeshift bed I'd set up for him in my living room last night. We'd gone for dinner together last night after saying goodnight to Lane and it had gotten late, so I'd convinced him a night on my couch made more sense than the trek to Lane's apartment.

The sun was barely starting to warm the sky, but I'd been up for two hours. He was buried in a tangle of blankets on my sofa, Walter purred contentedly on his chest as he spoke.

"Sorry, did I wake you?" I said.

"I've been up for a little while. Just didn't want to disturb the furball. Go ahead and turn on a light. We don't need you tripping on cat toys."

"Walter looks pretty happy. I was going to make some tea, but if I move toward the kitchen, he'll discard you like a dirty tissue. Might even leave track marks on your chest to get to his wet food."

My father laughed and scratched Walter behind the ears. He lifted the cat, moving him to the other end of the sofa, then sat up adjusting the pillows behind his back.

"I don't have any coffee," I said, switching on a floor lamp. "I forget to buy it. And Erik took the Nespresso machine when he moved out, anyway." It was funny how little details of our former life popped back into my mind at odd moments. Things like this didn't make me sad so much as it reminded me of how drastically my life had changed in such a short period of time. And that the legal details of his estate were far from resolved. "So, your choices are orange juice or tea."

"Nothing for me, I'll get a cup at the hospital." He paused. "You can tell me, you know," he said, looking a bit forlorn. The dim light cast shadows over the hollows of his face making him appear aged and tired. "I can tell when you're keeping something back. You always try to be so stoic, but I can see it. I can see that you're worried."

I didn't know how to answer. Should I tell him that two people may have died from an energy drink and his daughter might be next? That I'd lain awake much of the night wondering about the woman I'd seen Michael kiss? That I didn't know if I'd still own Link-Media a year from now? It all seemed too much to worry him with when his daughter lay in hospital bed.

Stoic wasn't how I saw myself. Practical, logical, yes. They were qualities that had served me well in my career; in my relationships, not so much. For me, sometimes the only way to move through life was to find tunnel vision on one issue and let everything else be ignored. This seemed like one of those times, both for me and my father.

"No, I haven't told you everything about Lane's situation," I said quietly. "But only because I'm still not sure what's true and what isn't. There's no point adding anxiety over something that may simply be an unconnected coincidence. I promise you I'm doing everything I can to find out, as is Dr. Lassiter." I smiled softly and looked down at him, pulling my robe tighter. "For now, the best thing we can do for Lane is to keep her spirits up.

She'll heal a lot faster if she's not worried, and that's more important. I promise we'll talk when I have some answers."

He didn't look entirely satisfied. I leaned over, squeezed his hand, and gave him a kiss on the cheek. "I'm going to go make that tea now, then take a shower. There are clean towels in the hall bath and an extra toothbrush. Dad, she's going to be okay."

My mind was on Lane and on Michael as I ran through my morning routine. Despite my trepidations about a relationship, I was hurt, and I was angry. Now I knew why he kept appearing at the hospital, he was juggling women who needed comforting. Michael's previous comments about "not sharing" came back into my mind in waves. What a load of shit. Obviously he was just another man, no different from Erik, who'd lie about anything to get laid, and to hell with who got hurt.

I stomped around my condo as the sun turned the sky orange, illuminating the Hancock Building outside my terrace. I busied myself with cleaning, email, anything to shift my mind off men behaving badly. Well, off men behaving badly in their romantic pursuits, the others were *exactly* who I needed to focus on.

It wasn't even 7 a.m. yet, so with over an hour to kill before even the earliest of birds was up and functioning, I moved into my makeshift office to clarify my thoughts on the VTF situation. It had been my habit as an ASA to plot out my cases visually on a whiteboard. Seeing the connections between people and events helped me think. Post-its on a blank wall in my empty office would serve the same purpose.

Right now, I had little to work with, just a handful of people and some accusations. But if the accusations had any teeth and the energy drink was either the cause, or an accelerating factor in the deaths, there would need to be an ingredient or specific contaminant at the root of this.

I popped open my laptop and went back to my previous

search on energy drink health issues, this time pulling up three websites, all by the same law firm, soliciting plaintiffs for a class action lawsuit related to energy drink health issues. The firm was a name well known to anyone who watched late night television or noticed billboards. They specialized in class action legal work and had offices around the country.

As I'd read earlier, these sites made connections between energy drinks and side effects such as kidney failure, cardiac arrest, and death. The issues circled around inadequate consumer warnings related to consumption levels, deceptive advertising, and effects on the body of specific ingredients such as high caffeine, taurine, and niacin, which could cause liver damage. I shuddered. Class actions were federal cases usually involving at minimum, forty individuals or more who'd been harmed. That meant attorneys were smelling blood in the water.

I noted a few other websites referencing civil suits and out of court settlements, adding a few notes to check into the details.

I stood and paced the small room. The claims in these cases were against disclosed ingredients that individually were not harmful, however the dosing or the combination of ingredients was at issue. I needed an analysis of the product. An independent analysis. I grabbed my phone, made a quick phone call, then headed toward my garage, Lane's confiscated bottles of VTF with me in a bag.

Thirty minutes later I walked into a nondescript building just west of the Roosevelt and Damen intersection, in an area known as the Illinois Medical District. The neighborhood housed a concentration of facilities for research, education, and government services such as the VA. The medical examiner's office was here, as was the FBI regional office.

A guy I knew from my legal days ran a small private testing lab. They were expensive and specialized in cases involving chemical analysis, therefore, as an ASA, it was a source used only on rare occasion. Given the second death, CPD would be running the energy drinks through their lab but I wasn't willing to chance the backlog. After all, Michael had made it clear I was on my own.

A small bald man met me in the lobby. He was thin and wiry with skin the color of burnt caramel and a smile that lived permanently on his face.

"Henry, it's good to see you," I said, extending a hand.

"I gotta say, I was surprised to get your call this morning. Didn't you leave law and order behind?"

"I'm here on a personal matter. In other words, I'm the one footing the bill," I laughed.

"Okay, friends and family discount it is. Come on back." He smiled and tilted his head toward the far corner.

We walked down a narrow hall and through double doors that opened into a small but well-lit room lined with cabinets and nonporous surfaces. Interior glass windows showed a portion of the lab in the next room where technicians in masks and goggles fiddled with complicated looking microscopes. I knew from previous visits that the space was a maze of rooms each dedicated to different types of testing. Including state of the art spectroscopy equipment, gas chromatography, etc., the lab held a massive amount of technology only a fraction of which I could even pronounce.

"I see that business is booming."

"Yep, the bad guys keep getting more creative every day. We're doing a lot of work on synthetic drugs. Bath salts, N-bomb, crap that can kill ya fast. You outta see the junk that's coming out of China. We get one formulation figured out, and before you know it, they got new stuff in the pipeline. I gotta admire the chemists, but these things are nasty. And even young kids can buy them at their neighborhood convenience store."

He leaned against a center island. "What do you have

for me?"

I opened the bag and pulled out several bottles of VTF from the stash in Lane's fridge. I'd given half to Lassiter and kept the remainder for myself. "I need an analysis of the contents of these drinks."

Henry picked up a bottle, scanned the ingredient list. "Okay," he said. "Are you looking for something particular? Or is this about verifying ingredients?"

I brought him up to speed quickly on my suspicions. "Basically, I want to know if there's anything in these drinks that shouldn't be there. Bacteria, contaminants, toxins. Or if the concentration of the ingredients is usually high. I want to know if there is any reason for these drinks to make people ill."

He scrunched his nose and held a bottle up the light. "We'll start with deformulation and see where that takes us. That's essentially the process of separating the individual components chemically. If we need to go deeper after we've got this stuff mapped out, that can be your call. No sense spending the bucks if you don't need to."

I agreed.

"What's your time frame?"

"Yesterday."

"You and everyone else. I don't know why I bother to ask." He laughed. "Good thing I like you."

He called over a technician standing at one of the computer stations. "I need a rush on these. Deformulation. Get started logging them and I'll be over in a minute to give you the details."

The tech smiled, loaded the bottles into a bin, and carried them to back to his desk.

"The product has a lot number and a use by date," Henry said. "I know you know this, but testing will only reflect the individual bottles that you brought in. It's a moment in time."

"I understand. It's all I've got to start with."

23

I was standing on the porch of Cavanaugh's three-flat. It was unlikely the man wanted to see me again, but so much had happened since our conversation yesterday there seemed no other option. He was an insider. He could corroborate Olivia's information.

Had it only been twenty-four hours? I pressed the doorbell, twice, no response. I reached into my bag for a business card and a pen.

"Can I help you?" a voice behind me said. Cavanaugh stood at the bottom of the stairs, his arms laden with grocery bags. A wool knit cap was pulled down over his ears and a thick down parka sheltered him from the weather.

"Oh, it's you again. Unless you're here, to tell me you put Bowman away, I think we've covered everything." He stomped the snow off of his boots as he reached the top, then set down his purchases to pull keys from the front pocket of his jeans.

"Mr. Cavanaugh, I know you want justice for your daughter. Let me help. I don't know why she died, but I assure you, I'm doing everything in my power to find out."

"And why would you do that?" he asked, with the flatness of a man who'd been disappointed repeatedly.

"Because I don't want my sister to be next."

He turned to me, keys in his hand, confusion spreading across his face. "She's sick too?"

"Yes. She's been in the hospital since Friday night. That's when she collapsed. She's experiencing arrhythmia. Her doctors can't find a cause."

"She drank that stuff?" I saw that he'd stiffened. Just hearing about VTF seemed to make him rigid with anger.

I nodded. "I don't know if you've heard, but there's another death being investigated. A young man died yesterday morning." I paused. "CPD is finally taking this seriously, but I don't know if it's fast enough for my sister. Please, I need your help."

He shook his head, unlocked the door, and motioned me inside. Shopping bags in hand, he disappeared to the back while I was drawn once again to the photos of Kelly. Every clichéd phrase of a life cut short came to mind. Somehow there seemed nothing more eloquent one could say.

I heard footsteps and turned.

"What do you want to know?"

I took off my coat, and we settled once again into the armchairs flanking the fireplace. I asked Cavanaugh if I could record our conversation. He agreed.

"I understand that over the last year there've been some significant demands on production at VTF. Can you speak to me about how that affected your process, your operations?"

The chronology of events was important but so was keeping Cavanaugh focused on less emotional issues.

"It's been a slow build over the last few years, nothing we couldn't handle, but about a year ago, everything got crazy. Bowman was working with some PR firm and they scored a few big stories. Before you knew it, everybody wanted the stuff.

"Of course, Bowman, being a sales guy, didn't really think about whether or not we could produce the stuff. Hell, he didn't even give me a heads up. If I'd had a couple months' notice, it was something I could've dealt with. But instead, I find out when I get an extra 50,000 units on order. And that was just the first two weeks." He leaned forward and shook his head.

"I added a crew for third shift, but before long we had problems getting raw materials. I pulled in every favor I had with my vendors but they were handcuffed too. Other clients, their own production issues, the usual. Bowman didn't care, we needed the goods. Things snowballed. We were delivering late. Retailers were bitching. I did everything I could, but without the cushion, without the planning, I just couldn't make it happen."

Cavanaugh ran a hand over the scruff of his beard and stared off, his face riddled with disappointment.

"Is that when things started getting tense, between you and Seth I mean?" I was keeping Kelly out of the conversation for now, I needed Cavanaugh's mind on the business.

"He blamed me. Expected me to pull a rabbit out of my ass. Hell, maybe I should've just put colored water in the damn bottles and called it a day. I'm not sure Bowman ever cared."

"Cared about filling orders? Or cared about his product?"

"His priority was looking good. Being the big man in front of the news. He likes the celebrity of success. Wants to control the illusion of VTF as this breakthrough force. Operations, that was always somebody else's job. Apparently, I was supposed to read minds."

"Was this happening right before you were fired?"

His face went dark, but he nodded. "This is what I was dealing with when Kelly died."

I set aside the reference to his daughter's death for the moment wanting to keep focused on the business. I was getting a clear picture of conditions as VTF, but also of Cavanaugh's state of mind. The disarray I'd seen at the plant told me that conditions hadn't changed much.

"I imagine that kind of growth took a lot of money," I said.

"Look, I don't know anything about the money side of this. Other than my key vendor stopped shipping me. He said we were sixty days behind for the fourth time in a year and he wasn't going to ship another order until we paid up. And going forward, he would no longer extend terms."

"I assume this is something you discussed with Seth."

"Bowman didn't want to hear about money, unless they were sales numbers. I submitted the invoices to the bookkeeper, as I always did, but she couldn't authorize the payment when the account was dry.

"We were screwed if we didn't pay this vendor. They supplied three of our core ingredients. Don't pay them, they don't ship. Then I gotta shut down the line. I had a lot of families depending that paycheck. I was desperate, so I went around Bowman. Called his partner. I explained the situation and next thing you know, my vendor's all paid up."

"Tell me about the partner. Is this someone active in the business?" I asked, thinking again about Aaron Nadell.

"He doesn't come to the plant. From what I hear, he focuses on the money side, more of a financial advisor who has to be consulted on the big stuff. Keeps Bowman in line financially. I had to send him monthly reports on inventory and production output. But aside from an email or two, we only had the one conversation."

"Can I ask this investor's name?"

"A guy named Aaron Nadell. Supposed to be some investment guy with a shitload of money whose only job is to make more. I hear he's been invested in the business for years but only gets involved when he has to."

Something else Seth hadn't mentioned when he'd had the

opportunity. Was this just Seth's ego and privacy issues or was I over-thinking? It was as if everything I was learning about my friend was through a back door.

"Mr. Cavanaugh, I have a question I need to ask that's uncomfortable."

He looked at me and crossed his arms. "You want to know if I had anything to do with the product being messed up. If I flipped out and accidentally poison my own kid?"

"It's very clear that you loved your daughter dearly," I said, softly. "But you've also been under tremendous stress. I can understand how a mistake could have been made."

I felt like a shit for asking and hoped that my voice showed the compassion I felt. I needed him to believe that I wasn't one more person piling on to the pain and the guilt and anguish he felt.

"Is that what Bowman says? That people died because I fucked something up?" Cavanaugh's voice was riddled with hate again and he sat back in the chair, glaring.

"If he's said that, he hasn't said it to me. I simply wouldn't be doing my job if I didn't consider all the logical options."

He leaned forward putting his elbows on his knees and his head in his hands. I stayed quiet granting him the moment of respect until he looked up.

"You think that question doesn't haunt me? That I don't lie awake night after night running through everything that could've gone wrong in production? You think I don't wonder if I had a role in killing my own daughter?"

His eyes were filled with an anguish I hadn't seen since my mother had died. He had the hollow emptiness that I remember seeing in my father, an emptiness I recognized even as a 15-year-old girl.

"The answer is no. But I imagine I'll spend the rest of my life asking that same question."

24

I felt like a schmuck. I'd left Cavanaugh alone with his pain, having opened his wounds all over again. I couldn't begin to imagine how he'd move on with his life. Seeing the ravages of his daughter's death, it was impossible not to think of my father. The years of emptiness, isolation, and grief. He'd moved through life as if by remote control having lost the ability to feel joy again.

Cavanaugh's torment brought me a tiny bit closer to understanding what my father might have felt after my mother's death. Grief, despair, endless feelings of guilt as he played back conversations and events in his mind searching for explanations. What had he done that had driven her away? What could he have done that would have prevented her from seeking solace in another man's bed? What could he have done that would've prevented her from being in that car that night?

At the time, I hadn't been mature enough to understand the dance that plays out in a marriage or to see my parents as individuals with their own needs, but the answer likely was there was nothing he could've done. Nothing, because it was never about him. Just as my husband had played out his emotional void elsewhere rather than dealing with it, so had my mother.

My heart ached for Cavanaugh and my heart ached all over again for my father. Suddenly the world seemed such a lonely place. My thoughts went to Michael and a pang of regret hit me. But regret for what? He'd sent me a text last night that I hadn't replied to. I hadn't trusted myself to respond so I'd said nothing, but that wouldn't hold for long.

I pulled my car into the garage near Link-Media and headed over to the office. After being attacked in the alley behind the building earlier in the year, I happily paid the monthly fee for a parking space that included security, even when it meant a wind-blown three-block walk.

Borkowski came barreling at me as soon as I entered the room. "Kellner, my office. Now."

I tossed my coat and bag on my desk and trundled after him once again being treated like a 14-year-old kid. What now?

I closed the door behind me and took a seat. This had been Erik's office and although none of his personal touches remained, his ghost still hovered around the edges. I was probably imagining it, but could smell his cologne.

"Where the hell have you been?" Borkowski said, not bothering to sit.

"Excuse me?"

"I asked you to stay away from working on anything having to do with your love life, but do you listen? No, you're out gallivanting around town trying to get into Bowman's shit when I assigned Martinez."

I opened my mouth to object but Borkowski shot me down.

"Save it. Martinez called VTF for an interview and was told you'd been there several times. Do you have any idea how idiotic shit like that makes us look?"

"For the record, I'm not romantically involved with Seth

Bowman. Never have been," I shot back, annoyed with the insinuation. "Two, why in the hell has it taken Martinez nearly a week to pick up the phone. He had what, three hundred words posted the day after the shooting, and nothing since? That's what makes us look idiotic."

"Where's your piece on Janelle Platt?" he fired back. "Where's our goddamn approval for the tech upgrade? You know, the work you're supposed to be doing."

Borkowski sighed and flopped into his chair.

"Stop making me look like an ass," he said, this time without the edge in his voice. "When you go off on one of your hunting expeditions, ignoring me and leaving me out of the loop, you're undermining my authority. The rest of the staff sees it. Before you know it, they're all going rogue and I'm worthless."

He was right. I'd been so wrapped up in Lane's illness and VTF, that I wasn't thinking about the position I'd put him in. It was exactly the type of thing we'd both been worried about, confusing the staff. I just hadn't thought I'd be the biggest offender.

"You're right," I said, humbled by his words. "I should have communicated with you. I'm consumed with worry about my sister's health and I can't help but think there's a connection with what's happened at VTF."

"All the more reason for you to stay out of it and let someone with a clearer head cover this."

Properly chastised, I returned to my office, left yet another pleading message for Ramelli inquiring about the budget approval, then opened my file on Janelle Platt. I had a few details to confirm but provided I could work some phone magic, I'd have the piece in decent shape by end of day. I made myself a cup of tea, closed the door to my office, and banged it out. It wasn't the deep dive that I liked to do, but showed where Janelle Platt's administration would likely direct its focus if she were to be elected. There would be many more opportunities between now and February.

I emailed the piece over to Borkowski for review, knowing he'd get back to me with feedback within the next hour or two and want it posted for the morning blitz. But I could do all of that from home. I was exhausted after getting so little sleep last night and needed some alone time to process the thoughts jumbled in my mind.

My phone rang just after I'd maneuvered my Audi out of the lot and onto Franklin Street. I punched the button on the steering wheel and the call came in over the Bluetooth connection.

"Hey, Andrea. It's Henry. Can you talk? Sounds like you're in the car."

"Hold on." I slid into an open parking space and pulled a note pad out of my bag. "Go ahead."

"We're just getting started on that analysis you ordered but I got a funny marker turning up that I wanted to get to you right away. It seems that I'm getting a hit on a botanical component."

"Why are you finding that unusual? My understanding, based on their marketing, is that herbal ingredients are part of the flavoring."

"I'll know more soon, but I think we've got something in the Solanaceae family in this sample. In other words, belladonna, and if that's part of their herbal concoction, that's a damn dangerous path to be taking."

"Belladonna? What's that?" I asked wracking my brain.

"It's an herbaceous plant in the nightshade family. Highly toxic. Back in the Middle Ages it was used as an anesthetic. And a poison. Some of the current alternative crowd use it as a pain reliever. Others get off on it because it can cause hallucinations."

A poison? I felt myself tense at the thought. Why would belladonna be in the drink? My mind jumped with questions

Henry couldn't answer. "I don't imagine something like that got into the bottle accidentally."

He laughed. "I've seen stranger things. Look, like I said, I don't have anything conclusive yet, it was one sample, but this was strange enough to bring to your attention. We'll keep working this. Give me a day or so."

"Thanks Henry. Call me when you know more."

I immediately phoned Lassiter and left a message asking him to look for belladonna in Lane's system. I also needed to tell Michael. Too angry over what I'd seen in the hospital last night, I hadn't answered his earlier text. But this I couldn't keep to myself, I sent him a text asking if I could see him tonight, then put in a call to Martin Vasquez.

It was time for another conversation with the crew at VTF. I pulled a note pad and pen out of my bag.

"This is Andrea Kellner again from Link-Media. I have couple more questions. Can we talk for a few minutes?"

"I was on my way out the door," Martin said. "Can it wait until the morning?"

"I'd really appreciate it if you could spare just a couple minutes now."

"All right. But I've only got a few then I really have to get going. My son has a basketball game I can't miss."

My head was swimming with questions, not the least of which was why? Accident? Part of the recipe? I couldn't fathom a rational explanation for what I'd heard.

"I'm curious about the raw materials," I said. "My understanding is that the recipe for each of the drinks is exactly the same, except for botanical flavorings and colorant. Is that correct?"

"Yes. Same base, it's all listed on our label."

"Some of the ingredients on the labeling could be interpreted as a bit vague. Can you be more specific about what you mean by natural flavorings?"

"We're not required to be more specific. I assure you we follow all labeling regulations to the letter of the law. Quite frankly, that question makes me uncomfortable."

"Uncomfortable? In what way?" His response was curious. I noted the avoidance. I hadn't asked about what he was required to disclose. I wrote down his words verbatim as well as my initial reaction.

"Well, the competition of course," he said, as if it should be obvious to anyone. "The specific ratios and components of our flavoring are things we consider trade secrets. We're in full compliance, exactly as labeled."

"Are you and Olivia the only people who order the raw materials?" I asked taking another tack.

"Yes, I handle sourcing, vendor relations, and production planning. Olivia writes the purchase orders and monitors delivery."

"Once the ingredients are onsite, how many people are handling the raw materials between receipt and use in a batch?"

"We have six guys trained, two for each shift."

"And for the ingredients not clearly specified on the label, the natural flavorings, are there multiple ingredients or is it a single?" Maybe working my question from the fringe would yield more information.

"It's a blend."

"And is that blending done in the plant or do you order a specific mix from your supplier?"

I was shooting out questions rapidly knowing that at any moment he would shut me down.

"I'm not sure I like where this these questions are going. What exactly are you getting at? It feels like you're insinuating something about how we do business." His back was up. I had one more question if I lucky.

"I'm just trying to clarify the process," I said. "Let me ask the question another way. Is there any possible way for something, a contaminant for instance, to get into a bottle? Is there any scenario where something you didn't want could get into one of the drinks?"

"The only people who know the full breakdown of our formula are Mr. Bowman, myself, Olivia, and my predecessor. Not even our vendors could recreate our formula. We blend our flavorings onsite. Every ingredient is coded and the people handling the raw materials have my ultimate trust. Our quality control is impeccable," he said, his voice rising a decibel.

"I don't know what you're suggesting, but I doubt Mr. Bowman would be happy with where this is going. If you have anything else, you'll need to speak to him." With that he hung up.

25

The heady scent of truffles and fresh pasta lingered faintly in the air as I entered the elegant restaurant. The clink of silver against fine china bounced at me over the low rumble of intimate conversations. A cascade of hanging lights glossed a warm glow around the room competing with the streetlights as they glittered in the park outside while Michigan Avenue traffic rushed past. I was led to a table next to the floor-to-ceiling windows where Michael sat waiting. My text late this afternoon had been returned with an invitation to join him for dinner at Spiaggia. Typically, I would have found it a lovely celebratory splurge. Tonight, it felt more like a *mea culpa.*

He stood when I approached the table giving me an appreciative smile and a quick kiss. "You look good in blue. I ordered a glass of the Cabernet you ordered last time we were here. I hope you're in the mood tonight."

I was surprised and impressed that he had remembered. But I already knew, from firsthand experience, that the biggest charmers were also the biggest liars. I settled into my chair and took a sip of the wine as our waiter handed us menus. May as well enjoy the drink, I suspected it would be an early evening.

"Shall we order? That way we can talk without interruption."

I nodded. The restaurant was busy for a Wednesday night. Good food always found its audience. Michael ordered a beet salad and the veal chop, and I, a mixed green salad and capellini with black truffles.

My head was a tangle mess of thoughts. The woman I saw Michael with last night. Whether Lassiter had found anything yet? And most importantly, how in the world had belladonna gotten into the drink? It made no sense. I'd agreed to meet Michael for dinner so I could tell him what I'd learned about VTF in person. It was too complicated for a phone call. But I hadn't expected him to suggest one of the most romantic restaurants in town.

I still needed his professional help. Whatever he was doing personally, was no longer my concern. At least that was the story I was telling myself.

"How's your sister today?" he asked.

The question was a perfect segue into who-the-hell-was-that-woman, but if we started there, we wouldn't discuss business.

"We're still waiting for toxicology reports to come in," I said instead. "You should know that I've hired a private lab."

Michael put down his scotch. "You did? For what exactly?"

"I've asked them to test the energy drink. It's a lab I know from my ASA days. They're the people I'd call in if I needed chemical analysis."

"And you've taken this on yourself instead of letting law enforcement do our jobs."

I ignored the irritation in his voice and the cold stare. "Of course, I knew CPD would be testing, but figured I could get it done faster by calling in a favor. You also made it clear that our jobs only intersect occasionally. So I'm going to share the early findings and you can confirm it with CPD forensics."

I paused for a moment waiting for his curiosity to surpass his irritation. He took a sip of his scotch then lifted a brow. "And?"

"Early analysis indicates belladonna in the drink. Testing is incomplete, but I'll know more soon."

The server arrived with our first courses, giving us a moment to let the information sink in. I saw the tightness around Michael's eyes change to confusion, and cop mode set in.

"Belladonna? You mean like the herb they used in that old Nicole Kidman movie. The one where she and Sandra Bullock were witches?"

"I'd forgotten about that, but yes. I think they used it to kill a guy who'd been bothering Kidman."

"That doesn't make any sense," he said. "Why in the world would the drinks contain a toxic plant?"

"That's the first question," I said, swirling the wine in my glass. "The next is, did it get there accidentally or intentionally? Apparently, it's used by the alternative medicine crowd as an anesthetic and a hallucinogen." I'd put Google through its paces after getting off the phone with Henry and had a little more background. "There are also indications for medical use treating bladder spasms and motion sickness. I called Dr. Lassiter, and of course, I'll send you the lab report when I have it."

"Any other investigation you want to tell me about, *detective*?"

"I've spoken with Cavanaugh, twice."

Michael tipped back his scotch and shook his head. "Jesus, Andrea."

"I know what you're going to say, but don't. We spoke about his daughter and his work at the plant. I didn't say anything about the lab testing. I know the assault charges haven't been dealt with, but I believe the guy."

"You believe what? That he didn't make a mistake? That he

didn't accidentally poison anyone while in the depths of his grief?"

Michael was annoyed and probably feeling insulted right now, but I didn't care about his ego. I kept my emotions in check even though Michael didn't seem inclined to.

"I believe that the man has extreme pride in his work, and that the idea of a poor quality product in any form, disgusts him. Look, the guy's been through hell and back and maybe things got out of control in his life, but I just can't imagine the man I spoke to being vengeful." I paused, recognizing the absurdity of the statement. "Strange thing to say after he shot Seth, I know. I mean it's a one-off. It's not who the guy is or was prior to his daughter dying."

Michael gave me a look that said, *really?*

"Okay, I'll correct that. He's angry at Seth and yes, he'd take a punch at him again in a heartbeat regardless of his current legal problems. The man is tortured wondering if anything that happened on his watch contributed to his daughter's death. A man in that condition does not put anyone else's life on the line."

"You mean not intentionally."

I shrugged and let the comment slide. Michael and I were both paid to be skeptical although the stakes were bigger for him. Investigation would reveal what was true and what wasn't. Provided everyone remained open to what developed.

"Apparently, VTF's financial situation is a little rocky," I added. "Cavanaugh indicated that they were making late payments to vendors and having trouble keeping up with demand."

Michael chuckled, a self-satisfied grin on his face.

"Is that necessary?"

Michael turned away. "I'll try to restrain my enthusiasm."

"Growth has been straining their financial resources.

They've had serious issues with vendors not shipping. I understand they've had to bring in some new suppliers last minute. Growth is pushing them and they're having a hard time keeping up. Common story."

I didn't add that I'd learned this from Olivia. My objective was to give Michael enough information to arouse his curiosity. His own investigative skills would take over if belladonna were confirmed.

"Okay, that starts to paint another layer for us. Money. What's that saying? It's the root of all evil?"

I cringed. The phrase brought back too much pain, too many memories. Memories that he knew were hurtful.

"Sorry, I wasn't thinking," Michael said, catching me wince. "I didn't mean to bring it all back."

He reached over and laid his hand on mine. I pulled away as our meals were delivered, shaking off the ghosts of my past.

"VTF has a financial backer. A venture capital guy who's been invested in the company for a number of years. His name is Aaron Nadell. He owns a firm here in Chicago called Nadell Capital. I don't know how deep he's into the deal, but they're the type who like big paydays. Could be someone to look into."

Michael had gotten that determined look he had when situations puzzled him. I could almost see the gears turning, forming questions in his mind that he would carry with him, pondering their meaning.

"I met him recently, Nadell, and his wife, Candiss. She's involved in the Drea Foundation. They hosted the gala where Seth was shot."

"Small world the rich run in." He finished off his scotch. "When do you expect to hear back from your lab guy?"

"I'm hoping for tomorrow. As I told you, I called Lassiter and let him know to look for belladonna. I'm going to the check with him first thing in the morning see if he found anything in Lane's system. I'm sure that will extend to the autopsy reports."

"Good. Now do we have to have another talk about your fondness for police work?"

"Michael, I have a job too. You asked me to share what I've learned, I've done that. So get over it."

"Are you upset with me about something?" he asked. "You seem distant, like you're not all that happy to be here tonight. Are you upset about last night?"

I looked down at my plate and took a breath before speaking.

"I saw you. I shouldn't care, I've pushed you away. I'm the one who's needed time, but I've told you about my marriage." I was rambling, trying to get the words out, any words without breaking down into tears. "I told you how hard trust is for me because of that..."

"Wait. What did you see? I don't know what you're talking about." Michael said, his voice urgent.

"You kissed her. The blonde in the hospital. You pulled her into your arms and kissed her."

I was shaking, holding back the flood of hurt and memories, not wanting to dissolve in a pile of weak female flesh. My father had called me stoic this morning, it was the furthest thing from what I felt right now as tears stung my eyes. I turned away, trying to regain composure.

"You saw me with my ex-wife. Her father's ill. She's terrified he won't make it and I went to see them. Yes, I gave her a kiss. We have a history, it was nothing."

He said it as if it were just any other small detail of his day. Michael reached for my hand but I couldn't take it.

I turned back to him, confusion flooded his eyes.

"And you've been stopping to see her for several days now?"

He nodded.

"If it meant nothing, you wouldn't have been keeping it secret. You've had days to share that with me. After everything I've told you about my marriage, about how I've been hurt by lies, you still chose not to tell me. And that means something to *me*."

I picked up my purse, laid some money on the table for the expensive meal, and left the restaurant.

26

My hands were wrapped around a travel mug of strong Earl Grey as I attempted to get feeling back into my frozen fingers. I'd managed to walk out of the apartment without gloves this morning. It had been a late night with little sleep and my mind was jumping, still distracted by Michael and worry for my sister.

Borkowski's edits on my Janelle Platt story had been waiting in my email when I returned from dinner, so I'd wrapped that up and loaded it into the queue for this morning's email blast. Michael had phoned about an hour after I'd left the restaurant, but I had let the call go to voicemail. I needed a clearer head before saying anything more to him. My history with Erik was clouding my thoughts. I didn't know if Michael was lying to me, but given everything I'd gone through, hiding the fact that he was seeing his ex-wife was essentially the same thing.

By the time I'd wrapped up the article, I'd been too wired to go to bed, and instead had stayed up well into the early morning digging deeper into my research on belladonna, and on Nadell Capital. Luckily, my father had gone back to Lane's apartment for the night and I'd been able to utilize my frustrations by working rather than lying in bed fuming. Not that it was helping my energy level this morning as I walked into the office.

My plan was to spend a little time with Brynn, see where she was on the VTF research I'd asked for, then head over to the hospital. I tossed my scarf and coat on a chair then picked up my mug and went looking for Brynn. I found her in the break room working on her own caffeine infusion. I cringed at the vending machine donut she was washing down, but since I hadn't eaten so much as an apple this morning, I was in no position to judge.

We had the room to ourselves, so I took a seat next to her.

"Anything on VTF yet?" I asked, shivering and taking a big gulp of my tea. "Damn, I can't seem to get warm. I wish I'd worn a heavy sweater."

Brynn held up the cellophane-wrapped pastry. "Sugar helps. I can see you want some."

"Ask me again when civilization has fallen apart and the only food left is Twinkies."

"Oh, come on, they're not that bad. Maybe you need to see someone about your food issues?" she teased.

"Yeah, a nutritionist. Let's both go." I laughed, quieting my inner healthy food preacher.

"I'm sure you know the basics. Company was founded seven years ago. Privately held, no bankruptcy filings. No existing litigation that I've come across, but I'm working a lead at a local ad agency who says VTF is stiffing them for a 200k bill. She says the modeling agency they used hasn't been paid either. And there are rumors about a bottle supplier who's pissed about nonpayment."

"Who needs litigation when you've got the rumor mill? Vendors can destroy a company's reputation quickly," I said. "That also corroborates some of the stories I'm hearing that cash is tight. I understand that Nadell Capital is backing them, quietly. Maybe they've closed the wallet."

"Or the parties aren't happy with each other. Pressure and money are a bad combo. The rumors about an IPO seem to be spreading like the flu. If that happens, speculation is that it could be as much as a $75-million deal."

"Whoa, that's life changing." I'd expected a healthy number, but that was staggering.

"Your friend will be very rich," Brynn said.

If the deal closes, I thought to myself. "That's enough money to change someone's behavior." Brynn and I looked at each other. How far Seth would go to ensure that windfall? How far would Nadell?

"It would certainly change mine," Brynn said. "I'd be sending you a sayonara text from a beach in Bali."

"And I wouldn't blame you. Look, I'm going to plead my case with Borkowski again. Just keep on this for now and I'll talk to you later."

I stood and returned to my office. My phone rang the minute I got back.

"Andrea, Henry. I've got the reports for you. Belladonna, in all samples. Atropa belladonna, if you want to be technical. I'm sending the report over now via email."

"Was the concentration the same in all the bottles," I asked.

"Within a minor variance, I'd say they were all in the same target range."

"So, could we then conclude the belladonna is being added during bottling?"

"Sounds like it to me. I don't know how else you'd get this level of consistency."

"If it's being added at bottling, then why isn't everyone getting sick?"

"Well, we have the batch issue. This is one moment. We don't know the extent of the exposure, in people or time. The other thing that comes to mind is that the parts per million are relatively small, consistent, but small, so perhaps there's some cofactor that's influencing who gets sick and who doesn't. It could be any number of things, including how much of the product the individual was drinking. We also have about 200 mg of caffeine and 40 mg of niacin per bottle, drink a few of these in a short period of time and your heart and your liver are going to be unhappy. Layer in belladonna, and we have a lot of unknowns. I just figure out what's in the stuff. You guys take it from here."

"Thanks Henry. Do what you can on that bill for me."

"I can probably shave a few pennies off the top," he laughed.

I told him I'd get back to him with questions after I'd looked over the report and had hard copies printing even before we finished our phone call. Scanning the screen, I sorted through the scientific jargon as best I could, then emailed a copy to Michael and to Lassiter. I also phoned the hospital and left a message that I had sent the toxicology report. I wasn't taking any chances that the information would get lost in the spam pile. I grabbed the printouts, my coat, and sent Michael a text that I was on my way to the hospital. As I drove, possibilities tumbled through my mind but the only scenario I could imagine was that the toxin had been added at bottling. The questions now were how long had this been going on and why?

Lane was awake when I entered her room, flipping mindlessly through the TV options while my father read the newspaper. She seemed to have a little more color in her cheeks today but maybe that was my mind convincing me to look for the positive.

After getting caught up on today's symptom check-in, I listened to her complain about the food and lack of access to coffee. The mundane request nearly had me in tears. I promised to bring up a tray of whatever the hell she wanted after Lassiter came in. I was trying not to panic, but it wasn't working.

Moments later he entered the room, report in hand. He nodded hello to each of us, then walked directly to Lane.

"We've been able to determine what's been causing you to be ill. Between the testing we've done and a toxicology report that your sister finagled, we finally have an answer." He held up a file.

Before Lassiter could say anything more, Michael rushed into the room. He was slightly out of breath and had a faint sheen of sweat on his forehead. We locked eyes briefly, but I quickly turned away while Lane and my father shot me confused looks.

"Well, are you going to tell us already?" My father said to the doctor. "You need to get on with fixing her."

"We've confirmed that you've ingested a poison called belladonna," Lassiter said to Lane.

"What the hell is that?" My father was getting irritated. I didn't often see his impatience come to the surface, but clearly he was exhausted emotionally and at his wits end.

"Belladonna is a poisonous plant. Part of the nightshade family. Both the foliage and the berries are toxic," Lassiter explained.

"Well, that makes no sense. Lane here doesn't exactly go foraging. I don't think she's ever been camping in her life."

Lane shot her eyes at us, a confused look on her face. I couldn't tell if it was the illness, or she simply wasn't following the conversation.

"No, Dad, the poison somehow got into the energy drink she's been using," I said. "We aren't sure how, but the testing lab I hired found the toxin in all six bottles they tested."

"That stuff isn't supposed to be there, is it?" my father asked, rubbing his hand repeatedly over his forehead.

"Unlikely," Lassiter added. "Belladonna is occasionally used in some alternative medicine circles as a pain reliever. But it would be unusual to add this as a normal course of business to a beverage."

"We aren't sure how the product came to contain the toxin," Michael added. "Nor are we sure how long this has been going on. But we will find out."

His voice was strong, determined, comforting. I was grateful for his presence as I watched Lane and my father grapple with the news and saw the waves of confusion and fear wash over their faces.

"It's deadly isn't it?" Lane said, her voice low and raspy.

"It can be." Lassiter added. "But now that we know what's causing you to be sick, we can treat you. I'm going to start you on a medication called physostigmine. It may make you nauseous while we flush this out, but trust me, you'll feel better in a couple days and we'll get you back home."

"So, it wasn't just me?" Lane asked, her eyes on me.

"No," I shook my head. "You're not the only one to have gotten sick." I didn't volunteer that we suspected two deaths from the product. This was enough for Lane and my father to wrap their heads around for the moment. They were frightened enough.

"I'll go speak with the nursing staff and see that your treatment plan is adjusted," Lassiter said. "And thank you, Ms. Keller," he said to me. "I'll check in later."

"Well, damn. Laney, time for you to eat some real food." My father gave her a hug and a kiss on the forehead. I could see the relief in his face. Finally, answers. Lane on the other hand looked shaken.

"I'll be back in a little bit," I said. "I need to speak with Michael." He followed me into the hall.

"Why didn't you return my call last night?" Michael asked, looking hurt and distracted.

"Because I needed some time and some distance." A nurse

interrupted us, rounding the corner, while she monitored a patient with a walker. I looked down at the floor, uncomfortable with the need in Michael's eyes. "And this isn't the place either. We're here to discuss the fact that my sister has been poisoned. Can we limit the conversation to work? Please? For now anyway?"

Michael, shot his eyes up at the ceiling before responding. "All right. But I didn't do anything to hurt you intentionally."

"Choosing not to tell me you were meeting your ex-wife was intentional." I forced my emotions down into the pit of my stomach. "When are you going over to VTF?"

"You're not coming," he said, his jaw locked down hard. "Nice work on the lab, but don't you dare say anything to your friend."

I stepped back. "I had no intention of speaking to Seth. I haven't forgotten all of my legal training," I said, feeling the sting of the accusation. "But what you'll need to decide is whether to tell him he may have been ingesting belladonna himself."

27

The nursing staff was back in Lane's room when I returned. Another round of vitals and one of the nurses was adding something to her IV bag. Lane fidgeted in her bed. Somehow the news about the belladonna seemed to have made her more agitated rather than calming her down.

"What are you putting in there?" She pressed the nurse.

"We need to flush out your system. I'm adding some medication the doctor has ordered to counteract the toxin. You should be feeling better soon."

"I don't want you putting anything in there without telling me what it is. I want to see the doctor. Now!"

"I'll send him in as soon as he's free."

She spoke to Lane like you would an elderly aunt. Part compassion, part this-is-for-the-best. But Lane wasn't having any of it. She pulled at the needle in her arm until the nurse grabbed her hand.

"Ms. Lane, I need to do this. I need you to calm down and let the medicine do its work. I'm sure you be much more comfortable without restraints."

I stepped over to the other side of the bed. "Lane, it's going to be fine. Everyone's here to help you feel better. Remember, the doctor told us he was adding a new medication. Now that we know what's wrong, you'll be out of here in no time." I smiled and followed the nurse's lead on voice control. "Can I get you something? Are you ready to eat?"

"How about a goddamn coffee? A real coffee, not the hospital crap."

I looked at the nurse, who shook her head. "Okay, I'll be right back." There was no way I was adding to her caffeine load, but I'd fight that battle when I returned. The idea seemed to calm her down enough for the nurse to finish the IV. "Dad?"

"Sure, how about a muffin?"

I looked at him as if to ask "you got this?" He took the hint and nodded. So I grabbed my bag and headed downstairs.

There was a juice bar in the food court where I ordered complicated concoctions for everyone with silly names like Mango Dance Off. Then headed to the neighboring stand and loaded up on bakery items hoping the carbs would distract Lane from the missing coffee. Morning snacks covered, I parked myself at a table and put in a call to my former boss, State's Attorney Denton Tierney, leaving a message with his assistant. No telling how many people had been exposed. Law enforcement would determine the course of the case, if there was one, but I knew Tierney would prefer the advance notice.

As I stepped off the elevator with the cardboard tray of drinks, my phone rang. Assuming it was Tierney's office, I set the tray on the floor and fished in my bag for the phone.

"Ms. Kellner?" A young female voice said. "This is Olivia. From the other day. At the diner."

"Yes, of course, how are you?"

"I need help. The cops are here. Do you know what's going

on?" Her voice trembled as she asked the question. "Am I getting arrested?"

Michael and his crew had wasted no time. They'd probably already been staked outside the VTF plant with a search warrant when he and I spoke outside of Lane's hospital room. Olivia sounded terrified. I could imagine the chaos as the staff watched with confusion and worry, not knowing what to do, while cops descended on their workplace.

"You're at the plant?"

"Yes, they just got here. They're in the office with Martin. They won't let me go in."

"That's okay. Just sit tight until you're told what to do. Is Mr. Bowman there?"

"No, but the receptionist called him as soon as the cops got here. I think he's coming. What's going on? I don't know what to do. Nobody knows what to do."

"There's no reason to believe that you're in any trouble. If the detectives have any questions for you, answer them as honestly as you can," I said, hoping to calm her down.

"Do I like, need an attorney or something?"

I knew it was likely that Olivia would be questioned, but probably not today. "You have the right to have an attorney present. If the police ask any questions of you that make you feel uncomfortable, stop the questioning until you have counsel. I don't think they'll need to speak to you today, but they'll let you know."

"This is because of that guy, the one that died, right? Are they going to shut us down?"

"The police are investigating whether there's a connection," I said, uncertain about how much more to say. Olivia was a scared kid who'd trusted me enough to reach out, but she also had information about operations at VTF and a police interview seemed inevitable.

"Is Seth getting arrested? Is Martin?" The tough young woman I'd encountered initially now sounded like a 10-year-old kid. Gone was the attitude, but so was adult leadership as her boss sat isolated with a couple detectives.

"Honestly, I don't know. That will be up to CPD. Right now they're simply gathering information to find out if there is a link and whether there is any risk to the public."

"You mean all of our product might make people sick?" Her panic was back, suggesting that the idea of the drink being dangerous was a new one. I tucked that away.

"CPD has to investigate all the possibilities." I kept my voice calm and my response vague, but regretting my word choice. Olivia seemed on the verge of losing it. She also seemed to be looking for assurances that I couldn't give her. There wouldn't be any charges today, but I certainly couldn't make any promises about what the future held, including what would happen as word got out.

"Olivia, CPD will tell you when you can go home, but there may be reporters calling or showing up at the plant. You have no obligation to speak with them. I just wanted you to be prepared in case that happens."

"Why would they want to talk to me? I don't know anything."

"They'll try to speak to anyone who leaves the plant. It's nothing to worry about, just say nothing and go on your way."

If they weren't on it already, the media would descend like the vultures that we were. Blocking exits, calling repeatedly, making accusations with their questions. Anything to get a quote or a bit of information that made the story seem different from the other news outlets.

I could only imagine how frightening it would be once the attack dogs picked up on the scent. Yet ironically, she'd chosen to call me, a journalist, for advice. I'd viewed our previous conversations primarily through the lens of a concerned sister.

Now, there was no longer an option but to treat this as the news story it was.

We ended the call after I told her she could call me again anytime. But where were the rules guiding me as I toed the line between journalist, a friend to Seth, and involved party? Link-Media couldn't sit silent on this; I needed to bring Borkowski up to date.

28

"What did I say? Your love life's going to be splashed all over the headlines. Again."

I was standing in Borkowski's office being chastised only half in jest. I'd rushed back to the office after my phone call with Olivia. Lane seemed to have calmed down by the time I returned with her food so I told my father I had to get back to work and asked him to call if there were any changes. Now I was bringing Borkowski up to date on the VTF situation and getting major shit for it.

"And as I've said, repeatedly, my love life is not part of this. I have no romantic connection with Seth Bowman. Period. End of conversation."

"Well, there's a certain photograph that is going to call *that* into question. Why the hell didn't Martinez bring this in?" Borkowski was pacing as was his habit when he needed to think. I stood just inside the door watching the Oriental carpet he'd installed go threadbare before my eyes.

"You'll have to ask him, boss," I said, not bothering to stifle the sarcasm. "Staffing is your responsibility, as I recall. I'm bringing you the story I have, and we need to figure out how to attack it. I have the contacts. I have the information. As far as I'm concerned, I've earned a seat at this table. It should be my lead."

Borkowski grumbled something I couldn't make out and then tossed his glasses on the desk.

"Fine, but no holding back. You and Martinez work it together. It's called cooperation."

"Shall I dictate for him?" I shot Borkowski a dirty look, but he knew what I meant. Martinez had been his pick not mine, and I'd promised to stay out of hiring decisions. It was one of those awkward lines Borkowski and I had drawn to clarify his position running day-to-day operations. Neither one of us wanted the staff running from mommy to daddy when someone's ego got bruised. But that didn't mean I had to be silent when we were in private, just like in any other marriage. I turned to leave.

"I'm glad your sister's okay," he said.

"Thanks. I guess this means I can expense the lab testing." I gave him a smile and left to find my charge. We could have the next round of the Martinez conversation another time. Eventually, the man would need to be fired or moved to something less taxing and Borkowski knew it, even if he wasn't ready to admit he'd made a mistake bringing him on board.

I found Martinez at his desk, head bopping to whatever was flooding his earbuds. He pulled them out when I sat down next to him and Sinatra floated out. Interesting. I wondered if he was the only male fan under seventy. Our conversation consisted of me downloading while he copied down every word as if he were a court reporter.

"Got it. I'll write that up," Martinez said, apparently believing that's what he was being asked to do. Don't you even want to check the source? I thought to myself.

"You know what, on second thought, don't worry about the

story." I tore his notes off of his pad and left him at his desk, a confused look on his face.

I made a beeline for Brynn's desk. Borkowski wanted Martinez on this story, I assumed out of some misdirected loyalty, either that or he was afraid of firing people, which was a problem for another day. But as far as I was concerned, the man was a doofus perhaps qualified to write classified ads, but even that jury was still out. I agreed that Borkowski needed to have full responsibility for staffing, but I hadn't agreed that I would work with fools. I'd deal with the business implications later; right now I needed a pro.

"What's this?" Brynn asked as I placed the notes in front of her. She picked up the pages and scanned. "These are VTF notes but it's not your hand writing. And what's this about poison?" She looked up at me briefly, then went back to the pages, her mouth dropping open as she read.

"It appears that the drinks, at least some batches, have been contaminated with a botanical toxin called belladonna. It isn't clear how the contamination occurred or when. But I suspect we've got a big story on our hands."

"Kelly Cavanaugh and Jeremy Wolanski?" I nodded. "And your friend owns the company. Have you spoken to him?" She looked at me, eyebrows raised.

"Not since I learned about this. But you're going to."

"What? Me?"

"The story's suspect if it's me alone. My reporting will appear as either too soft or out to get him depending on who's interpreting. That's why you and I will work on it together; we'll share the byline, and mitigate any of the favoritism issues."

She pursed her lips, then brought her coffee cup up to her mouth. I could see her mind pinball from excitement to fear. I knew which would win out.

"Borkowski?" she asked.

"He's partially on board, just thinks I'm working with Martinez."

Brynn broke into a chuckle.

"That's not helpful." I smiled and laughed myself. "See what you can do about getting this mess organized." I tapped on the notes. "I'll email you the lab test and we can talk later."

"Andrea, thanks for doing the this." Her smile was broad and sincere.

"Thank me after," I laughed. "You might want to go back to covering the dog shows by the time we're done with this."

As I returned to my office, I saw Olivia standing in the reception area, tentatively scoping out the space. She seemed to relax when she saw me. I walked over.

"I hope it's okay that I came here. I'm just so freaked out by the cops that I need someone to talk to."

Her eyes darted around the room as if afraid she'd see someone she knew. Her head was bare and loose pieces of wind-blown hair had come loose from her ponytail and brushed against cheeks pink from the cold. A thick hand-knitted scarf was wrapped multiple times around her neck and glistened with snowflakes that had melted.

"Of course it's okay. Let's go to my office."

"Is there someplace else?" She paused. "Someplace without so many reporters?"

"There's a coffee shop nearby. Give me a second to get my coat."

She waited in the hall while I grabbed my things and we rode down the elevator in silence. The coffee shop was three doors down on the corner. I paid for our drinks while Olivia grabbed a table.

I set cups in front of us and tossed my coat on the chair. Olivia didn't seem ready to unwrap her neck. Instead, she twirled her hair and stirred her coffee for what seemed like an eternity. At least twenty questions jumped around in my brain, but she hadn't come here to be grilled. She came because she was scared. So, I sipped my tea and waited for her to talk.

"They want our computers. All of our records, production records, batch numbers, dates. Martin wasn't going to give them anything without Mr. Bowman saying it was okay, but they started taking stuff, anyway."

"And did Seth, Mr. Bowman, show up?"

"Yeah, and boy was he mad. He stormed in while the cops were unplugging our computers. Started yelling about his rights and about calling his attorney. The cops said something about having a subpoena. I didn't understand what that was all about, but it just made Mr. Bowman even madder. Then he started yelling at Martin as if it were his fault for letting the cops in the building. They're cops. What did he think Martin was going to do?" She shook her head. "The whole thing was out of control."

"What happened from there?"

"This attorney showed up. At least everyone was saying she was Mr. Bowman's attorney. The two of them went into the supply room to talk. I didn't see them again. That's when Martin told everybody to go home. He shut down the plant. I don't know what I'm going to do if I lose this job. Everybody's scared, including me."

I was imagining the employees frozen by the chaos and fear, uncertain what to do as their boss lost it. I was also wondering about Seth. He was barely a week past his gunshot wound, likely still on pain meds and antibiotics, and I was uncertain if he, too, had ingested the belladonna. I had the urge to tell him, but that was in Michael's lap.

"Did he say anything about why the plant was being shut down?" I asked.

"Martin, you mean?" I nodded. "To the crew, he said it was so they could clear up the confusion. But to me, he said it was so no one could mess with anything."

"Company records?"

"I guess. He told me he didn't want the cops saying we'd messed with anything later. You know, changed records or something, deleted files. Said that he would talk with Mr. Bowman and sort everything out so we could be back to normal tomorrow morning."

I doubted everything would be sorted out by tomorrow morning, but hopefully the staff would have some guidance on business operations. I had no doubt that the attorney Olivia referenced was Cai. And that right about now she was giving him referrals to other attorneys more appropriate for this new development. What a time to not be able to talk to her.

But I could talk to Olivia.

"Why do you think Martin would worry about files being changed or deleted?"

I laid the question out as simply as I could, following her lead, curious about whether she'd speculate. It wasn't an unusual first reaction for someone who'd had a previous legal encounter, but seemed odd coming from a plant manager. Was he particularly cautious or had there been a previous incident?

"Um," she paused, taking another break by swallowing some coffee. "He's probably thinking about our backer. They've had some fights."

"What do you mean?"

She fidgeted in her seat like a 5-year-old who had to pee and played with the fringe on her scarf as she decided how to answer. "The money guy. Sometimes he complains, well, more than complains from what Martin tells me. He's cheap, I guess he's supposed to be. Thinks we spend too much. Anyway, they've had a couple knockdown drag-outs when the guy tried to do our work for us. Martin doesn't trust him. Apparently, he caught him a couple times coming in after hours and going through our records. Martin says he even cancelled an order once."

29

I stepped off the elevator on the 32nd floor of a Loop high-rise having decided a conversation with Aaron Nadell was appropriate, although he didn't know it yet.

Olivia's comments about "the money guy" had sparked my interest big time. Particularly if Martin was worried the guy, whom I knew to be Aaron Nadell, might mess with records. Did that mean Martin was worried there was something worth deleting? Or just that he didn't want himself or his crew to be blamed for anything? Hard to tell, but if Nadell was showing up at night unannounced and poking around on their computers, he not only had a key, he operated as if he was far more than just a banker.

My research into his firm told me it was on the smaller side as far as venture capital went, five employees, focusing on seed to early-growth stage, up to series A investments. That meant they were into their deals for between one to five million dollars per investment. But the real money was made later in the IPO. Unlike most VC's, Nadell Capital didn't seem enamored with the latest greatest tech companies that their peers found sexy, instead they put their money into stable, boring stuff, like small manufacturing. According to their website, they were invested seven companies right now. Strangely, VTF Industries wasn't listed in their portfolio.

I pulled open a door and found myself in a small reception area that hadn't been decorated in easily twenty years. Patterned carpet, dark wood reception desk, paintings produced a hundred at a time in a printing factory. It was tasteful but conservative and completely in line with the impression I'd gotten of their investment strategy. More banker than Silicon Valley chic.

I announced myself to the receptionist and asked to see her boss not certain Nadell was even in the office.

"I'm sorry," she said. "He doesn't normally take unannounced meetings." She looked at me as if to say "honey, you know better."

I smiled sweetly. "Oh, I understand. Mr. Nadell and I met recently at the Drea Foundation gala. I was in the building and thought I'd stop in and say hello. You don't mind just checking with him do you. I promise I'll only take a moment."

"Oh yes, the gala. Mr. and Mrs. Nadell are huge supporters of Drea." She smiled and punched in a key, getting someone on the phone. It was amazing how often one little fact allowed people to fill in connections for themselves even if they weren't real. She probably assumed I was one of the big donors. She relayed the information to whoever was on the other end of the phone and a second later said, "He'll be up shortly Ms. Kellner."

I settled into one of the stiff chairs flanking a coffee table loaded with the obligatory financial papers. Unlike the younger VC's, the office held no trophy wall of video footage or company logos screaming their coolness. All Gold Coast instead of West Loop. Must have been Candiss's influence.

The door behind the desk opened and Aaron Nadell stepped out.

"Oh yes, Andrea, how nice to see you again." He extended a hand. "What an evening?" he said conspiratorially, referring, of course, to the shooting.

Gold cufflinks and a wrist chain adorned his bankers uniform of a white dress shirt, gray slacks, and a neutral tie. The highly starched shirt strained to fit his bulging mid-section as if he were in denial about his increased girth.

"I hope you were unscathed by our little incident. Candiss is mortified by the whole thing. Me, I thought it added a little spice." He laughed. "Please, come back to my office."

Nadell's voice was deep and theatrical, calling to mind a prosecutor I'd worked with, who seemed to enjoy playing a trumped-up TV version of the role. I thought he was more sizzle than skill and wondered if Nadell was the same?

He escorted me down a long hallway to a corner office. As opposed to the reception area, someone had made an effort to decorate. Framed prints, silk plants on top of a stand. A large walnut desk was carefully placed in the corner, in front of floor-to-ceiling windows where I could glimpse gray white caps on the lake. Two computer monitors set side-by-side on the desk. They were some of the largest monitors I'd ever seen. Probably close to thirty-two inches each which didn't leave much room for anything else. But if your job was managing money, what else did you need? He directed me to a brown leather club chair in front of the desk, and then joined me.

"So, Ms. Kellner, what brings you down here? I hope you're not here to complain about my wife hounding you for money?"

He chuckled. I got the sense that this was a well-used joke. The one he pulled out at every opportunity, thinking he was being cute.

"Please, call me Andrea. I understand we have a mutual friend, Seth Bowman."

"Yes, Seth's a great guy. Candiss has known him for years.

Boy, did he dodge a close one the other night. It's been a singular topic of conversation at our home while Candiss dealt with the aftermath. Donors have been calling nonstop, the girls families, the media. This type of thing just doesn't happen in our crowd." He shook his head. "I doubt I'll ever get Candiss back into the Peninsula, she's so annoyed with them. Which means I'll have to sneak into Shanghai Terrace alone."

The situation seemed to amuse him as if it were all a game of who's-to-blame instead of someone's life having been hanging in the balance.

"How long have you known Seth?" I asked, smiling as if there was nothing but polite curiosity behind the question.

I wasn't clear on the timeline or the depth of Nadell's investment in VTF. And the big question in my mind was why wasn't it front and center on their portfolio page? VCs loved the world to know where they'd taken a position. It was a show of confidence, a look-how-smart-we-are marketing move for both the VC and the firm they were investing in. When a big name VC put his money behind you, it was like having Harvard Law on your resume. Doors opened, vendors extended credit, and the business world watched, waiting for the anticipated IPO that usually was the end-game prize.

"Let's see, at least a couple of years. My wife introduced us somewhere along the way at one of her social engagements. Hard to keep track of all that. She's quite active in her charities."

He pulled himself up in his chair, then tugged on his cufflinks. Already I had the impression of a man who defined himself by his career and his connections. I didn't know if it was the affected posturing or the slightly dismissive tone when he spoke of his wife's pursuits. But I distrusted him immediately.

"I understand that you are an investor in Seth's business, VTF industries. The shooting must be quite a blow to the company."

He paused, clearly taken aback by the comment.

"That is correct, isn't it? Nadell Capital has a stake in the business?"

Again he hesitated for a fraction of a second.

"I gave them a little seed money in their early stages," he said, as if it were the equivalent of buying a friend lunch.

"Interesting. I hear it's more than a little." I kept my tone light and my smile soft. One of the many reporter faces in my bag of tricks.

I saw a flash of something in his face that disappeared just as quickly. Surprise? Irritation? Fear? Had Seth called him yet about CPD's interest in the plant? If he didn't know, he would before the day was out.

"I'm not sure where you're getting your information. As I said, we gave them some seed money because I thought it was a good investment. It's what we do around here." He held up his hands and smiled, trying to make a joke of it.

"Are you saying you have no involvement in business decisions?" I flipped open a notepad. Nadell narrowed his eyes and stared at me. "Because I've been told that you receive monthly reporting directly from personnel at the plant."

"What exactly are you suggesting, Ms. Keller? I think I've been quite clear. And I certainly don't need to defend my investment choices to you."

He'd taken on an indignant tone but it felt forced, as if that was the emotion he thought he was supposed to portray. The bombastic TV prosecutor image came back into my mind. So did the phrase, "false outrage." What was that all about? Why was he minimizing his involvement? It seemed out of character.

"No, of course you don't," I said. "As you know, Seth is a friend of mine as well and I understand that there may be some, shall we say, tough business issues coming up. I thought you might want to clear the air on your role in the company before people asking tougher questions are at your door."

This time I could see the confusion in his face or was it fear? It didn't appear that he knew VTF had been served a subpoena.

"As I've said, I was an early investor in VTF. I gave them money to get things off the ground and that investment has rewarded me. Now, you'll need to excuse me. I have an appointment."

He stood, adjusted his French cuffs again, and puffed up his chest before walking over to the door. A power move. We're done. His tone had changed and the actors smile was back. But I could still see the flash of anger in his eyes. His so-called appointment was most likely a panicked phone call to his partner asking what the hell was going on.

"Then I won't keep you. Nice to see you again and my best to Candiss."

I left the office feeling like I'd scored a win for getting the admission of seed money. But I was no closer to understanding why Nadell was being secretive.

30

I was on the phone as soon as I hit the lobby. First a check-in with Brynn where I clarified a couple of details, then a call to Candiss Nadell. She'd been asking me for a meeting to discuss my involvement in the Drea Foundation. Now seemed like the perfect moment to chat. Candiss had been involved in her husband's company a few years back and likely knew a lot more about the inner workings than my research could reveal. If I was lucky that would include information about the VTF investment.

Candiss suggested we meet at the Waldorf again. I agreed, assuming it was her version of a neighborhood haunt. She arrived before me and I was escorted to the same booth we'd shared at our last meeting. Compared to the other day, the crowd had shifted from morning power brokers to ladies-who-lunch-then-pop-over-to-Barney's-for-a-$1000-pair-of-shoes. Pots of tea or white wine were the drinks of choice, with a salad as an accompaniment. The occasional whiff of poached fish with herbs and butter sauce floated past me.

She was scrolling her phone as I approached and as usual, she looked perfectly coifed. I couldn't imagine what it took to maintain such precise polish. I was no schlump in the grooming department, but my world didn't end if I chipped a nail. This woman must have standing appointments at the salon for hair, nails, and makeup. Even in this weather, she looked unruffled. Although I didn't imagine she'd walked the ten blocks from her Gold Coast greystone to the hotel. Like any proper fashion gal, I was also lusting after her ivory Chanel jacket.

"Andrea, how lovely we could finally get together. Please, sit," she said, setting her phone back in her bag and smiling warmly. "I remembered that you were a tea drinker. I hope I wasn't being presumptuous by ordering."

"How very thoughtful of you," I said, settling into the role of a woman who frequents luxury hotels for afternoon tea service instead of standing at Starbucks with a paper cup.

I hung my wool coat on a hook at the end of the booth and took a seat. A waiter appeared immediately and opened a mahogany box for me. I pulled out an organic Earl Grey and thanked him.

I could tell Candiss took satisfaction in anticipating my preferences. It was the kind of thing an attentive hostess made sure to know. She'd ordered coffee for herself and the table was set with an assortment of pastries and a plate of fruit, perfectly ripe and beautifully arranged, garnished with mint.

"How are your fundraising efforts from the gala coming along?" I asked, choosing an easy segue.

"Despite the unfortunate incident, we managed to raise nearly $1.5 million. One of our most productive evenings. Perhaps the incident made everyone feel a little guiltier." She leaned in with a little bit of a smile.

Unfortunate incident? An interesting choice of words. Or maybe I was just feeling cynical after speaking with her husband.

"Good to hear. Drea is such a worthy cause. How long have you been involved?"

"Oh, for quite a number of years. Initially it was simply as a financial contributor. I'd occasionally host a luncheon, cajole my friends into making a donation, small things. I didn't really have time back then. As my work situation eased up, I was able to get more involved. I took over as the director about four years ago."

"I understand you were involved in your husband's company prior to your time at Drea," I said, smiling and keeping my voice light. I was also allowing her to speak openly in hopes of getting closer to learning more about VTF.

"Yes, I was the chief operating officer for a number of years as Aaron found his footing. He's essentially a salesperson at heart, and salespeople, well, let's just say, they have their strengths and weaknesses." She smiled the way wives do when they really want to call their partners a lovable dumbass. "I came in to give the organization a more stable footing operationally."

Somehow I sensed there was a story behind her involvement. Some instinct perked up my ears, but I couldn't be sure if it was her tone, her eyes, or just knowing how often women were called upon to fix messes. Or maybe it was a reaction to the impression I'd gotten of her husband as arrogant.

"I know exactly what you mean," I said, taking a drink of my tea. "There are always the rainmakers and then the people who actually make things happen."

"Exactly. Aaron just can't seem to be bothered with the how of getting things done. I swear his attention span is about fifteen seconds," she said, pursing her lips. "But then again we all have our talents."

"How did you get him to realize he needed your, ah, special brand, of help?"

I got the sense Candiss was a woman who didn't suffer fools

or foolishness. The fact that she'd had an operational role at her husband's firm didn't surprise me, but I wondered about the dynamic.

"These are the things men like him only realize when they're deep in the middle of a mess and don't know where else to turn. Since I have both an accounting degree and a JD, it was a pretty easy skill set to match. The hardest issue for me was it meant walking away from a position as General Counsel. But I didn't really see that I had much choice. Aaron needed me. Nadell Capital needed me."

"I didn't realize we had that in common, both former attorneys no longer practicing."

"I think there are a lot of us." We both laughed knowing exactly what she meant. The long hours, the endless stress, the lack of a social life, were all particularly hard on women. At least women who were unwilling or unable to put in the 120-hour work weeks many of our male counterparts did, or simply didn't use the proper locker room at the East Bank Club. Outside of family law, it was still largely a boys club.

"I suspect were both happier now," I said. "Or do you miss the law?"

Accountant, lawyer, and COO. The woman had an impressive resume. She could probably run rings around her husband intellectually.

"I did at the time. It wasn't an easy transition for me personally, but one makes sacrifices for one's family. And this was one of those moments where I was the one who needed to sacrifice. I was the one who needed to give up something for the greater good of my family."

I thought back to the years after my mother died. To the years I had sacrificed being a carefree teenager, being forced, well, that wasn't really accurate, no one forced me. I took it upon myself to try to fill in as a stabilizing force in my family. I knew it changed me. I knew I'd missed out on those carefree days while friends worried about prom dates and dresses. And I worried about my father's mental health and whether my sister was going to make it home in one piece or at all.

"I think most women can relate to a moment of sacrifice in their life. Particularly when families are involved," I said, admiring her strength and commitment, but also wondering if she had regrets. "Something must've changed so you felt that you could move on and work with Drea?"

"I'd spent six years working with Aaron. I set up an organizational process, a solid accounting system. Basically, I felt that he had a structure in place that could operate on its own. All they had to do was execute the plan. And that's when I moved on. That's when I joined Drea."

A waiter arrived to refresh our drinks. As he poured, I looked more closely at Candiss, wondering about her resilience, scanning her expression for emotion behind the practiced face.

"And were you involved in any of the financial investments at Nadell Capital?" I asked. "It must be fascinating to watch the growth of new companies. To see them blossom, given the right financial freedom and guidance, of course."

My legal training was useful once again as I navigated the conversation toward my agenda. A natural opening had occurred and I pounced, hoping for a tidbit.

"Of course, I was aware of how our assets were invested, but I played no role in those relationships, beyond monitoring the performance."

Candiss stirred cream into her coffee, then waved at a woman three tables over who was trying to get her attention, imagining that wasn't uncommon.

"Does Nadell Capital specializes in startups?" I asked, spearing a piece of pineapple and continuing to keep the dialogue light.

"A better way to put it would be we specialize in high-growth opportunities."

"In other words, high-risk, high-reward opportunities." It wasn't lost on me that Candiss had used the word we, instead of referring exclusively to her husband.

"Well, that's where the money is, isn't it? Aaron thrives on the adrenaline rush. He just gets excited by the possibilities," she said, smiling again and clasping her hands in front of her on the table. "I'm the moderator in the family. I encourage him to be a little more balanced, to mitigate risk for the long term."

"The way I see it," she continued, her face now pensive, "the power of patience goes a long way in building our dreams. But, sadly, discipline is a lost art today in this world of immediate gratification."

"Are there specific industries that he focuses on?"

"Goodness, how did this conversation turn into background on my husband's company?" She laughed. "You're not letting me do my sales job. I'd really love to have you on the board Andrea. Is that a possibility? You'd be a great asset, both as a role model to the girls, but you'd also bring your business leadership to the board. As you know, nonprofits tend to have, shall we say, people with a lot of time on their hands versus business experience." She had leaned in and lowered her voice.

"It would be an honor, Candiss."

"Terrific. I'm so pleased. I know it's short notice but I'm hosting the board for cocktails tomorrow evening. Very informal. I'd love for you to join us. It would be a good opportunity to meet everyone. I'll send you an email with the details."

I let the conversation stay on the Drea Foundation and the near-term objectives of the organization but I wasn't done with my exploration into Nadell Capital. As we were finishing our drinks, Candiss made reference to the post-gala work she was doing, and I saw another opportunity.

"I understand your husband was an early investor in Seth Bowman's company."

"Yes, as a matter of fact, we were," she said, drawing back a little with the comment. "I forget that you've known Seth for a number of years as well. I knew him to be ambitious, smart, and quite frankly, early to catch a trend. So I introduced the men. They got along, and one thing led to another. Aaron saw the potential in the business."

"So that means Aaron will do quite well with the IPO."

She looked flustered for a second. "I wasn't aware that information was getting out."

"I wouldn't say it's public knowledge, but given what happened at the gala, Seth chose to share that with me."

"Oh? Does he feel there's some connection? Beyond the terrible publicity, I mean? Although, I guess some ascribe to the view that any publicity is good publicity."

I wasn't quite sure where I was going with this. Seth had thrown competition out as an explanation for Cavanaugh's action. Maybe I wanted to see whether Aaron Nadell had said the same to his wife? Our conversation would certainly get back to him. How would he react knowing a journalist had spoken to his wife? I decided to push the envelope.

"He thinks it's a possibility. Perhaps competition trying to influence whether the IPO is successful."

"He's suggesting that the shooter, Cavanaugh, is working for the competition?" She looked appalled.

Not exactly what I said, but I noted her response.

"I'm sure you know that Cavanaugh believes there's a connection between the drink and his daughter's death. What you may not be aware of is that CPD has found contaminated product."

"Contaminated?" Her face went pale. "With what?"

"A botanical ingredient, belladonna. It's a toxin. What isn't clear is how it got there. And whether Seth Bowman was aware of it."

How long would it take Candiss to phone her husband in a panic? Seemed like a good time for Brynn to call Nadell Capital for a comment on the situation. Pending litigation was often a good way to get people to talk.

31

I was back at the diner in the loop where I'd met Olivia earlier in the week. This time the early dinner crowd was in full throttle. Plates of pot roast and thick Ruben sandwiches, oozing with corned beef and sauerkraut floated by. While the smell was divine, it had been years since I'd eaten beef and my stomach cramped at the thought. I ordered a chef salad, skipped the ham, and sipped an iced tea while I waited for Olivia.

She'd sent me a panicked text an hour ago saying the plant was going to be closed again tomorrow. But it wasn't her work schedule that I was interested in. She and Luke Cavanaugh were my inside view to VTF, and I wanted to keep the conversation going.

How long had the belladonna been in the drink? And why? As I waited, I considered the situation and how to proceed. Seth hadn't been honest about much of anything, so expecting straight answers from him was foolish. Michael would be scouring company records for explanations, but I couldn't be certain what he'd share with me or when. All of that meant I needed to keep my own sources active and see what played out first.

Given the pending assault charges against Cavanaugh, Michael had a revenge theory on his brain and I was certain that CPD considered Cavanaugh the primary suspect. I understood that from a logical and legal standpoint, but my gut said Cavanaugh wasn't the guy. But gut feelings weren't fact.

Then there were the legal challenges. There were any number of potential legal challenges ahead, depending on what the medical experts had to say about cause of death for Jeremy Wolanski and Kelly Cavanaugh, in light of the new information. I didn't know enough about how belladonna metabolized to know if it could be traced back to Kelly were her body to be exhumed. Or how litigious the parties might be. Although, a good class-action attorney would have no problem bringing a case, when anyone who ever drank VTF product came out of the woodwork and claimed to have been caused harm.

Any way you looked at it, this was a PR nightmare for VTF. With the plant closed, mouths would be flapping with speculation. Whatever Seth had been hoping to accomplish by minimizing the issue, he'd better wise up and start talking. This IPO was toast. If he wasn't smart, his company would be as well.

Olivia arrived as my salad was being delivered. I pushed a menu at her. "Go ahead, my treat."

Meatloaf, mashed potatoes and gravy, German chocolate cake, and a Coke to wash it down. I guess she was right when she'd said she didn't follow the VTF diet.

"Have you heard anything from Martin today?" I asked. "Other than don't come in to work tomorrow."

"He's totally freaked out. Mr. Bowman won't tell him what's going on and it's driving him nuts. We've got shipments that were due to go out today. Employees are calling every five minutes and he's got nothing to tell anyone." She looked up at me, her eyes damp. I was reminded how young she was, I guessed twenty-one, maybe twenty-two. Even people much older would be terrified by CPD invading their workplace. With Seth immersed damage control and Martin on his own to figure out how to handle operations and the staff, she had to be flailing.

"Has he spoken to CPD?" I asked, aware that the question might be crossing the line. I wasn't going to quote her, but it would give me information I could feed to Brynn, who could then press CPD.

"He said they questioned him for about an hour, mostly about where we get our materials, who handles the product. Basic stuff I guess, but he would've answered the same even without six guys wearing guns tearing his shop apart."

She dug into her meal as if it were the first one of the day. Perhaps it was. She'd said her mother had passed away and her father wasn't part of her life. I pushed around some limp iceberg lettuce in my bowl and gathered my thoughts. Olivia, Martin, and Cavanaugh were the three people who knew the production process best. If anyone had a clue about how belladonna had gotten into the drinks, it would be one of them.

"It sounds terrifying," I said. I wasn't sure if she just needed a shoulder to cry on or if she thought I had some information because of my relationship with Seth. The best course of action seemed to let her talk, for now.

"Nobody knows what to do." She dragged her fork through the potatoes, watching the trail of gravy as it formed. "The cops didn't speak to me but they took my info, you know, to talk to me later if they needed to." Her voice was back to the frightened little girl I'd heard earlier. "Are they going to shut us down?"

I felt bad for her. It was too much legal drama for someone her age. I imagined she'd be wondering soon about whether to start job hunting if she wasn't already. Kids her age rarely had financial cushions, tending to live paycheck to paycheck, and she had no parents fall back on. It wasn't clear how VTF would handle this set back.

"I don't know. But I do know is that there will be lots of people asking questions and trying to figure out if there's any cause for concern. I'm sure Martin and Mr. Bowman will communicate when they can."

I paused and took a sip of my tea, knowing I wasn't being much comfort.

"Can you help me? I feel like I need a lawyer or something. What if they accuse me? What if I say something wrong?" Her eyes were wide, expectant, as she looked at me and there was a slight tremble in her hand as she fiddled with the straw in her drink.

"I'll make a few calls," I said. "But let's not jump the gun. CPD hasn't asked to see you yet." I paused. "When we met the other day, I mentioned that my sister was in the hospital. She got sick from the VTF drinks too."

Olivia stared at me, mouth open. Then ran her hand over her forehead.

"Can I ask you a few questions about VTF?" I said. "Maybe we can figure out how this happened." She nodded.

"Can you think of any reason that a contaminant would get into the drinks?" I asked.

"A contaminant? You mean like bacteria or something?" she said, dropping the straw. "Our sanitation process is really strict. Martin makes sure of that. The bottles and caps are sterilized. We keep a log at every stage of the process. Gloves, hats, wash your hands three times after you pee. If you're thinking something happened to the product, while it was in the plant, I can't imagine how."

"What about a contaminant in the raw materials delivered to you? Is it possible that you didn't get what you ordered or that one of your suppliers substituted an ingredient?"

How the belladonna had gotten into the drink was the central question in my mind. If I could figure out how, then who and why become easier to answer. She was quiet for a moment contemplating my question.

"I suppose it's possible something weird happened at one of our suppliers. But if Martin caught it that would be the end of their business with VTF. Why would they throw away such a big account?"

"I don't know that anyone has, it could have been accidental, but one possibility would be to increase their own profits. If they could make a little more money by substituting a cheaper ingredient or a filler, they might be tempted."

"You mean like street dealers cutting coke with corn starch?"

"Exactly. What is your testing process on raw materials? How do you know that you've gotten what you've ordered? Or you've gotten the quality you ordered?"

Again she was silent, and her eyes searched the restaurant as she ran through the possibility in her mind. I chewed on a cherry tomato, washing it down with some iced tea as I waited for her response.

"I guess we wouldn't know. Not really, it's not like we test every batch," she chewed on her lower lip as she thought. "That would take a lab. We certainly don't have time to send everything out. Is that what all this is about? The cops I mean?"

"I'm just speculating about possibilities. CPD will be looking into all of this."

The waitress came over, delivering Olivia's cake and topping off my iced tea. I squeezed some lemon into the glass and resisted the urge to order a slice of my own.

As Olivia dived into her chocolate, I said, "I know we talked about this before, but to be clear, Martin, and his predecessor Luke Cavanaugh, were responsible for sourcing the raw ingredients. Correct?"

"Yeah, they found the vendors. They had the relationships with the salespeople. They did the production planning. You know, how much to order, when to bring it in, price negotiation, things like that. I wrote up the purchase orders and sent them to the vendors, tracked that everything was going to show up on time, and confirmed the receivables so that accounting could pay the invoices."

Talking about the basics of her job seemed to help her relax, or maybe it was the heavy meal.

"And how many vendors were you buying raw materials from?"

"We had three vendors for each of the primary ingredients in the drink. And two that supplied flavoring and coloring."

"Why multiple vendors?" I asked.

"It didn't start that way, but our first company wasn't able to keep up, so over the last year we decided to bring in more. You know, as back up. Don't want to put all your chickens in one basket."

"So how many vendors in total would you say there are?

"At last count, I think we had seventeen."

I mentally filed that away. That complicated narrowing down the source, although, given what I knew, lowered standards seemed inevitable.

"When the raw materials come in, do you have any way of identifying which vendor supplied that particular raw ingredient or do they all get mixed?"

"I'm not sure I understand your question," she said, scraping the last bite of frosting off her plate.

"I guess what I'm asking is can you track raw material A from a vendor, once it's in the final product or does raw material A become mixed with the supply from vendors B and C?"

I envisioned testing of raw materials as the next step and was curious about how far back into the timeline and the pipeline the contamination had occurred. It was entirely possible that the bad raw materials were long since used up which meant determining the source might be impossible.

"You can tell the supplier from the packaging as we receive it," she said. "But when we are filling a hopper, we don't really care which vendor supplied the ingredient. Everything would be mixed."

"So the control numbers on the bottle would identify the batch which would tell us when the product was made, but not who the supplier of that ingredient might be. All three could potentially be mixed in the hopper and therefore mixed in individual bottles," I said, restating the process.

"That sounds right. I never thought about needing to keep track. I don't know how we'd ever track it back to a vendor."

Michael had his job cut out for him, I thought, wondering about the production calendar and how quickly he could get forensic analysis on the raw materials.

"What do you know about the financial investors? You said there was someone who had some pull with Seth." I intentionally left out a name wanting to see where Olivia went with the subject.

"The money guy?" Olivia said, but her eyes went flat, as if he were someone she disapproved of. "What about him?"

"Did you see him around much? Any idea how active he was in the business?"

"See him?" she scoffed. "No, he never came around. Not when we were there, but I heard enough to know he's a money hungry pig."

My ears perked up at her tone which was harsh and judgmental. What was that about? It sounded personal.

"What do you mean?" I watched her face closely. She'd turned away, staring out in the room as if daring the man to walk through the door. She turned back a moment later, her eyes hard.

"He's been hanging in the background for a long time. At least that's what I hear, but he's only been showing his face around the plant for the last year or so. Not that he pays any attention to any of us. Martin says he slinks in after the second shift is gone. Probably doesn't want anyone to see his cowardly face."

She drained the last of her Coke and let out a breath before continuing. "He's the guy that got Luke canned. I think they ousted him so they could pay Martin half his salary. Martin's a nice man, but he's getting screwed over too. Ever since Luke got the axe, all we hear about is budget cuts. It isn't Martin's fault there's nothing left to cut but the payroll. These bottles aren't going to fill themselves."

"I thought sales were extremely strong, why the budget cuts?" This wasn't the first time I'd heard about finances being tight, but nothing that explained why.

"It's not like they tell me, but Nadell, Natell, whatever his name is, is a financial guy, right? All they care about is getting every damn dime. I know I told you that we started adding extra vendors so we could balance out our shipments, but these new vendors are also about 30% cheaper. Not the same quality. Hard to believe that he didn't have something to do with that."

I needed to understand the timing. "Olivia, can you get me into the plant? Tonight?"

32

Walter purred contentedly, limp in my arms. There was nothing like the simple pleasure of a happy cat. If only human life could be so easily satisfied. I was in the pantry pulling out a bag of Greenies, Walter's favorite. He squirmed anxiously for the treat. I tossed two pieces into his bowl, then went to my bedroom to change into jeans and a sweater.

Kelly Cavanaugh had been the first to become ill, at least as far as we knew. Since I could pinpoint when she'd gotten sick, I thought maybe I could connect the timing to one of the new vendors. And hopefully trace the source of the belladonna that way. CPD had taken the computers, but Olivia thought hard copies of purchase orders might still be in the office. She'd agreed to give me access, provided I didn't remove anything.

We'd arranged to meet outside the plant at 7:00, after she was certain the cleaning service was done for the night. As I changed and pulled my hair back into a low bun, I ran over the day in my mind.

Conversations had fueled my instincts, but the details were sparse. VTF was a high-growth business struggling to keep up with demand and in the process, letting supplier standards get lax. Its CEO had lied to me repeatedly. The company had a financial investor that seemed to want to stay in the background, yet felt emboldened enough to cancel orders in the dark of night. And there was a shitload of money dangling in their future if they could make rumor and accusations go away. But so what? Lots of businesses were sloppy and greedy.

Could the company survive the PR disaster they seemed unable to avoid? It seemed the only way to do that was to figure out the source of the belladonna, eliminate it, and fall on the mercy of the public, the courts, and the bankers. Doable, but hardly a cakewalk, especially for a small company with limited cash. The more I thought about it, the more I kept going back to behavior. Something Seth had told me flooded back. He said he suspected tampering around the time that Kelly got sick. That they'd isolated the batch, recalled product. That was months ago. Yet just days ago, I was able to pull a dozen contaminated bottles out of Lane's fridge. Was Seth lying about the whole thing?

I was searching in vain for a pair of oxfords when I heard the familiar ping of a text coming in. As I walked to my bag to retrieve the phone, my foot tagged the corner of a box of tile, sending shooting pain from my little toe up my ankle.

"Damn!" I shouted, momentarily frozen with the agony, then hobbled to the kitchen for a bag of ice, leaving a trail of blood as I walked. I then sat on the sofa, foot raised, packed in ice, with a kitchen towel underneath to protect the furniture. Walter sat at my feet smirking.

The text I'd rushed to get had been from Michael. *"Can I see you tonight?"* I sighed, leaned my head back on the cushion debating, then replied. *"My place at 9:00?"*

———

OLIVIA WAS LEANING against the door when I drove into the parking lot. Shadows hid her face, but I recognized the army jacket and thick knit scarf wrapped around her neck. I parked, double checked that my phone was fully charged, and walked over to meet her.

"What happened to you?" she asked as I got close. "You weren't walking funny this afternoon."

"Dinged my toe. It's nothing that a minor amputation won't cure. Lead the way." Each step felt like a shard of glass burrowing into my flesh.

She looked at me and laughed. "And I thought I was a klutz." After unlocking the doors, she walked quickly through the reception area to the hall on the far side and flipped a light switch, then continued toward the production office, not waiting on me.

I limped after her, feeling my toe swell. The plant was eerily quiet. Gone was the bustle of the production line, the hum of the conveyor system. The hulking machinery sat ominous in the dark recess of the warehouse. Olivia had turned on two desk lamps in the office and I followed her, parked myself into the first desk chair I saw.

"That bad?"

I shrugged and took off my coat. "You said you might have purchase orders in hard copy. Correct?"

Olivia undid her scarf, and then pulled a 3-ring binder out of a desk drawer.

"We try to run paperless," she said. "But I got caught in a bind a few times when our system fritzed out, so I started making copies and putting them in a binder for backup. I'm the one who gets the phone call when the accountant is reconciling billing so I figured it's kinda essential to my job. Martin would get on my case about the cost, so I just don't tell him."

She laid the binder on the desk between us and opened the cover.

"What do you want to see?"

I pulled myself closer to the desk to get a look at the contents. "Kelly Cavanaugh died in the middle of August so we know that the drink had to be contaminated prior to that. What I'm wondering is whether we can figure out which raw material vendors might have been new to VTF in the months prior."

I hadn't identified the deadly ingredient to Olivia, nor did I intend to. Not now.

"You think one of the new guys gave us bad stuff?"

"Maybe. It's just a theory. I want to start with the things that changed."

She flipped pages scanning the dates.

"So this PO was received August 10th. It's the flavorings shipment closest to when she died. But I don't think the timing works."

I looked at the document, thinking about a reasonable calendar. "I agree. Production, shipping, getting it onto the shelves. There wasn't enough time. But we can use this as the cutoff point. Do you have any little Post-its or flags?"

She pulled open a drawer and handed me a pad. I flagged the page.

"Okay, so let's work backwards. Flip through the POs from here back through March, and read me any names of vendors that were new, or established, but providing a new ingredient."

I pulled out a notepad and my phone while Olivia began scanning the purchase orders. As she identified a new supplier, I photographed the purchase order, and logged the date and company name. The identifying item numbers, what Olivia called SKUs, were undecipherable to me. Once we'd narrowed our list, I'd have her translate.

Moments later she paused on a page, her eyes narrowed.

"Something odd?" I asked.

She opened the binder and pulled out the document, handing it to me. "See this," she pointed at a line of text. "This line that's crossed out and a new SKU handwritten below? That's not me. It's not my handwriting."

"Luke?" She shook her head no. "It was marked as received June 6th. Does the SKU mean anything to you?"

"No. And I was out that week."

––––––

MICHAEL WAS WAITING for me in the lobby of my building when I returned at 9:05. My head was so focused on the altered PO, I almost didn't see him sitting in a chair, elbows on his knees.

"Ms. Kellner, what have you done to yourself now?" Norman the night doorman asked. He'd arrived for his shift while I'd been at the plant. At this point, my toe felt swollen to twice its size and my limp was impossible to hide.

"Just a dumb accident."

Michael stood, looked at me, then my foot, and shook his head. I shook my head and gave him a kiss.

"I'll tell you upstairs," I said.

I tossed my coat and bag on a chair when we got into the apartment, then plopped onto the sofa to remove my shoes. Michael stood over me, scowling as he noticed the trail of blood I hadn't bothered to clean up earlier.

"Can you get me some ice? And help yourself to the scotch."

I pulled off the sock and the Band-Aid. Yep, purple, puffy, getting bigger by the minute. Michael returned with an ice pack and a towel. He propped my foot on a throw pillow and played nurse. Then returned to the kitchen, this time bringing back a glass of Cabernet for me and a scotch for himself.

"Thanks." I raised my glass, and then took a much appreciated drink.

"What happened?" Michael nodded at my foot.

"Jammed my foot into a box of tile. A reminder that it's time to finish this damn reno, I guess." He held my eyes for a moment as if he wanted to say something. Or do something. Something I had a feeling would confuse me.

"And you rushed out of here so quickly after, that you didn't even wipe up the blood?"

"I, uh, had a meeting." I didn't see a reason to give him more detail.

He took a drink of his scotch but didn't press. We sat in silence for a moment toying with our drinks. Walter sat on the floor between us looking up and eyeing Michael suspiciously. He seemed to be suffering from an even worse case of caution than I was. Erik had never shown him the time of day, so I assumed he was making a judgment about men in general. Smart cat.

Michael pulled a catnip mouse out of his pocket presenting it to Walter who promptly turned on his heel, ignoring the gift.

"Is he ever going to like me?" Michael asked, confused, not for the first time, by Walter's indifference. At least he'd realized it wasn't the toy.

"Hard to tell," I said. The man was bribing my cat, I was in trouble.

"I've been thinking about what you said the other night," he said, his voice low. "But I'm having trouble understanding your reaction. Nothing happened. That part of my life is over. It's not something I want back. Explain to me why you're so upset."

"You chose not to tell me you were seeing your ex," I said. "That was a conscious decision. A lie of omission. Lies, of any kind, aren't something I'm willing to have in my life anymore. I'm coming from a relationship where my husband thought explaining and lying were interchangeable concepts. I've used up all the benefit-of-the-doubt I have in me. When, I saw you kiss her, that's where I went." Michael was silent.

"I thought you knew enough about my history to have understood that, but maybe I was wrong." I could hear the sadness in my own voice, as regret and memories flooded back.

Michael stared at the floor and worked his jaw. "I guess I don't have an answer. Don't you trust me?"

He took another drink of his scotch and scrunched his eyes, clearly unhappy with how the evening was proceeding. Welcome to the club. He'd been here all of ten minutes and already it seemed as if the evening would not end well, but I wasn't in the mood to massage his ego or anything else for that matter.

"That's exactly the point." I was trying hard to control my emotions. Michael clearly didn't understand the impact of the devastation I'd experienced. "If you're comfortable omitting this, I can only wonder what else you won't tell me."

Michael seemed confused. But I wasn't. There was no room in my life, or in my heart, to let in more hurt.

"I didn't tell you because I thought I'd be opening a wound," Michael said, his voice low. "That I'd be reminding you of everything you went through." I heard him sigh. "Obviously, I'm an idiot, but it never occurred to me that you'd draw the conclusion that I was hiding something."

"Then your detective skills are slipping," I said. I sipped my wine, thinking about lies, and who else might be telling them.

33

Ouch! For the first time, the three-block walk from the parking garage to the Link-Media office seemed an excruciating distance. My toe had swollen to the size of a walnut overnight and was starting to turn a beautiful shade of eggplant. Finding a pair of shoes in my closet that didn't pinch had been an impossible task. The best I'd been able to do was a pair of square toed oxfords. So, I'd chosen a pair of skinny black pants and an oversized sweater to go with, hoping it could pass as today's fashion look.

With a messenger bag slung across my body, I held a travel mug of Earl Grey in one hand and clamped the collar of my jacket closed with the other. As I pulled open the door to the building, a delivery guy brushed past me, dinging my injured foot. I winced with pain nearly dropping my drink.

The day was off to a bad start.

My evening with Michael had ended abruptly. He was confused and hurt, but also couldn't explain why he'd been secretive. And I was shutting him down, projecting my experience with Erik onto him. Was it fair? Maybe not, but self-protection was the best I could manage without going back into therapy. I threw my coat on the hook on the back of my door and settled in with my tea and email.

I zeroed in on a note from Janelle Platt. She was calling a press conference back at 1871 to address women and technology. Looked like our conversation last week had either given her an idea or had been a practice run. I took a quick glance at my calendar. Good, nothing I'd have to reschedule. That gave me an hour to make some calls.

I was still trying to understand where the belladonna had come from. Without the lot numbers, and therefore, the dates of the associated batches, it was difficult to pin down the source. The musical chairs that had been going on with VTF's suppliers didn't make it any easier. Olivia had been helpful last night with names of the new suppliers, and the altered PO felt like a step forward.

I uploaded all the photos I'd taken of the purchase orders to my laptop, then printed them out, scanning the documents for patterns. I concentrated on the altered PO, looking for other occurrences of the specific handwritten SKU.

An unknown number flashed on my cell phone and I picked it up.

"Ms. Kellner, this is Luke Cavanaugh. You said you wanted to help me find out what happened to my Kelly. Is that still true?"

"Yes, of course," I said, hearing the challenge in his voice. And realizing that he didn't know about the belladonna. What was the protocol for telling him I might know what killed his daughter? He could also help me shed light on the supplier list. "I'm glad you called," I let out a breath. "I just received some information that might explain what happened to Kelly."

I heard an intake of air on the other end of the line, whatever he'd called about now forgotten. "Go ahead." His voice broke as he responded as if he wasn't sure he was ready to know.

"I hired a testing lab and brought them product, product from my sister's stash. A contaminant was found."

"What? What kind of contaminant? That can't be." He seemed offended by the thought and what I imagined to be implications on his quality control process.

"It's a botanical toxin called belladonna. We aren't sure about the timing, so this may or may not be related to Kelly's death," I said, feeling the need to inject caution. Without lab confirmation of cause of death, I was projecting. "Until CPD has a better handle on lot numbers, timing, and can figure out when the toxin was inserted into the process, we shouldn't jump to conclusions, but I'm sure CPD will be in touch as they investigate."

"In the meantime, I'm looking at your vendor list. I want to see if I can figure out where the material might have come from. Would you be willing to look over a list of the suppliers that you worked with? Specifically, the suppliers of the botanical raw materials. Did you ever see belladonna on their product list? Anyone who might have been sloppy in filling orders? When did you first order from them? Things like that."

"Sure, I can do that. Email it to me." He read off his address. "But I'm a little confused. Are you saying Kelly was poisoned? Why wouldn't they know that when she died?"

"Autopsies don't always show everything at first glance," I said, thinking about a difficult case I'd handled as an ASA. "I don't know how this particular toxin reacts chemically to routine blood testing. Sometimes the ME has to be looking for that needle in the haystack. But it's a good question for CPD and the medical examiner." I made a note to myself to ask.

"And you were the one who ordered this test, not them?"

"Yes, as I told you, my sister is ill as well, so I hired a private lab. The forensic backlog can get pretty heavy."

"Then you can send me a copy of those lab results. I was

calling to tell you I've hired an attorney. We're filing a personal injury lawsuit against VTF."

Damn! The bad start to my day had just gotten worse. I was going to be dragged into being a witness in the legal proceedings. I told Cavanaugh I'd email him the vendor by the end of the day, then grabbed my coat to head over to Janelle's press conference.

By the time I'd arrived, twenty or so journalists and a handful of the film crews were gathered in the auditorium. The room on the corner of the building was flooded with light. A vivid orange wall adorned with a graphic mural contrasted with the exposed pipes and air ducts, increasing the manufactured cool factor.

I said hello to a few of the journalists I knew, then took a seat in one of the molded plastic chairs. The rumble of conversation quieted as Janelle entered the room once again sporting the female version of a power suit.

She glad-handed her way to the podium a warm smile on her face. I hadn't figured out how I felt about her candidacy, but she sure had the polish and moves of a natural. I wondered if the public could get past her husband's drama long enough to hear if she actually had positions on the local issues. And in this political environment, big city mayors had obstacles coming at them from all sides.

She welcomed the group and wasted no time jumping into her agenda. Good. No-nonsense played well in Chicago.

"Back in 2011, when 1871 was just an idea, a group of people gathered to discuss what it could be. A Brand Summit where Chicago's entrepreneurial and city leaders gathered. They came to the simple conclusion that Chicago is a city of builders. That is our history, our DNA. And they wanted a place where business was built. But Chicago is also a city of immigrants. A diverse and wonderful city of neighborhoods. We have our issues, no doubt, and one of them, from my point of view, is that economic opportunities haven't been equally distributed. Where are the women? Where are the people of color?"

She paused, looking around the room, her gaze intense as phones recorded her words and quotes were written.

"Shouldn't women and minorities have the same opportunity to be builders?" she said. "Shouldn't they have the same access to education, funding, mentorship, and entrepreneurship? That's why I'm running for mayor."

She continued, outlining a five-point plan that would be the core tenet of her administration. She spoke with conviction and passion, more campaign speech than press release. I had to admire her strategy and hoped the TV news made good use of their clips. She wrapped up, not taking any questions. Again, good strategy. That way, no one could ask her about her husband, the schmuck.

I jotted a quick note on the back of my business card and slipped it to her assistant. I knew she didn't want the peanut gallery to throw her off message, but thought maybe I could get her alone. So, I did an end-around and requested five minutes in the conference we'd been in last week.

Fifteen minutes later, Janelle walked in.

"Nicely done Madam Mayor," I said, giving her a smile. "You may have a future here."

"Did you like the 'sorry, no questions today'?" she laughed. "Even you journalists have to be herded now and then. Unfortunately, you're like herding cats. Present company excluded, of course. What's on your mind? Race relations, budget deficits, sanctuary city status?"

"None of the above. Although, I'll take a rain check on those subjects."

She raised her brow and took a seat. "I'm all yours."

"When we spoke last week, you said something about Aaron

Nadell being shady. Can you tell me what you've heard?" I leaned back in my chair and watched her face.

"Can you tell me *why* you want to know?"

"All I can say is that it appears his name may be in the news again related to a company he's invested in. I don't know if he'll be on the sidelines or digging his own trench. I'm curious about the rumors you mentioned, and whether the past might be repeating itself."

"Aren't you tired of men being assholes?" she shuddered. "Seems to be a genetic defect in most of them." She smiled and shook her head.

Although she didn't say it, I imagined that we were both thinking about our ex-husbands failings right now.

"Tawdry was the word I used, but I was being polite," she said. "Rapacious and unscrupulous would be more accurate. About ten years ago, his company nearly went bankrupt. Turns out he had invested big into a software start-up that was spending their dough like they had a personal ATM into Warren Buffett's bank account. Aaron being Aaron, he was so excited by the potential upside, that he didn't manage them, didn't hold them accountable to budgets. Before you know it, the money's gone, mostly on things the IRS wouldn't approve of, and they're nowhere near having a product."

She glanced briefly at a text that had popped up. I perked up at the word bankruptcy. Interesting timing. It seemed a safe bet that this was the situation that pulled Candiss into the business.

"A sane business person would have taken the loss, tucked his tail between his legs, and shut them down. But that's not Aaron, his ego won't let him. That would have meant admitting to the world that he'd fucked the whole thing up. So he starts moving the shells and pulling money out of one deal and into another. Eventually he has to play fast and loose with the books to cover his tracks." Janelle pursed her lips. "That's the power of compounding lies."

"How did he get out of it?" I asked, my mind still on Candiss's role.

"I don't know. But that's when he switched his focus away from the glamour and glitter of the sexy tech sector and into the boring stuff."

"And how do you know all this?"

"Because I know the guy who owned the software start-up. Part of his exit arraignment included a legal gag order that prevents him from discussing the details."

So, left to his own devices, Nadell's business investment strategy matched his personality. Fast, loose, and blustery. With Candiss not around to reign him in, had he returned to old habits?

34

I pushed through the revolving door of the Merchandise Mart onto the street at the corner of Wells and Kinzie. Five feet out a blast of wind slapped me in the face, blinding me with dust for a moment. I cleared the debris stuck to my lipstick, pulled my scarf tighter around my neck, then fished out my gloves.

Seth had left a phone message while I'd been meeting with Janelle. He'd been nearly incoherent, mumbling, asking me for my help. The situation he was in at VTF was far too complex for anything other than a high-priced legal team. If he was thinking I could get involved or smooth things over, he was quite mistaken. But I was frightened by the sound of him.

I phoned the receptionist, who told me he was holed up in his office and had asked not to be disturbed. Something was wrong. The shooting, the legal pressure, the thought of whether he had been ingesting belladonna, all crashed through my mind. Was he ill or having a breakdown?

After my last conversation with Cai, I'd been hesitant to call. Our conflicting interests had put tension in our relationship for the first time, but this wasn't the time for pettiness. I punched in her cell.

"Your client's losing it," I said, when she came on the line. "I need your help."

"What?"

"Bowman, he's having a breakdown or something. Hold on." I paused as the "L" rumbled overhead.

"Where are you?"

"Kinzie and Wells. I'm heading over to VTF. Seth is either horribly sick, on something, or about to go off the deep end." I relayed the tone and contents of the message. "I suggest you, or any other attorney you've helped him retain, meet me at their office before he does something stupid."

"Shit! Okay, I'm on my way. And I'm putting in a call to Turow."

"Turow? Oh, that's cozy. I'll text you if it looks like I need to call an EMT."

Harlan Turow was the attorney from Cai's firm who had unsuccessfully defended Janelle Platt's husband in the casino deal, and a total ass.

Although it was only six blocks to the old brick warehouse, I hailed a cab as quickly as I could. Texting Brynn that I'd taken a detour. The building was now an office loft space, that housed VTF industries, and a handful of other creative businesses.

In the five minutes it had taken me to get to the loft, the receptionist had moved from nonchalance to thank-god-a-grownup is here. Her panic was obvious in her inability to stand still.

"He told me he didn't want to be disturbed, but he's like yelling, and like, throwing things. I called him a minute ago, and he was like, really rude to me. I'm afraid to go back there," she said, twisting her long ponytail.

Rude was not what I was worried about. "I'm going to go check on him," I said to the young woman. "His attorney is on the way as well. Send them back when they get here. It will best if you can keep everyone else away from Mr. Bowman's office right now." She nodded vigorously, and I wrote down the attorney's names. As I moved down the hall, I heard voices from an open door to a conference room.

Martin and Olivia were inside having taken over the room. They looked at me blankly, seemingly as confused as the receptionist. Spare laptops, an extra printer, and a stash of office supplies filled the conference table. It looked like they'd settled in to keep operations moving as much as they could.

"Do you know what's going on at the end of the hall?" I asked, shooting my eyes from one to the other.

"Bowman's gone bonkers," Olivia said with her usual tact.

"Mr. Bowman is agitated," Martin added, giving Olivia an eye roll. "He's been in his office since early the morning. I got here at 7:30. We were supposed to review the budget, talk about what we were going to do about the orders for this week. He was already closed up in his office by then. I knocked for our meeting, but he told me to come back later."

"Ha, he threw a book at the door and screamed profanities at you. Playing like this is normal ain't going to help," Olivia said.

"Has he been out or let anyone come in?" I asked, my concern ratcheting up.

Martin shook his head. "The door's locked."

"Any idea what set him off?"

"Beyond the obvious?" Olivia said.

"Stay here. I'm going to see if he'll talk to me." I said, ignoring Olivia's commentary.

The other doors along the corridor were closed, I assumed because of the ruckus, but I could see faces turn my way through the slim side lights as curiosity won out.

Seth's office was wedged into the back end of the office space facing Erie Street. Flooded with light, its walnut door was flanked by wide glass side lights. I didn't see him at first, but heard movement. I stood in front of the glass where he could see me and knocked. Nothing. I knocked again. He stomped over toward me and stopped. His face was the hollow shell of a prisoner who hadn't seen daylight in months. His eyes looked at me but couldn't focus. I didn't know if I would have recognized him on the street if I'd seen him in passing. Then realizing I was there, he turned and paced the room like a caged animal. I knocked again and tried the handle, locked.

"Seth, it's Andrea. Please let me in, let's talk about this."

No response. He continued to pace as if not hearing me.

"Seth, why don't we go get a cup of coffee. A walk might be good for you." Coffee wouldn't be but a slap of the cold weather might be.

My presence seemed to agitate him even more. He was moving faster now, his gait more erratic.

"Seth?" I knocked again. "Talk to me."

"Go away! I changed my mind. You're just like the rest. Trying to destroy me." He picked up a ceramic vase of flowers off his desk and threw them at the door. Startled I stepped back as it crashed against the wood. Water began to seep under the door into the polished concrete floor.

Doors opened an inch with the sound and frightened eyes looked back at me. I told everyone to go back inside and lock themselves in. What the hell was wrong with him?

I headed back down the hall away from Seth. My arrival was aggravating him further. Martin stood outside the conference room a horrified look on his face. Olivia was just behind him, a smirk hid the fear in her eyes. The receptionist was nowhere to be found.

I grabbed my phone and dialed Michael.

"I'm at VTF's River North office. We have a situation. Seth Bowman is suffering some kind of breakdown. He's locked himself in his office. Throwing things. Incoherent. I've tried to talk him down, but it made things worse. Can you send a team?"

"Weapons?" he asked, ticking off the risk assessment.

"Not that I'm aware of."

"Stay out of his way. I'll be there in five."

I hung up and said to Olivia and Martin, "Lock this door. CPD is on the way. I'm going to wait for them at reception. Is there another exit beyond the main door?"

"The windows," Olivia said.

I sighed and left them in the conference room, frightening images flooding my head. I tossed my coat on the receptionist's chair but kept my phone in my back pocket, then locked the door. The last thing we needed were unexpected visitors.

As I waited for the cavalry, I ignored the endless ring of the phones, and wondered about Seth's condition. He's looked ill for over a week now and clearly was deteriorating rapidly. Was it a side effect of the gunshot wound? Or could the belladonna be causing this? I racked my brain for answers trying to remember what symptoms other than arrhythmia were common. Would high doses cause someone to become violent? Lane had been incoherent before she collapsed.

"No cops yet?" Olivia stood next to the desk.

"You should go back in the conference room," I said, "Just until we calm Mr. Bowman down."

"What's wrong with him?"

"I don't know." I looked at her, seeing a young woman confused and uncertain.

"The drink?" she asked, her voice wavering.

I shrugged and squeezed her hand. "I know that VTF views the recipe as a trade secret, but it seems to me that you'll need to divulge that information to authorities." She nodded, deep in thought. "How many people know exactly what's in it?"

Olivia avoided my question. I tried another tact.

"I understand that caffeine is used in energy drinks for a quick boost. Hits the blood stream fast."

"Caffeine is a short-term high," she said. "The lazy way out, according to Mr. Bowman. He believes that herbal supplements can provide a safer and longer lasting jolt of energy. We use caffeine because people expect the quick hit. It's the first layer, then the botanicals take over."

Someone rapped on the glass. Cai and Turow

I stepped over and flipped the lock.

"What's going on?" Cai asked as soon as they walk inside.

"Seth is locked in his office. He seems to be suffering a breakdown. I've told the staff to remain in their offices and lock the doors, CPD will be here momentarily," I said, rattling off the high points.

"Oh, come now, that seems a little melodramatic. Is it really necessary to involve them?" Turow said, condescension dripping from his voice.

"It became necessary when your client threw ten pounds of pottery at the glass I was standing behind, after I asked him if he wanted coffee." That wiped a little of the smugness off his face.

"I'll go talk to him," Cai said.

"No," I put my hand on her arm. "We need to wait for CPD." She nodded. "I don't want to chance this escalating and someone getting hurt."

We heard the cops before we saw them. Michael, and three others fully equipped with bullet-proof vests and all the gear. Seemed excessive but who was I to judge?

"He's in the last office on the left," I said to Michael. "It's been quiet for the last few minutes." We looked at other, words unsaid.

"Do we know if there's a key?" He looked at Olivia who shrugged.

I pulled open drawers in the receptionist's desk but found nothing.

"Everyone stays here and out of the way," Michael said to the group. "Guys, lets move." He nodded to the officers. Then to me, his eyes deep on mine, "You okay?"

I nodded, and he walked down the hall.

We could vaguely hear the officers from where we waited. Knocking, talking, but it was impossible to make out what was being said or who was saying it. We waited, looking at each other with shock and confusion over what was happening. Eventually the voices got louder. I couldn't tell if they'd picked the lock or Seth had opened the door, but Seth's was the voice piercing the silence.

"You can't do this!" he screamed. "Don't touch me. It's not safe. You're not clean. I can see them, I can see the maggots that have infested your soul. Eating away at the decay inside you."

Two officers held Seth by the arms as they marched him, handcuffed down the hall. He twisted in their grasp. Another followed behind. Michael stopped in the reception area as the officers moved to take Seth from the building.

Turow stepped over to speak with his client but was met with a string of obscenities. "Okay, I'll follow you," he said to the cops, shaking his head and not knowing what to do any more than the rest of us did.

Michael stayed behind as the officers led Seth to a waiting police vehicle, and likely to the hospital. Cai, Olivia, and I stood open-mouthed, shocked by the scene and not sure what to make of any of it.

"Any idea when this break from reality started?" Michael asked.

Before anyone could respond, we heard voices in the hall outside of the office.

"What is this? Where are you taking him?" a male voice, loud, insistent, and familiar.

A moment later Aaron Nadell burst through the doorway.

"What in the hell is going on around here?" he demanded, looking immediately to Michael for an explanation. "Why isn't anyone answering the phones? Where is the girl? The desk girl?" He threw out questions, irritated that we weren't answering fast enough.

"And you are...?" Michael said.

"This is Aaron Nadell. Seth Bowman's financial partner," I said.

Nadell looked at me for the first time, recognition and confusion crossing his face. As I swung my eyes to Michael, I saw Olivia seizing with anger. Her eyes were slits, her mouth drawn into a tight line, her hands clenched into fists. I stepped toward her. She swatted me away.

"It's him! He's the one to blame!" she screamed, her voice filled with rage. Everyone turned in stunned silence, the confusion even deeper, all eyes on the young woman.

Nadell stepped forward coming at Olivia. "What the hell are you talking about? Who are *you*?"

Cai put a hand on Nadell's arm cautioning him to stay calm, while Michael moved to get between them if needed, and I tried to figure out what craziness had overtaken everyone. Olivia however, would not be silenced.

"All you've ever cared about was money. Your position," she said, her voice dripping with accusation and hatred. "You're the one who swapped ingredients for the cheaper product. You've been lying and hiding it from Mr. Bowman. Just to make more money. Just so your stupid IPO could make you millions more.

You've never cared about anyone. You haven't cared about your customers. And you haven't cared about your daughter!"

Nadell stopped, his face changing from confusion to awareness in an instant before he looked longingly at the door.

"That's right, you coward. Your daughter. Me. The one you've refused to acknowledge for the last twenty-two years."

35

The morning had just become an episode of Maury Povich.

As Olivia ranted, Nadell shot back his denials, accusing her of being as insane as Seth. The room erupted in a mass of voices and bodies.

Michael stepped in front of Olivia to prevent the incident from escalating further as Cai ushered Nadell out into the hallway.

"Coward," she screamed as he left, flailing at Michael's chest, an immovable object in her path. As he attempted to calm her down, I saw that Martin had left the conference room and was now standing back, shell-shocked at the scene before him. Others poked their heads around doors trying to understand the chaos.

Weren't we all? I stepped closer to Olivia and put my hand on her back.

"Olivia," I said softly. "You need to calm down. This is Officer Hewitt. He's my friend. He'll listen to anything you have to tell him. But we can't hear you if you're screaming." I said, gently putting my arm around her shoulder. "Let's go somewhere and talk to him."

She slumped forward against Michael's chest, but stopped fighting. Sobs shook her body. And she nodded, allowing me to take her under my arm.

Michael looked at me, eyebrows raised, as confused as I was. "It okay, I've got her," I said.

He nodded. "Bowman's being taken to Northwestern for evaluation. I want Nadell and her in for a chat. Let's sort this mess out." Michael said to me. "You'll bring her in?"

"We'll be right behind you, but first I'm getting her an attorney."

I led Olivia to a chair and gave her a box of tissues and a bottle of water.

"Martin," I said. "I'm going to take care of Olivia. Give me five minutes to get her out of the building, then send everyone home. Do you still have my card?" He looked at me blankly. I pulled another out of my bag and handed it to him. "Pull yourself together." He nodded.

Keeping an eye on Olivia, I stepped into the hallway. No sign of Cai or Nadell. I then phoned an attorney friend and explained the situation as best I could in three sentences. Luckily, he agreed to meet us at police headquarters.

Olivia and I walked the two blocks to my parking garage and headed south. She was quiet on the ride, her anger and tears had morphed back into the attitude that she normally carried as her mantle. I wasn't sure which was more helpful. She said nothing as we made our way out of the Loop and I let her sit silently with her thoughts. It was better if she said nothing further to me. Given the anger that she'd clearly harbored for a long time, I couldn't help but wonder how far that anger had taken her. Her description of her father as a loser who walked away before she was born, came back. Was it possible that Olivia was the one extracting her revenge? How had Nadell not known she was his daughter?

We were led to a small beige conference room in police headquarters after we arrived. Michael was nowhere in sight. And neither was my attorney friend. Olivia plopped down in the plastic chair crossed her arms over her chest and stared at the floor. I excused myself, sent Brynn a text that I wouldn't be back for another few hours, I'd explain later, and then went to find Olivia a Coke. She had a feeling she was going to need the caffeine. A few minutes later I returned, a soda in hand for her and hot tea for myself.

"Andrea, there you are." My friend Scott Price stood in the hallway looking for our conference room. He was a tall, spindly guy, who carried an old briefcase, that wouldn't close and looked to be half his weight. I led him further away from the room, so we could speak with a tiny bit of privacy, then fleshed out the details of the situation.

"She sounds like one angry young woman," he said, speaking factually not in judgement.

"Sullen, certainly. Moody. But outright hostility that's not something I've seen until this morning." But clearly she was capable and probably deserving.

"Parental abandonment. Withdrawn love. Classics." He lifted his eyebrows.

"That doesn't mean she's done anything. I've heard from a few sources that Nadell has been putting pressure on the company to tighten its finances. Let's not jump to anything just yet," I cautioned.

"You don't think our friends at CPD are going to jump there?" He let me answer the question for myself. "Why don't you introduce me to my client?"

Price was already two moves ahead and like it or not, he was right. He opened the door, and I followed behind him. Olivia was in the same position I'd left her. Slumped in her chair. Petulant, angry, foot bobbing restlessly.

"I figured you could use a drink," I said, setting down the can in front of her. She nodded, noticing we weren't alone. "This is Scott Price, he's an attorney and a friend of mine. He'll sit in with you while the detectives ask their questions."

"So, I'm the guilty one now?" Olivia shot back, her voice full of hostility.

Price pulled out a chair at the head of the table next to Olivia. "It's nice to meet you Olivia. I'm here to make sure that you say what you want to say and don't inadvertently say something you didn't mean. That you're not pushed into saying anything and, in case you happen to need it, you have legal protection. I'm here to work for you and only you."

Good. Price was treating her with respect and kindness, just as I knew he would. It was important that this first impression be the start of trust between them. Many attorneys would either treat her like a dumb kid or as if they were waiting to rush out and plug the meter because the next client was waiting. Hopefully, she wouldn't need him beyond today.

"How much do you charge?"

"Today, nothing. Let's get through this conversation with CPD, see if there's anything unexpected, and we can decide from there if you need my services any further. Does that sound okay?"

Olivia nodded and mumbled thanks as she popped open the soda and took us swig that had to be half a can. I guess I should've gotten two. The door opened, and Michael entered, accompanied by one other detective. Introductions were made, and the detectives took seats opposite Olivia.

"Good, I see you found something to drink," Michael said to Olivia, smiling and trying to keep the tone light. "Olivia, you made some allegations at the office. I think it would be helpful if we could talk about that in more detail. It sounded like you have information that you wanted to share about Mr. Nadell's instructions. Can you tell us about that?"

Again, Olivia nodded. Michael turned to me. "I'll wait outside," I said.

"I want you to stay," Olivia said.

"It's better if I don't. Mr. Price will take care of you," I said, trying to keep my voice light and upbeat. But I knew that Olivia had made herself a target. What I didn't know was how aggressively Michael would pursue that line of questioning.

36

I sat in the reception room nursing my tea, my mind tangled with thoughts. Had people really died because of cost-cutting? Olivia's accusation had been about swapping ingredients. Either she knew something and hadn't told me, or she was letting her anger get the better of her imagination. I thought about Seth, how he had seemed out of touch with reality. Was he having a reaction to his antibiotic? Was he hallucinating? Was he experiencing the side effect of belladonna poisoning?

I pulled out my phone and dialed my friend Henry at the lab.

"I've got a few more questions about the testing you did for me. Can you spare a minute?"

"We on the clock?" He laughed. "Just kidding. What do you want to know?"

"We're trying to figure out how and why belladonna got into these drinks. Is it possible that it might have been confused for something else? I guess that's the first question. Or would it have been added for a specific effect on the body?"

"Well, it's hard to know what the intent was. In terms of

confusing belladonna for something else, I guess that would depend on the form it was in. Was it belladonna in plant form where both the leaf and the root are used? Or some kind of processed tincture? My first assumption would be it was in a liquid form because the drink itself was the delivery mechanism. This wasn't some kid who ate a couple of the berries out in the forest. Occasionally, ointments are made using belladonna, but my guess is were talking about a tincture."

"So, drops of some kind added to the bottles or into the ingredients during processing," I said, confirming what I'd already assumed.

"That's what I'm thinking. Process of elimination would be to separate the raw material and test those. If you find belladonna, then you go deeper into how that was processed. Basically, reverse engineer the stuff. If you want to test raw materials, we'll need to get you help with the sampling."

At this point that would be better left to CPD's crime lab.

"Is there any legitimate reason for ingesting belladonna?" I asked, wondering about Olivia's accusation. She'd specifically said Nadell had swapped ingredients. "I believe you said it's historically been used as a pain reliever and a hallucinogenic. What about today?"

"This is outside the realm of traditional medicine, but my understanding is that some in the alternative health world, and I'm talking people who are pretty out there in their views, are using it as a sedative. I've heard of people using it to stop bronchospasms—which happens in asthma and whooping cough, Parkinson's disease—things like that. It works to block some of the functions of the nervous system. Which I guess, in some cases is thought to be a good thing but obviously that's dangerous territory. I wouldn't go DIY on that although some in the homeopathic crowd seem unconcerned."

"Can you tell me about the hallucinogenic effect? Is this seeing things, or does it lean more toward paranoia?"

"Oh, you want to get specific with your high," he laughed. "What I understand is that the high is described initially as euphoric but then there's a crash. Like everything, it depends on dosage, body weight, the usual."

Euphoria? Interesting. A terrifying idea crossed my mind. Was it possible that was the intended effect? Could belladonna be not a contaminant, but an active ingredient? My mind raced. It was an ugly thought, but given the lies, and the amount of money at stake I couldn't dismiss the idea.

"Do you know if this poison would come up in an autopsy tox screening?" I asked, thinking of Kelly Cavanaugh.

"Verify this with the ME, but probably not unless they were looking for it specifically."

"Henry, I want to go back to another aspect, and you may not know the answer, but do you have any sense of whether this is an inexpensive stimulant? I guess I'm wondering if it's possible that belladonna was substituted for something else, whether that was to save money or because another ingredient that did the same thing might have become difficult to get? I know it's asking you to speculate, but humor me, help me brainstorm a little. I won't quote you."

I heard him exhale as he considered the question.

"That's hard to say; I guess that depends on what effect you're trying to get. There are a number of compounds that could be used for either the hallucinogenic quality or pain relief if that was the desired result. As far as pricing goes, that's relative and I'm not up on the market, but when you can walk into some of the big-name pharmacies and find homeopathic remedies containing belladonna for a couple of bucks, it can't be that pricey. I know I'm not being very helpful, but I don't have enough data to answer that."

I thanked him and ended the call. I needed to speak with Michael again about Kelly's autopsy. Cai and another attorney I didn't know were walking toward me, deep in conversation. They stopped speaking the minute they saw me, then stood huddled before going their separate ways. Cai walked over and sat down next to me with a sigh.

"This isn't going to screw up our friendship is it?" she asked.

"No, of course not. Obviously, it's going to fuck up Seth's situation, but you and I will be fine."

"I miss you. I haven't been to Nico in almost two weeks. I've got five cases I haven't been able to tell you about. And," she leaned over to whisper. "I'm dying to know if your cop friend has been able to use his handcuffs, off-label."

Only Cai could choose a day like this for innuendo. "Miss you too." We laughed. "Well, we should be able to get back to normal socializing soon because it looks like your client list is about to get shorter," I said.

"It does, doesn't it? Turow's walking into a mess. Whatever the hell is going on here is not my forte."

"Nope, I don't see any IPO's in VTF's near term future. Speaking of acronyms, what about Nadell? I assume he was on the horn to his high-powered legal team in about half a second." She nodded. "Did he know? About Olivia I mean?"

"Hell if I know. By the look on his face, I'd say this was a problem he thought he buried long ago. Look, I'm going to go through withdrawals here pretty soon so let's figure out when we can come out of our respective corners."

"Looking forward to it." I smiled back at her.

Michael stepped into the reception area. He'd ditched the jacket, loosened his tie, and rolled up his sleeves. I had the urge to tell him how cute he looked, and might have, if I hadn't been mad at him.

Cai and I stood.

"Time for me to get back to work," Cai said. "I'll speak to you later."

"Detective." She nodded and took a few steps, but when she was certain Michael's back was to her, she lifted her wrists together in a "cuff-me" gesture and winked.

I cleared my throat with a fake cough and tried to keep my mind on anything but Michael's bedroom maneuvers, whether that was with me or anyone else. Nothing good would come of those thoughts.

"You okay?"

I nodded. Not trusting myself to say anything.

"I'm done with Olivia for now. But I want to keep her in the conference room a little bit longer. We're wrapping up with Nadell and I want to make sure he's safely out of the building before we have another incident on our hands."

He looked at me as if wanting to say something more.

Best if we didn't go there. Too much craziness had happened today, too much emotion. "Thanks for letting me know. Can I speak with her now?"

"It's fine with me, as long as her attorney agrees. But wait here until you see Nadell leave."

As if on cue, Nadell and Turow, stormed through the lobby. I could see that Nadell was still seething by his get-out-of-my-way stride. He didn't give anyone a glance. Michael and I headed down the hall toward Olivia.

As we entered the room, attorney and client sat next to each other speaking in low tones but looked up when we entered.

"Olivia, you're free to go now," Michael said. "Thank you so much for your help." He nodded to me and left.

"Do you want to talk about it?" I asked.

"No, I want to get the hell out of here. Can I go now?" she said to Price.

"You heard the officer." He pulled a business card out of his breast pocket and laid it in front of her. "I'd like you to come into my office tomorrow and we can spend some time digesting what's happened today." She mumbled she would, grabbed his card off the table, and her bag, then headed out the door.

"Well?" I said. "What do we know?"

"We know that your young friend has some serious daddy issues."

37

"Olivia, wait up." She was out of the police station and halfway to the bus stop before I caught up with her. Her trademark chunky scarf coiled her neck against the cold and heavy wool socks were pulled over her jeans, peeking out of the top of her Doc Martens.

She swung on her heels at the sound of my voice. "Are you here to find out what's really happening at VTF or to set me up as a scapegoat for your friend? Right now, it feels like I'm the one who's got a target on my head. Why the hell are you here?"

Her anger hadn't lessened. But this time I was the one in the line of fire. I pulled the collar of my coat tighter to my neck, shivers starting to kick in.

"I'm trying to find out who or what is poisoning people. Just as I've told you all along. I want the truth. I need the truth. My sister was a victim too."

Olivia's expression softened lightly. "Sorry, I'm just messed up right now. Is she okay?"

"She's going to recover because we were able to figure out what was making her ill. There's a medication that counteracts the effects of the poison, but how many others have been affected? We don't know how many bottles are still in circulation or how many are sitting in backstock on retail shelves? Others could die. I'm doing everything I can to prevent that, but we still don't know the full picture."

I shuffled my feet and pulled my coat closer to my neck, trying to control the shivering.

She seemed to calm down. "Look, I just want to go home. I'm all talked out. I can't even think any more." She looked at her phone. "My bus should be here in a few minutes."

"Can I give you a ride?" A cold blast of wind hit us in the face. The weather wasn't improving. This unusually early cold snap showed no sign of ending anytime soon. Snow flurries had been picking up steam all day and threatened to become an all-out storm with over a week to go before Thanksgiving. But this was Chicago; it could be 65 again next week.

"Okay, I'm out by Midway. Is that too far?"

"Not at all."

She followed me to the parking lot. I turned on the engine, cranked up the heat, and let her get in, and then pulled out the scraper to clean the snow frozen to my windshield.

We both were quiet on the drive. I sensed Olivia's need to process her thoughts, so we drove in silence. According to the WXRT traffic report, there were two accidents on the Stevenson, so Olivia directed me west on Archer, south on Cicero, and ultimately to a small one-story brick bungalow just south of the airport. The yard was tidy with simple shrubs lining the stoop as was every other house on the block. They only varied in the amount of holiday decorations that were already enhancing the decor.

I pulled to the curb and turned off the car. Olivia made no move to exit.

"Do you feel like talking about any of this? Nadell? VTF?" I asked.

"I guess. Come on inside."

I followed her up the three steps to the front door where she pulled out keys and undid the lock. The door opened to a small living room. A deep comfortable sofa and loveseat loaded with pillows and afghans rested in the corner. A shelving unit filled with books and photos anchored the room. And a newer TV rested on a small oak stand. It was warm and comfortable and homey. It also surprised me. I didn't seem like student digs.

She unwrapped her neck and hung the scarf and coat on a hook near the door, then held out her hand for mine. "Do you want water or something?" she asked.

"A glass of water would be great." As she walked to the back toward the kitchen, I scanned the bookshelf. Mary Higgins Clark, Danielle Steel, Agatha Christie. Interesting. Not what I would have expected from a 22-year-old. I looked around the room again. Was this her mother's home? The photos were mostly images of a happy, smiling young girl who I assumed were Olivia in her childhood. A larger photo framed in silver sat in a prominent spot in the center. It was of the young girl and a woman in her early thirties. Heads together, they smiled brightly at the camera.

"Here." Olivia held out a glass.

"Is this you and your mother?" I held up the photo. I could see the resemblance in their eyes, the shape of the nose. I could feel their happiness.

"Yeah, I was six. That was taken on my birthday. We went to the Field Museum. I wanted to see Sue." She smiled at the memory. "I was really into dinosaurs back then and the idea of seeing a real-live T. Rex was the coolest thing that had ever happened to me. I didn't want to leave. I guess I told her was going to stay there and live with Sue. She had to take me to the gift shop and buy me a plastic one so I would go home."

"She sounds like a good mom. When did she die?"

Olivia moved over and took a seat on the sofa so I put the photo back in its place and followed.

"She died two years ago. Cancer. This was her house, well, our house. It's the only place I've ever lived. I inherited it when she died. I haven't really changed anything. I guess I still want it to feel like she's around."

"I'm sorry. I lost my mother when I was a teenager. I know how it turns your life inside out." I was getting a glimpse of where Olivia's tough-girl attitude was coming from. She was angry, angry at the world for taking her mother, angry at Nadell for a whole host of things better left for a therapist to untangle.

I sat on the loveseat, my body turned to face her. The afternoon sun streamed in, glinting off the picture frames. Olivia looked drained, depleted of energy. It was as if the events of the day had drained her of emotion.

She grabbed a throw pillow and pulled it to her chest, then tucked her feet underneath her. "Growing up it was always just my mom and me. She didn't have any other family, so neither did I. Not in the U.S. anyway. I think there are some cousins back in Ukraine, I'm not sure. Anyway, it didn't bother me or anything, it was just normal. She was amazing. We were happy."

"What did she tell you about your father?" I asked.

"When I was a kid, nothing. I didn't start bugging her about it until I was in high school. She was working two jobs and money was always tight. I didn't mind that we didn't have money, none of my friends did either, but she was exhausted all the time. It was making her sick. She was doing everything for me to have a good life and not taking care of herself. It seemed like he, whoever he was, should help. I only cared about the money because she needed it."

"And did she tell you?" I kept my voice soft, conscious of not adding to her burden.

"At first, she just said that he was someone who didn't want a family. And if he didn't want us, then she didn't want him. I let it go. But at the end, when she knew she was dying, she told me the whole story."

Olivia turned away, her focus on some spot on the carpet. Clearly the memory was still painful.

"She'd had an affair with a man named Aaron Nadell. At the time, he was her boss. Her married boss. When he found out she was pregnant, he told her he'd pay for an abortion. She said no way, she was keeping me. So he bought her this house. Paid cash. Made sure it was about as far away from his as he could get, then fired her, and told her never to get in touch with him again. That's the kind of royal prick he is."

My gut clenched and a new level of loathing for the man seeped in. The image of his face earlier this morning when he realized Olivia was his daughter flashed in my mind. And still he denied it. I felt my own body tense, imagining the rage Olivia had carried with her the past two years, seeing her in a new light. Underneath was a strength few her age possessed.

I paused for a moment, gathering my thoughts. "Do you know if your mother honored that request?"

"As far as I know, she did."

"So this morning was the first time Nadell knew who you were?" Why had Olivia waited to confront him?

"Yep. Not exactly a warm welcome, was it?" her voice was getting steely again as she relived the incident. "It's not like I expected him to be anything other than the shit he was to my mother."

A new thought came to mind.

"I don't know how to ask this question other than to be direct," I said, watching her face. "Did you seek out a position at VTF because you knew that Nadell was involved?"

"You're damn right I did. That S.O.B. doesn't get to ignore me anymore. He needs to be held accountable for being an asshole. Even if it's just by his wife."

"But you didn't confront him. Not before today," I said, puzzled by the lag. "Your reaction today seemed to just burst out of you. It wasn't planned." I looked at her and leaned forward, putting my elbows on my knees.

She hugged the pillow and pushed back a loose strand of hair. "I've been waiting, trying to figure out how and when. Planning what I would say to him. I even went to his office once, but they wouldn't let me see him. I wanted to nail him, expose him for what he is as publicly as possible. But today, when I saw him finally, I just couldn't take it anymore."

A tear ran slowly down her cheek while I wiped away my own.

38

The drive back from Olivia's had been brutal, not just because of the awful traffic on the Stephenson, but also because of my inability to sort through this VTF situation. It was getting messier by the moment.

I'd used the time taking advantage of my Bluetooth connection to check in with a number of people. I phoned my father who told me Lane was reacting well to the new medication and would probably be released tomorrow. Phoned the hospital, which wouldn't give out information on Seth's condition, so I then tried Michael, but just got his voicemail. After that, I put in a call to Martin who only had time to tell me that CPD was back, this time with a search warrant to take samples of raw material.

By the time I was back to the office, it was 3:30. I was hungry, tired, and desperate for a couple of Advil. I picked up a sad-looking pre-made salad from the corner deli and headed upstairs.

I waved to Brynn, tossed my coat on the top of the file cabinet in my office and flopped into the desk chair.

A nagging thought had kept me company on the drive. Had Olivia intended to do something other than expose Nadell as her father? Her anger and hatred seemed deep-seated. I could only imagine the blame she placed on him for her difficult life, and more importantly that of her mother's. Like it or not, I couldn't help wonder about her desire for revenge.

I took a drink of my Pellegrino, a few stabs at the iceberg lettuce, and opened my laptop. I'd been so preoccupied lately with my sister's health and the situation at the VTF that I had all but neglected any other work. Borkowski was breathing down my neck for another installment on the mayoral run.

Brynn rushed into my office. "Turn on your TV."

As I hit the clicker, Michael Hewitt's face filled the screen.

"At this point, we've linked two deaths to the consumption of VTF energy drinks. We believe the product has been contaminated with a plant-based toxin. At this time, we have not isolated the contamination to a specific lot number or date. We're working with VTF Industries to determine that information and will provide it to the public as soon as it's available. Therefore, we are strongly encouraging consumers to discontinue consumption."

Martin stood to Michael's left, visibly shaken. He stepped up to the mic, a sheet of paper in hand. Where was Nadell? With Seth hospitalized why wasn't he playing spokesman?

"As Officer Hewitt said, the drinks may have been contaminated. So, to be safe, please do not consume the product," Martin said, his voice cracking. He looked down at the paper in his hands and read. "We're asking all retailers who may have back inventory to set it aside and not sell it to the public. We've set up a hotline for anyone concerned about their own exposure and we will work with our retail partners to deal with their existing inventory. VTF is dedicated to resolving the situation immediately and will do everything it can to regain the trust of the public."

Short, sweet, and written by an attorney.

Brynn turned to me. "Now I know where you've been all day."

"You don't know the half of it yet." I looked at her and flopped back in my chair. We turned back to the screen.

A reporter called out, "Is this sabotage? A disgruntled employee? Or a dishonest vendor?" Another said, "Do you have a suspect? What's the toxin?"

Michael took the mic. "The toxin is a botanical material called belladonna. We are interviewing employees, past and present. Vendors. Anyone who might be able to shed some light on the subject, but at this point we don't know why it was found in the drink. VTF and its CEO, Seth Bowman are cooperating fully."

"Make you thirsty?" Brynn teased.

I rolled my eyes. And I wondered if Michael had intentionally tied Seth directly to the investigation. It was completely obvious to me he failed to mention that Seth himself seemed to be a victim.

"Wait, a second?" I squinted at the screen "They're in the Loop, standing on the sidewalk outside of Nadell's office. Damn." I jumped to my feet. "I gotta go. I think they're about to arrest him."

"How does Nadell fit into this?" Brynn asked, tilting her head to the side as she watched me flit.

"He's VTF's money guy," I said, grabbing my coat and bag. "We have a lot to get caught up on. I'll call you after I know what the charges are. Nobody knows about him, so we'll have the story first. Fill Borkowski in, clear your schedule, and stay near the phone."

"Will do," she said as I dashed out the door.

I jumped in a cab, making the trip in just under fifteen minutes. Two cop cars were parked in front of the building, empty. So I headed inside.

Stepping off the elevator, I walked down the hall and opened the frosted glass door of the Nadell Capital office. Inside I found a flustered receptionist but not a cop in sight. She barely glanced at me as she flipped through some documents on her desk while juggling the phone in the other hand. Her hand was shaking and the only thing she was saying to the caller was "I don't know."

As I stood waiting for her, the interior door opened. Michael stepped out followed by two officers and Aaron Nadell in handcuffs. The receptionist was now in tears seemingly unable to comprehend what was happening. I hit the recording app on my cell.

"Mrs. Nadell will be here any minute," she said to no one in particular.

"Call my attorney," Nadell said, to the stunned woman. "Have him meet me at police headquarters."

She nodded vigorously and grabbed for the phone again.

Michael paused when he saw me but said nothing, tightened his jaw, and moved his charge toward the door. As he did so, Candiss Nadell walked in.

"What is going on?" she demanded, running her eyes around the group assembled here. She stopped when she saw me, furrowed her brow, then directed her gaze at Michael. "What are you charging my husband with and where are you taking him?" Aside from the urgent tone in her voice, she gave no hint of being flustered. Not even her husbands arrest impacted her impeccable appearance.

"For starters, your husband is being brought in on reckless endangerment in regard to his involvement with VTF Industries," Michael said, then explained that Nadell's attorney could fill her in on the details. He then escorted his suspect out of their office.

"Meet me in Aaron's office in ten minutes," she said to the

receptionist. "Call any clients he has scheduled for today and tomorrow and reschedule for next week. I want an update on the status of any open issues or projects. And a cup of coffee. Did you get to the attorney?"

The young woman nodded. "Right away ma'am."

Candiss opened her mouth to say something to me, then thought better of it after noticing the phone in my hand. Instead, she turned heading toward her husbands office while the receptionist got to work.

I made a quick exit, phoning Brynn on my way downstairs. I dictated the basics of the arrest as I jumped in a cab directing him to police headquarters. Then I called Cai.

"Nadell's been arrested," I said. "Did you hear me? Your client has been arrested."

"Not my client," she replied. "If he were, I don't think I'd be answering your call right now. I was just in the wrong place at the wrong time this morning. You should be calling Turow for a comment."

"Did you know they were going to charge him?"

"Andrea, I'm not his attorney."

"But you're the tort queen. Why reckless endangerment against an individual versus negligence or a product liability charge against the company? From a legal strategy I mean? This says he knew and did nothing, or that he took direct personal action. Aren't you curious? Is Seth going to be charged?"

"Can't talk to you honey, not about this. You know that. Try your boyfriend."

"Ouch, that was a little bit mean."

"You can take it. So, is pumping me for info the only reason you called?"

"For now... Talk to you later."

I sent Olivia a text letting her know Nadell had been arrested. The news would make her day if not her lifetime.

Only one truck was parked on the street in front of the building. Good, I'd beaten the crowd. Inside, I saw the Channel 5 crew prepping their equipment. The reporter was engrossed in her phone. As I walked past them, two other crews entered the building. Damn.

I saw Michael crossing the corridor with a cup of coffee and made a beeline toward him. Hopefully I could get in a few questions before the rest of the contingent knew what was going on. He stopped when he saw me approach, but looked nervously at the journalists setting up behind me.

"Why are you charging Nadell?" I asked.

He brought his coffee up to his lips. "Do you ever let up?" he said.

His eyes were a mix of apprehension and sadness, as if he wanted to say something, as if he were asking a different question. Part of me wanted to hear what he'd been thinking about since our last conversation, part of me wanted to block it out. The push-pull hadn't stopped.

"Hey, you told me I'd get first shot when you had something. Hauling Nadell out of his office in handcuffs seems like a development to me." I took the easier path.

Whipping out my phone I hit the recording app. "Do you care to comment on the charges that have been filed against Aaron Nadell?"

He looked down at the floor for what seemed like an eternity. When he looked up, only sadness was left in his eyes. Before he could respond, other reporters saw that I had Michael cornered. They scurried over with cameras and microphones at the ready. Michael stared at me and clenched his jaw.

The rapid-fire questions flew at him. He let out a breath and addressed the group.

"We're speaking with Aaron Nadell in connection with the situation at VTF Industries," he said.

"Are you telling me that when I saw you lead Mr. Nadell out of his office in handcuffs, you simply wanted to ask him a few questions?" I shot back.

Michael kept his calm but didn't elaborate. Interesting tactic. Why was Michael evading? Can't arrest a guy without a warrant. Sounded like Nadell's attorney was trying to alter appearances. The other reporters picked up on the thread and started throwing out questions of their own.

"Why was Nadell in handcuffs?"

"What did you ask him about?"

"What are the charges?"

The reporters were relentless, but Michael wasn't playing the game.

"Sorry folks, we had a few questions for Mr. Nadell, which he has answered," he said smiling. "If we have new information, we'll let you know."

Michael backed away signaling an end. Nothing more to report. Bullshit. The pace and volume of the questions only grew more urgent as Michael tried to leave. A commotion behind us caused me to turn. Aaron Nadell and his attorney marched angrily toward the exit. He made bail already? That was some quick lawyering. If they had intended to sneak out quietly, those plans were out the window as two additional news crews filed in.

I shot Michael a look. We stayed, eyes locked for a moment. He had a job to do, and I had mine. We'd both known that from the beginning. We'd also known it would get in the way. I turned and ran after Nadell.

Good try guys, I thought to myself, but Nadell was not going to be able to slip out unnoticed. A posse of journalists surrounded them. Hesitating for only a moment, the men stopped and whispered to each other. Turow stepped forward doing what good attorneys do in the situation, he took charge.

I swung around to a spot between two new cameras where I could get a clear line of sight and started a new recording.

"My client is just as anxious as you all are to move past the unfortunate incidents at VTF. As a show of good faith, he came in to police headquarters voluntarily to share everything he knows of the situation. He is cooperating fully with CPD's investigation and we look forward to being able to assure the community of the safety of the product very soon. Mr. Nadell is heartbroken by the news of the unfortunate deaths and his heart goes out to the victims and their families."

Yeah, right. Nadell was anxious all right. Anxious to pretend he had no connection to VTF. Nadell stood sullen behind his attorney, his hands clenching repeatedly as if ready to punch out the next person who challenged him. I had a feeling Turow was going to have his hands full keeping his client gagged.

Questions came fast and furious as reporters angled for one more morsel. I also imagined Nadell was wishing Seth were the one with microphones in his face. Whatever cooperation Nadell was or wasn't giving, it hadn't happened today. Turow had simply finagled bail creatively. Latitude was given to the wealthy. Turow wanted better timing so he and his client could talk before the justice system took charge. I had no doubt he'd be back in the morning for a deeper conversation with CPD.

I was also mulling over the choice of a reckless endangerment charge. That in itself was telling. What did CPD know?

"That's all we have for now," the attorney said, starting to usher his client through the crowd.

As reporters jostled and yelled questions at their back, a flash of movement on the left drew my attention. Olivia. She ran into the lobby, breathless, stopping when she saw Nadell. Her eyes were wide with anger and confusion. She swung her head from Nadell to his attorney, then to the group of reporters behind him. I rushed over around the back of the group trying to get to Olivia. I didn't know what she'd planned, but instinct told me it wasn't good.

"You're letting him go?" She screamed in disbelief.

Nadell turned toward her, pausing for half a second, then continued his path toward the door as if she meant nothing. As I reached Olivia's side, I laid a hand on her shoulder.

"Olivia, let's go somewhere and talk. I'll explain what's happening." She looked past me toward Nadell as if not seeing me, then brushed away my hand. Before I could stop her, she ran full out. In seconds she was on him, knocking him to the floor. Her arms pounded at his head while she screamed angry, unintelligible words.

39

Three officers ran toward the commotion as reporters gleefully took in the scene. Nadell's attorney stood stunned shaking his head. Or maybe he was just afraid to get his suit dirty. Two of the officers grabbed Olivia by the arms and pulled her up, but her feet kept kicking at the man as she continued to yell obscenities. The third officer helped Nadell get to his feet, a bloody gash dripped on his forehead and he was rubbing his jaw where his head had landed on the tile floor.

Scott Price wasn't going to be happy receiving another phone call from me. I wondered if Olivia could afford to pay him. It seemed unlikely that she'd escape the need after drawing blood.

"She's crazy, I bet she was the one who poisoned our drinks," Nadell shouted.

The press was loving the outburst. They were like German Shepherds salivating because a steak was on the grill. I should have been part of the feeding frenzy, but I was too close to the situation. I forced myself into observation mode trying to be objective about the whole mess.

Could Olivia have acted in some way to take revenge? Would she have done something so dangerous? I wasn't sure. Anger could force people into behavior they'd never recognize themselves as capable of. But what about Nadell? I had no problem imagining him as a penny-pinching S.O.B. unaware of the consequences. Janelle's account of his history only confirmed that view.

Nadell and Turow were following the officer out of the lobby, most likely to determine if they intended to press charges while Michael pushed the reporters out of the space.

"Thank you folks. Nothing more to see." As he moved out of their line of fire, he whispered to me, "Nice mess you've gotten yourself involved in."

He left, walking into the bowels of CPD headquarters and I returned to my car, phoning Price and Brynn with updates as I walked.

Before I pulled out of the lot, I glanced at my phone; Lassiter had sent me a text confirming that Seth too had been suffering the effects of belladonna. So, I merged into the city traffic, maneuvering toward the hospital to check on both he and Lane. At the very least, I felt relieved that he was safe and being treated.

After two weeks of visits, the nursing staff simply waved as they saw me arrive.

"You have a little more color in your face today," I said, seeing Lane alert and sitting up in bed when I entered her room. She was scrolling through something on her laptop, the TV playing in the background.

"I'd be better if someone would've brought me my makeup and a decent change of clothes." She looked at me disapprovingly, wrapped in the pink terrycloth robe I'd brought from her apartment. Feisty. That was more like the Lane I knew.

"If you recall, you were too sick to care about whether you were wearing mascara," I said. "You should feel grateful you have clean teeth. Anything beyond that is a luxury that can wait until you're home in your own bed but I'm glad it's starting to bother you."

I sighed quietly, soothed by the normalcy, and surprised by how much I associated that spark with who she was.

"I'm damn sick of being in this room," she grumbled. "If they don't hurry up and let me out, I'm going to need you to run back to my apartment and at least get me yoga pants. I'm tired of my ass hanging out when I get out of this damn bed. The 90-year-old guy next door caught a flash of skin this morning and now I can't get rid of him."

"Better than seeing *his* ass."

We both laughed. It was good to hear, not only the laughter, but the impatience. The drug was working. I never thought Lane's attitude would actually make me happy.

"Where's Dad?" I asked, throwing my coat on the door hook.

"Walking the floor. Said he needed to stretch his legs."

"Did the doctor say you could go home tomorrow?"

"Yeah, yeah, yeah. Every day it's the same thing, maybe tomorrow."

"I know it's not as exciting as blush, but I did bring you a smoothie." I handed her a pineapple concoction. She shrugged, probably wishing it was coffee, but took it in both hands and drank.

"Okay, you are a good sister."

A familiar voice caught my ear, and I turned toward the television. "Turn that up," I said. "The TV, turn up the volume."

Candiss Nadell filled the screen.

"My husband, Aaron Nadell, was brought in for questioning earlier today in connection with contamination of products manufactured by VTF Industries, a company Nadell Industries has invested in. I'm certain that this misunderstanding will be cleared up shortly and that the true cause of the contamination will be identified."

She was calm, poised, and spoke with authority. I admired her self-control in response to the pressure.

"We are cooperating fully with CPD and analyzing our vendors to identify any potential issues that might have occurred. While my husband is devoting his energy to resolving this issue, I'll be taking over operations of Nadell Capital. I want to assure our customers that we have a strong team in place and we are prepared to move forward with this structure for as long as it takes to bring the issues at VTF to their conclusion."

This was a speech for their investors. It was a smart move, but just a starting point. There would need to be transparency and plenty of mea culpas as the case progressed if Nadell Capital was going to come out of this.

"So, that's Nadell's wife?" Lane said. "I would've expected he him to be with someone less, I don't know, prissy? But what do I know? I only met him once. Do you think she was involved with VTF as well?"

"I don't think so, but they all seem to be liars so, maybe." I shrugged. "Do you need anything thing else right now?" I asked, picking up my things.

"Vodka would be nice."

"Funny. You're lucky I bring you fruit drinks." She flipped me the bird. Now I knew she was feeling better. "Give me a call later if you hear anything more from the doctor. If it's going to be another day, I'll make a run over to your apartment tonight."

I gave her a hug goodbye then checked in at the nursing station to find Seth's room.

He lay asleep in his bed, an IV dripping into his veins and

various monitors flashing quietly beside him. A sheen of sweat glossed his forehead but a little color seemed to have returned. I stood next to his bed watching him sleep, wondering what had happened at VTF, wondering if he knew.

He woke with a jerk. Leaning over the side of the bed. "Pail," he said. I shoved it under his head as he retched. I took the bucket, handed him a glass of water and some tissue. Then rinsed out the pail in the bathroom and waited.

"Welcome back to the land of the living. You gave us a scare."

"This is living?" he said, downing more water. Then leaning back against the bed. "What the hell happened? Everything is fuzzy."

I took a seat next to him and placed my hand on his. It was clammy and warm.

"You've been poisoning yourself," I said gently. "Your drink, it contains a toxin called belladonna."

"What are you talking about? We've been through this." He took another swig of water, then wiped his mouth. Blinking hard a few times he adjusted his bed to more of an upright position and looked at me.

"Seth, I'm serious. The lab has confirmed it. You're taking a drug to counteract the effects and that's why you're nauseous. I'm sure the hospital staff told you some of this earlier, you just don't remember. It's been a rough day."

He stared at the wall with bloodshot eyes, blinking again, as if to clear his head. I could see him processing the news.

"Everything is still murky. They could have told me I had just given birth and it wouldn't have registered." He pinched the bridge of his nose trying to shake it off. "I don't understand. We don't use belladonna. How could that happen?" He seemed genuinely confused.

"I don't know, Seth, but people have died, starting with Kelly.

This is serious. And CPD will be in here asking questions as soon as they know you're coherent."

He reached for his water, again draining the cup. I took it from him, refilled it, and handed it back. After making a dent in the refill, he rubbed his hands over his eyes. Looking a little more awake, he responded.

"Andrea, you know me. You know I wouldn't intentionally hurt anyone, nor would I jeopardize my company. Help me figure this out."

I hesitated, contemplating his request. I didn't trust him any longer, but I certainly didn't think he was a killer.

"Then how could belladonna have gotten into the drinks? You know the process, the raw materials, surely you have some idea of how it might have happened." I said, watching his face, his body language. I chose not to mention Olivia's assertion that Nadell may have swapped ingredients. Better to see if the last six hours had given him a come-to-Jesus moment.

"The drink is a mix of performance enhancing botanicals—guarana, taurine, rhodiola, some B vitamins, caffeine of course —our secret, if there is one, is in the ratio and specific strains of the plants. Our suppliers have growing methods that enhance certain properties. It's not inexpensive, but the results are a superior product and therefore, superior performance results. I would never compromise quality."

Sloppy vendor management and vetting contradicted that claim. As did Cavanaugh's assertion of being left out of the advance planning. Seth's reference to the expense of higher quality botanicals however, did arouse my curiosity. It also over-lapped with Olivia's claims. Given how the day had played out, I hadn't been able to understand the specifics of her allegation, but perhaps I could tease something out of Seth.

"How is Aaron Nadell involved in your business?" I asked, getting a surprised look in return.

"I didn't know you knew about his involvement. He's been funding me."

Seth shifted in his seat, looking momentarily at the bucket. I moved it closer, but he waived away after the moment passed.

"We've tried to keep the investment under the radar. Aaron thought it would make his other clients uncomfortable. There are some losses in his past he's trying to distance himself from and I'm risky compared to where he normally puts his money."

"And what's that relationship like?" There would be plenty of time for Seth to learn details of the formal investigation, for now I was wondering whether the two trusted each other.

"It's tense at times," he said. "Aaron and I disagree, usually about money, but that happens in these relationships. Profits vs. quality. That's the dance. But production is under my control. His job is making sure we keep the red ink off the balance sheet."

"Has Nadell ever pressured you to use lower quality materials?" I was still watching Seth trying to gauge my instincts on whether he was telling the truth.

He laughed. "All the time. It's one of our standing arguments." He looked away for a moment, staring at the wall as if something horrible had just come back into his memory. "No." He looked at me, eyes wide.

"What? Are you remembering something?" I asked.

"Months ago, in one of our endless disagreements over cost, he suggested we try other actives that would accomplish a similar natural high, was insistent about it. Said the customers really didn't care about how, they just wanted to feel good. He'd even found some internet research to try to validate his point. I told him to stick to spreadsheets and never thought about it again."

"Belladonna?"

He stared at me, mouth agape, shaking his head. "It can't

true. Would he have gone behind my back and substituted our botanicals with belladonna just to save a few cents?"

"I need to know the date of that conversation and so does CPD."

40

I scrolled through my phone as I left Seth. My foot was throbbing, I had a headache that felt like a drum quartet, and I desperately needed something to eat. I was also worried about Olivia. Seeing a couple emails that needed an immediate response, I sat in the waiting area and tapped out an answer before going down to make the rounds in the cafeteria.

I dialed Michael while I was waiting for the elevator. As the doors opened, he stepped out, phone to his ear. We smiled and put away our devices.

"Obviously, I was thinking about you" I said, my voice soft. "I was calling to see what's happening with Olivia."

There were fifty additional questions swirling in my mind but Olivia was foremost.

"Nadell's pressing assault charges," he said. "I came over to see what Bowman has to say about all this. How's your sister?"

A group of touring med students descended on us lining up for the elevator. A tipped my head toward the seating area and we stepped over. I sat on an open sofa and rested my foot on the wood coffee table in front of it.

"Still hurts?" Michael asked, sitting down next to me. He ran his hand over his chin, then unbuttoned his coat.

His eyes were tired and a bit sunken. Was it work or us? Or just the florescent lighting that made everyone look peaked?

I nodded. "Too much standing today. Lane's supposed to be released tomorrow. The drug is working." I pulled a water bottle out of my bag hoping to calm my growling stomach. "Tell me about Nadell."

"You didn't really think a guy like that would suffer public humiliation or physical abuse silently did you?" he scoffed.

I hadn't, but I'd hoped the fear of exposure would've knocked some sense into him, even if Olivia hadn't. And the man clearly had exposure risks with both his wife and his financial situation. If there was even a chance that he was Olivia's father, and he'd brushed her off like yesterday's crumbs, assault charges seemed like a dumb bet or a diversion.

"Sounds to me like he deserved humiliation," I said. "Somehow ignoring that you fathered a child tends to piss people off. I don't blame her. I'm sure she'd love to get in front of the camera and talk about what an ass her daddy is."

"That may be true, but she'd have been better off airing their dirty laundry on reality TV. At least everyone would know what to expect. I'm not sure what she hoped to gain out of that stunt. There are other ways to take him down."

Michael sounded a little cagey about the whole thing but maybe it was just the tension between us and I was reading into his tone.

"Acknowledgement. Validation." I shrugged. "Olivia told me he bought her mother a house. Abandoned them both before she was born."

Michael nodded.

"There are any number of ways Olivia could make his life miserable if she chooses to," I said, considering the options.

"There has to be a paper trail on the home purchase. She's over twenty-one so trying to sue for back payment of child support would be tricky, but she could make it ugly in public. And the Nadells run with an expensive crowd. But I don't think it's about money for her." I was speculating, but the real question was what *did* she want?

"The kid seems like a fighter to me," I added, thinking about the tough couple of years she'd weathered. "We probably haven't heard the last of how she intends to make his life hell. And if he wants to bring assault charges, he'll open himself up to the charade of her paternity. But that's up to them. Have you released her yet?" I asked, thinking about how alone she must feel.

"Her attorney arranged bail thirty minutes ago." Michael was silent for a moment. "How in the hell do you keep getting sucked into these messes?"

The same question was going through my mind. The only problem with this mess is that it overlapped with my personal life. "Isn't that like asking a cop why he spends all his time chasing bad guys?"

Michael laughed but didn't say anything. Wise.

"So, you knew about Nadell?" Michael asked, when the silence became awkward, but his tone was a bit vague as if he were feeling me out.

"Not everything. But it's possible Nadell went around VTF's production staff and changed at least one purchase order. Apparently, belladonna was a cheaper substitute for the botanical ingredients. I've seen an altered PO and Seth can pinpoint a date when he and Nadell had a fight about it. He'll cooperate fully with you," I said, filling him on how I knew.

"Proof?"

"Not really. Just the PO. You'd have to match the handwriting."

I thought about the chronology. The substitution would've occurred while Cavanaugh was the plant manager. I didn't imagine he knowingly swapped the product, but hadn't Olivia said something about Nadell having cancelled an order? It was conceivable that he'd had changed the order himself.

"If Bowman can give us a date, that'll help us narrow down the lot numbers. At the very least, we can be certain the contaminated product will be out of circulation. The lab is processing the raw materials so that will help as well," Michael said, but we both knew that wasn't a quick process.

A pair of nurses walked past, giggling about their children's antics, and distracting us for a moment.

I turned back to Michael. "You've charged Nadell with reckless endangerment, tell me the details of the charge. What do you have?" I asked. I was still confused about how that happened and felt something was missing in my knowledge of the situation. "You obviously had a reason to bring him in, and I might add in a dramatic fashion, although it seems the legal eagle was a better negotiator, because he barely stayed long enough to set up a charging document."

Reckless endangerment charges required the extreme disregard for harm. Or had he brought Nadell in on some other issue? That depended on what Olivia knew and what she'd withheld from me.

"You forget, we know how to fuck with people's heads too. Maybe we staged our little catch and release so that we could watch what he did next."

"I can see that working with Nadell, but you can't get him in the door without life-endangering conduct, so how did you yank him out of his office?"

Michael paused and looked at me before responding. "I have a witness that claims he laced Kelly Cavanaugh's drink with belladonna."

"What?" I snapped my head up, pulling my foot back to the floor and staring at him. "Who's your witness?"

"Your friend Olivia."

I could feel Michael's eyes on me as I stared at the floor, processing what he'd just told me. Olivia had that information and hadn't told anyone until now? She hadn't even hinted at that in our conversations. Why? My next thought was why was she telling CPD now?

I looked at him and lifted my hands. "What the hell?"

"According to Olivia," Michael said, "Nadell, Bowman, and Kelly partied late one night at the production facility. Nadell was intrigued by the young woman, jealous of Seth's relationship with her, and decided that he had a better shot of getting into her pants if she was high. He'd done his research on belladonna as a product ingredient and knew it could have a hallucinogenic effect. As you've learned, he'd already finagled the product substitution to cut costs. They were in the plant, it was convenient, all he had to do was pull a little off the stock shelf and lace her beer. Olivia wasn't certain if they'd had sex, but two days later Kelly was dead. The toxin hadn't shown up in her autopsy, in part because no one looked for it, and in part because the congenital heart issue distracted the medical examiner."

"Wait, a minute. I can't wrap my head around this." I ran through every impression I'd had of Olivia, of every word I remembered her saying. If she'd had this info the entire time, and not told anyone, she was the biggest liar in the bunch.

"How would she know and how long has she known it?" Michael's claims had me grasping. Every instinct I'd had about Olivia had been wrong, dead wrong.

Michael leaned forward. "She claims she overheard Bowman and Nadell fighting about a month ago. It was the first she knew anything about Kelly or the belladonna."

"Do you believe her?"

He shrugged. "She claims to have a recording of their conversation. She'll turn it over, in exchange for immunity. Of course, Tierney's office will handle the negotiations."

I let out a sigh, my mind surging with thoughts. What in the world was Olivia up to?

41

Olivia. She'd known about the belladonna and about Kelly and said nothing. I couldn't get past the thought that I'd been played, that we'd all been played. Nothing that seemed real actually was. Seth, Nadell, Olivia? Where did the lies end? Olivia was the part that I just couldn't reconcile, in large part because I felt manipulated and hadn't seen it coming. Was that because I didn't expect a 22-year-old kid to have the skill? Or was it my own bias? I'd be replaying this one for quite some time.

The other thought that hit me long after speaking with Michael, was where had she gotten the bail money?

To add another bizarre aspect to the day, the Drea Foundation cocktail party was still on schedule for tonight. I assumed it was Candiss's way of pretending everything was normal or having one last shindig before her husband was confined to a cell. I hadn't planned on taking her up on her invitation to join the Drea Foundation party, but it suddenly seemed like an interesting idea, journalistically speaking, anyway. An unfettered opportunity to see how Nadell and his wife handled themselves on the eve of him being charged with rape and murder. I could see the headline now "Gold Coast Elite's Last Meal" or something equally tacky.

Although I couldn't imagine what the small talk would be like considering Nadell's arrest this morning. Although the news coverage never hinted at anything other than a financial connection between Nadell and VTF, surely even their crowd had heard the news, despite the whitewashing. But what would anyone say to the guy? "Pass me a cheese puff. How will you spend your time in jail?"

These were the thoughts that rolled through my mind as I slipped on a black sheath and my favorite pair of burgundy stilettos. My toe still hurt, but this was one fashion sacrifice I felt compelled to make.

The Nadell home was a Gold Coast brownstone on State Street, supposedly built for some German beer baron in the late 1800s. I imagined it was a regular stop on the neighborhood walking tours. Ostentatious was the word that came to mind as I entered. If you were into ornate, overdone, highly carved status architecture, this was your place. Intricate wood panels lined the foyer and extended up the grand staircase. A marble mosaic punctuated the floor in the entrance before transitioning to wood inlay. I could see four large, crystal chandeliers just from my vantage point. Seemed like the perfect home for the Nadells.

A maid took my coat and ushered me out of the foyer into a front parlor. Small groups of people huddled, sharing light banter, crystal glassware in hand. A waiter rotated through the room offering canapés.

Candiss stood near the fireplace having her ear bent by a white-haired woman who spent as much time at the salon as she did. She smiled when she saw me and excused herself.

"I'm so happy to see you," she said without even a moment of awkwardness. "And your timing is perfect. I'd heard as much about the poor font choice for the gala invitation as I could stomach. Mrs. Anderle is a lovely woman, but she does drone on about the two things a season that sit in her craw. Let's get you a drink and then I'll introduce you."

I wasn't sure if I should be stunned or impressed by her complete lack of acknowledgement of the day's events. Surely it was as pressing on her mind as it was on mine. I accepted the offer of wine and stepped aside to observe the festivities from a neutral vantage point. Had I just joined an organization that spent their precious time embroiled in debates over the attributes of Times New Roman when there was a criminal in their midst?

Candiss tapped on the side of her glass with a spoon to silence the group.

"Everyone, may I have your attention for a moment. I just want to make a quick introduction and then you can get back to discussing your plans for the Bears vs. Packers game this Sunday. Notice I didn't say it was a debate over which team would win." The room laughed politely and the jazz pianist in the corner paused his play.

"I'd like you to meet Drea's newest board member, Andrea Kellner. Andrea joins us from Link-Media, with a background in journalism and the law. Please introduce yourselves, give her a warm welcome, but don't scare her away," she chastised.

Candiss smiled graciously, and I felt twenty pairs of eyes searching to form a first impression. Aaron Nadell stood next to the baby grand, a practiced smile on his face, but his eyes sent another message. I shot my eyes to his leg, wondering about an ankle monitor and the power dynamics playing out in their marriage right now. What had he told her? And how in the world were they getting through the evening pretending everything was hunky-dory when a legal nightmare waited in their future. I imagined social power couples like the two of them had

had a lot of practice swallowing emotion but this had to be seen to be believed.

I also noticed that Candiss had chosen to be vague in describing my previous legal career. I imagined it was a subject she didn't want highlighted tonight.

As the room returned to my pre-entrance banter, I introduced myself to my fellow attendees, trying hard to remember names, their pedigrees, and even harder to overhear conversation. I also kept a close eye on Nadell. I hadn't decided what I would say to him if I got an opportunity to speak to him alone, but it was my primary focus. Drugged any young girls lately was a cocktail party favorite. I doubted that Nadell had shared that tidbit yet with his wife, however, she'd know soon enough, as would everyone in this room.

As I sipped my wine, I flitted from cluster to cluster curious about the scuttlebutt, while keeping an eye on Nadell. Despite Candiss's head in the sand approach, the whispered conversation was all about her husband's predicament. The gossip seemed centered around two issues, whether Aaron had made the proper choice of attorneys and whether Candiss was going to divorce him. Both issues seemed to be at fifty/fifty odds. Personally, I was betting she'd stay married to the guy. She seemed like the type to entomb herself in their lifestyle and stand by her man for appearances. Although with jail in his future, it might be the best of both world.

A man in a red sweater, whose name I'd already forgotten excused himself, leaving Nadell alone near a cafe table that served as a staging spot for napkins and silverware. I made my move.

"Lovely home you have Aaron. I imagine you really need that whisky after the week you've had. Do you care to comment on your role in the death of Kelly Cavanaugh? Is your wife aware that you've been accused of drugging her for sex?" I smiled sweetly at him as if I'd said nothing more than comment on the weather.

His eyes flared at me and red crept up the skin of neck as anger took hold. He opened his mouth to respond when Candiss moved to join us. I had the feeling she'd been watching for a sign she needed to referee. Rather than speak, he closed his mouth and took two steps back.

Behind him, a flash of movement caught my eye. Olivia.

She barged into the room a wild look on her face. Her eyes were red and swollen as if she'd been crying for hours. She beelined toward Nadell, oblivious to her arrival, leaving the maid in her wake. I swung my head my head from Olivia, to Candiss, and back to her husband. Candiss saw her first, a look of horror on her face. Did she recognize Olivia or did she simply feel the anger that exuded from her presence?

"Did you think you could ignore me forever?" she screamed. "You treat people like toilet paper. Use them, discard them, never think about them again."

Nadell's face had gone cherry red and the surrounding guests stared in confused silence, appalled by the outburst. Candiss got to Olivia three steps before me. She leaned close, taking Olivia by the arm, trying to avert the disaster. I had the sense that they weren't strangers. But Olivia was consumed by her rage. Pushing aside Candiss's grasp she continued to rail against the man.

"Aren't you going to introduce me to your friends? Too bad my mother couldn't be here to help you celebrate. She's dead. Did you know that?"

Olivia continued her tirade, moving closer. Nadell scanned the room, not seeing his guests horrified faces, but instead looking for an escape route.

I stepped in front of Olivia and took her gently by the shoulders. "Sweetie, you've accomplished what you came to do. Come with me. Let's talk this through. He can't ignore you anymore. CPD won't let that happen," I said, trying to get her off the ledge she'd put herself on.

Olivia barely heard me. She pushed my hands aside and made a run at Nadell. Guests shouted, screamed, and moved out of the way, as I went after her and Candiss toward her husband.

Candiss stood between Olivia and Nadell. "Olivia," she said. "Put down the gun. He knows what he's done to you. We've punished him."

Watching in horror at the events playing out before me, I dialed 911. Nadell huffed, sweat dripping from his red face, and possibly on the verge of a heart attack, as his wife tried to diffuse the situation. Candiss stepped closer, easing her way toward Olivia, her hands up and open in front of her.

My heart raced as I watched, frozen in place, reliving the incident with Seth, reliving Erik's death. The past raced through my mind as if it were all happening again. All I could see was the gun firmly in Olivia's hands. The voice of the 911 operator, pulled me back to the present. Sirens wailed faintly in the background.

"Olivia, please, put down the gun," I said, my voice shaky. "He can't hurt you anymore." She turned to me as she heard the sound of my voice, but her face was a mask of pain and rage. In that moment of distraction, Candiss rushed forward, reaching for the gun. A shot rang out jolting me with its intensity. I watched Candiss fall to the floor, as if in slow motion, a pool of blood growing around her.

Her husband stared at her with blank eyes as CPD burst in seizing Olivia. EMT's rushing in behind them. I fell to my knees, my body no longer able to support itself.

Candiss lay on the floor, contorted in pain as the EMT's worked to control the bleeding from a bullet to her stomach. Her eyes locked on mine as they attended to her, and her mouth opened, releasing only hollow gasps. I found myself unable to turn away as if maintaining the bond in our gaze would somehow give her strength.

Around us I could hear conversation, sense movement out of the corner of my eye that told me Olivia had dissolved into a puddle of sobs as she was cuffed and led away, so wracked by pain I could hear the shuffling of her feet as walking became difficult. Additional officers arrived, corralling the guests, moving them out of the way of the technicians. Nadell was silent refusing to speak as he too was escorted to CPD headquarters. His bail would be revoked and the reality of the charges facing him would set in as he spent the first of many nights in jail.

An EMT leaned over Candiss, cutting away her dress, applying pressure to the wound as she wheezed, reaching out a hand toward me. I stayed on the floor, my eyes still fixed on hers, and willing her to live as her body shuddered and her eyes flickered closed.

She was alive, but it seemed barely.

42

It had been twelve hours since I'd shown up at the Nadell's home last night and I was now nursing some weak tea in a waiting room at Northwestern Hospital. Candiss had been rushed immediately into surgery in critical condition and I had come over first thing this morning hoping for an update. The hours after the incident had been an endless parade of questions by detectives, and phone calls from Borkowski, Brynn, friends, and family as the news got out. Sleep became more a wish than a reality.

Sorting through the backstory of these overlapping lives was going to require visual aids. As I thought about the connection between Olivia and Nadell, I imagined a complex family tree of people and companies and greed all intersecting like a bad made-for-TV movie. But there was something about the exchange between Candiss and Olivia that had haunted me all evening. Candiss had said, "we've punished him." Could she have had a role in this? I also remembered Olivia telling me that one of her customers at the Waldorf had helped her get a job at VTF. That certainly sounded like Candiss. A staggering thought crossed my mind. Was it possible that she had known about Olivia all along?

I sat on a sofa, my head in my hands, eyes closed, thinking about the implications.

"How are you?"

I lifted my head. Michael was kneeling on the floor next to me. His face tired and full of worry. I sat up and opened my mouth to speak. Instead, Michael pulled me into his arms. Neither one of us needing another word. Not right now. I stayed in the comfort of his embrace, feeling his warmth, and my body relax into his.

"I'm waiting for some news about Candiss," I said, pulling away. "Have you gotten an update?"

He nodded. Running his hand through his hair. "The surgery was successful. They've upgraded her to stable condition. I'm waiting to see her."

I let out a breath feeling the tension in my body release. "Thank goodness."

A nurse approached. "You can go in now, but keep it brief."

"Thank you," Michael said, getting to his feet. "Would you like to join me?"

I nodded and followed him down the hall.

We found Candiss in her bed. Pale and disheveled. Her eyes were closed, but she opened them when she heard me.

"Lovely party wasn't it?" she squeaked out, her voice wavering. "My guests will be talking about this one for years. Every hostess' dream." She gave us a weak smile.

"How are you feeling? Can I get you anything?" I asked, looking around for a water bottle, not knowing what to do.

She shook her head. "They tell me I'll be fine. Maybe I should ask for a room adjoining Seth? We can nurse our wounds together.

Michael and I looked at each other endless questions between us. But was she strong enough? I'd follow Michael's lead.

"Have you locked up the despicable man I'm married to?" she said, addressing Michael.

"He's behind bars." Michael didn't elaborate. "Are you up to a few questions?"

"Only a few?" A small smile curled her lips. "Go ahead. I'll let you know if it's too tiring. But help me lift the head of my bed first."

I stepped over and pressed the control.

"Did you know about the belladonna?" Michael began.

"Goodness, no. And quite frankly, I doubt Seth did either. Aaron's greed and poor judgement are his alone. We'll spend a couple years issuing our mea culpas, institute an outside testing program for quality control and transparency, and over time, win back the trust of our customers." I noted that her voice seemed to have gotten stronger talking about the business. But her commentary was confusing.

"Tylenol did it. We can too," she added.

"We?" I looked at Candiss then at Michael, confused by her words of ownership and how quickly her thoughts had gone to her husbands' business.

"We, as in VTF and Nadell Capital. I'm Nadell Capital," she said. She motioned for a water bottle.

I pulled the tray over so she could reach it. "So you're going to continue to filling in for Aaron, should he face jail time," I said, trying to make sure I was hearing her accurately.

"I won't be *filling in* for anyone ever again. The ownership of Nadell Capital is 100% mine, in fact, all of our assets are in my name. Homes, cars, investments, all of it. Aaron doesn't have much more than the clothes on his back unless I decide to give it to him."

Michael and I looked at each other again, confusion obvious in our faces.

"I can see you've missed some of the important details in this drama," she paused for a drink. "Let me bring you up to speed. Ten years ago, when Aaron made the inevitable mess of the business, I had to come in and clean up after him. I know I told you a little of that story," she said to me.

I nodded. A nurse came in to check on her IV as the heart monitor beeped quietly in the background. After she left, Candiss continued.

"Part of that cleanup was something I orchestrated, the transfer of assets. All of our assets to me individually. To protect us you see. Because obviously the impulsive prick I was married to was incapable of controlling himself or his business. We were going to lose it all. The assets are held in a trust. So the company is mine to do with what I like." A satisfied smile spread across her face.

Awareness hit me as I contemplated her words. She'd used the near bankruptcy to manipulate him.

"Did you know about Olivia?" Michael asked.

"When I was going through the books, I found old records of a home purchase. Something I knew nothing about. Imagine my surprise when I traced it. My husband was not only unable to control his company but where he put his dick."

Even through the post-surgery malaise, I could see her face was filled with a mixture of disgust and strangely, a sense of pride.

"Do you know why I'm so passionate about Drea?" she asked. "It's because I was one of those girls. Aaron didn't rescue me, I rescued myself. But he showed me that there was another life. He, of all people, knows how close to my heart the subject of child abuse is, yet he tossed aside the woman he'd impregnated and abandoned his child as if they meant nothing to him." She shuddered with the memory. "The irony of me being involved with Drea when my husband himself disowned a child..." Her face was hard now, the years of revulsion, showing themselves.

"Why didn't you divorce him?" I stared at her, unable to wrap my head around what she was telling us. She'd known about Olivia and she'd known for years.

"Because then I wouldn't get to see the look on his face when he finds out he's going to jail. And that I'd gotten payback for his betrayal. His betrayal of me and of his illegitimate child. I didn't know how it would happen, but I knew he'd make another risky move. He can't help himself. Patience and discipline would get me there, it always does. All I had to do was sit back and watch him do what he does best, fail. But this time I wouldn't clean up after him. I'd be the one putting my foot on the scale."

A shadow of regret crossed her face while Michael and I listened, stunned by the revelation, stunned by her control, her planning, the willingness to wait.

"Of course, I never imagined people would die because of my husband's greed."

Her thoughts about her husband, the planning required, it seemed so compartmentalized. I couldn't fathom how she'd live with the deaths. Would that be isolated and stored in a box too?

"And what about Olivia? Did she have a role in this?" Michael asked, his face had remained unmoved, but I saw the shadow of revulsion in his eyes.

"Only in a minor way. She simply became my eyes. Unfortunately, she struggles to control her anger. She's young."

"What happens now?" I asked Candiss. My mind was shooting all over trying to understand but the cold, hard, manipulation was beyond me.

"Aaron goes to jail. I divorce him, leaving him with nothing, and run Nadell Capital properly."

"That leaves Olivia in quite a mess." Michael said.

"She's a lovely girl who hasn't yet learned self-restraint," Candiss said. "There will be some cleanup needed, of course, after last night. I'll cover her legal bills, make it as easy as I can, and I've also set up a nice trust fund for her. She'll be fine."

I looked at Candiss and said sadly, "So you both got what you wanted. Revenge."

My next thought was a wave of sadness. No man was worth the years she'd lost to all-consuming rage.

———

I SAT in the Link-Media conference room three days later, listening to Borkowski beat up the staff for more content. Brynn and I smiled at each other across the table feeling slightly victorious with our co-authored lead story gracing today's news blast. Suddenly the charges facing Aaron Nadell were far more serious than reckless endangerment. And with more to come as Luke Cavanugh had just authorized the exhumation of his daughters body.

Lane was out of the hospital, and out of danger, while my father had returned to his home in Milwaukee. For the first time in weeks, I was relaxed, happy, and looking forward to a leisurely dinner with Cai tonight at our favorite hangout, Nico. When I made the reservation, I warned them to expect a long, slow meal with lots of wine.

Things with Michael were still in flux but we had plans for tomorrow. Dinner only. Beyond that, time and lots of conversation would tell.

"Kellner, ya wanna pull yourself outta dreamland," Borkowski bellowed. "I know you're basking in the glow of another, kick-ass story, but can ya bring yourself down to earth long enough to get back on the horn with Ramelli about our budget approval?"

I looked around the room at the staff, watching me expectantly. Then giving Borkowski a big smile, I said, "Yes, boss. I'm on it."

Feet firmly on the ground was exactly where I wanted to be.

DID YOU ENJOY THE BOOK?

Thank you so much for reading THE LAST LIE. I'm truly honored that you've spent your time with me.

Reviews are the most powerful tool in an authors' arsenal for getting attention to our books to other readers. If you've enjoyed the story, I would be very grateful if you could spend a moment leaving an honest review.

You can leave your review by visiting Amazon or Goodreads.

NEXT IN THE SERIES

GET INFORMATION ON THE NEXT ANDREA KELLNER
STORY
   Sign up for my Mailing List at www.danakillion.com

I love to hear from my readers. Did you have a favorite scene? Have an idea for who I should kill off next? Jot me a note. I occasionally send newsletters with details on the next release, special offers, and other bits of news about the series.

Also by Dana Killion
   Fatal Choices - a free prequel short story
   Lies in High Places - Andrea Kellner Book 1
   The Last Lie - Andrea Kellner Book 2

ACKNOWLEDGMENTS

Writing a novel involves months, sometimes years, of plotting, planning, and fretting over every word, and mine was no different. It also involves the support and dedication of good friends and loyal fans.

Many thanks to my writing pals Kari Bovee and Shelly Blanton-Stroud for your support. Anxious to see your books on the shelf!

Thanks to editors Nancy LaFever and Andrea Hurst for tightening my prose and my story.

To my boys, Alex and Zach, I hope you live dreams of your own. And finally, to my husband Theo, thank you for keeping me well supplied with fake sauce these past few months. You've become quite the chef. xoxo

ABOUT THE AUTHOR

Dana Killion grew up in a small town in northern Wisconsin, reading Nancy Drew and dreaming of living surrounded by tall buildings. A career in the apparel industry satisfied her city living urge and Nancy Drew evolved into Cornwell, Fairstein, and Evanovich.

One day, frustrated that her favorite authors weren't writing fast enough, an insane thought crossed her mind. "Maybe I could write a novel?"

Silly, naïve, downright ludicrous. But she did it. She plotted and planned and got 80,000 words on the page. That manuscript lives permanently in the back of a closet. But the writing bug had bitten.

The Last Lie is her second novel. Dana lives in Chicago and Florida with her husband and her kitty, Isabel, happily avoiding temperatures below fifty.

www.danakillion.com

Published by Obscura Press

ISBN-13: 978-0-9991874-3-2

www.danakillion.com

74978759R00178

Made in the USA
San Bernardino, CA
23 April 2018